T0156552

GOOD-BYE, GADSDEN

A novel of World War II

A. A. Jackson

iUniverse, Inc.
New York   Bloomington

Good-Bye, Gadsden
A novel of World War II

Copyright © 2009 by A.A. Jackson

All rights reserved. No part of this book may be used or reproduced by any means, graphic, electronic, or mechanical, including photocopying, recording, taping or by any information storage retrieval system without the written permission of the publisher except in the case of brief quotations embodied in critical articles and reviews.

This is a work of fiction. All of the characters, names, incidents, organizations, and dialogue in this novel are either the products of the author's imagination or are used fictitiously.

iUniverse books may be ordered through booksellers or by contacting:

iUniverse
1663 Liberty Drive
Bloomington, IN 47403
www.iuniverse.com
1-800-Authors (1-800-288-4677)

Because of the dynamic nature of the Internet, any Web addresses or links contained in this book may have changed since publication and may no longer be valid. The views expressed in this work are solely those of the author and do not necessarily reflect the views of the publisher, and the publisher hereby disclaims any responsibility for them.

ISBN: 978-1-4401-1335-2 (pbk)
ISBN: 978-1-4401-1336-9 (cloth)
ISBN: 978-1-4401-1337-6 (ebk)

Library of Congress Control Number: 2008943163

Printed in the United States of America

iUniverse rev. date: 3/18/2009

For my dearest friend, Howell Carter, whose reminiscences helped shape this work. He was one of the greats of the Greatest Generation.

1

It seemed a lousy end to our war. That thought played in my mind as the yellow raft bobbed lightly on the smooth surface of the Pacific. In the panic-filled moments after our B-29 was hit and the crew rushed to bail out, there was no time to check navigation charts for the nearest land. Not that I had thought to do so anyway. Nor had Bill Deems, who was sitting across from me, so close our knees nearly touched in the cramped space. All we could surmise was that we were somewhere south of Japan and well north of Saipan, from where we had taken off yesterday morning. That seemed a millennium ago, and there was no sign of a rescue submarine.

Bill had nodded off, his head hanging down as if in prayer. Sleep had not come easily, mostly in snatches, since the first sharks appeared yesterday just before sunset. The bastards must have put us on the menu for their evening meal. They circled off and on throughout the night. Another even bigger shark rocked the spare raft from underneath, ripping a scream of raw terror from both of us. The sharks left about dawn, probably in search of easier prey, although a couple reappeared from time to time.

Neither of us had ever seen a shark, except in the penciled illustrations of what to watch out for if you had to ditch over water, courtesy of the Army Air Corps. What those warning drawings did not tell us was how big the suckers were. The biggest fish I had ever seen was the twelve-pound catfish I caught just below Noccalula Falls outside Gadsden when I was eleven. It was big enough to get my picture taken by the *Gadsden Times*.

Nostalgia gripped me like a vice. I had to choke back the tears which threatened to betray the fear that gripped my soul. Would I ever see those falls again or pass by the sign, just outside town, that read "Welcome to Gadsden, Alabama"? The bottom part of that wood sign has been painted over—the part that stated *Colored not living here must leave by sunset*. The war had brought many changes to Gadsden. That was one of the better ones, by my thinking.

At least we were alive. It was lucky Bill remembered to toss me a raft, or I would not be sitting here now. We were the last to leap out from the big belly of the *Lydia Sue* as she sputtered perilously toward her ocean grave. I never lost sight of Bill after his parachute opened. Still, it was a long hour before we finally hooked our rafts together. Neither of us spotted any of the other crew who bailed out ahead of us. By nightfall our voices were raspy from yelling, and we gave up any hope of connecting with any survivors. We were alone, adrift, surrounded only by an azure vastness and the curious sharks.

Bill was the first to hear the distant airplane engine, even before we spotted the small, dark object in the clear sky, pinpointed by the burning afternoon sun reflecting off one of the wings. Bill, facing the western sky, had the best view of the approaching plane. Maybe it was the same navy reconnaissance plane that dipped its wing to us some time ago to acknowledge help would be on the way, or maybe it was another plane sent to guide the rescue ship to our location.

"Can you tell if it's one of ours, Bill?" As I asked the question, a foreboding prickled hairs on the back of my neck.

Shading his red-rimmed swollen eyes with one hand, Bill strained to identify the enlarging object as the noise of its engine subtly increased. "It doesn't sound like one of ours, Johnny. I think it's a Zero. And he's coming right for us." Bill's voice was rising with alarm. "He's bound to see us in a minute, if he hasn't already."

Squinting was painful. The merciless sun beating down on us from a cloudless sky, intensified by the reflection off the calm ocean, had burned red rings around Bill's brown eyes, giving them the appearance of two dark chunks of coal. I could feel the lids and skin below my own eyes, raw from many hours of exposure to the relentless, rainless daylight.

After ripping off my helmet in the haste of bailing out of our foundering B-29, I'd forgotten my cap. Bill had alertly stuffed his billed cap inside his leather jacket before parachuting from the disabled aircraft. He had shared the cap with me at frequent intervals since we secured our rafts together and struggled into the same raft sometime yesterday afternoon. The second raft would be our back-up if the first raft began to deflate.

The selfless act made little difference. Neither the olive cast of my skin nor the thick brows shading my deep-set eyes deflected the sun. Painful blisters had formed on my nose, on the high ridges of the cheekbones below my eyes, and on my square chin creased by a deep cleft. Bill stared at me; the same naked fear I felt was written on his face and betrayed further by his anxious breathing.

"What are we going to do, Johnny?"

It was natural for Bill to look to me in a crisis. We had been friends since sharing a desk at Dwight Elementary School in Gadsden, Alabama, through our first four years of grammar school. A prim second-grade teacher, who wielded a worn wooden ruler like a riding crop, separated us for a time, ordering me to remove myself to an empty desk at the back of the room. Distance proved no deterrent to our mischief. After finding we behaved better together than apart, she finally revoked my ostracism, and I was seated beside Bill once again.

"He's headin' right toward us, Bill." My tone mirrored Bill's alarm. His eyes were trained on the western sky and on the shape, now distinctly an aircraft, although still some distance away.

"Should we get into the water? Maybe he won't spot us if he think the rafts are empty." Bill looked at me intently, awaiting my answer, his sunburned freckled face paled by the growing danger of our situation. Japanese pilots were notorious for attacking life rafts on the open ocean. We were sitting ducks—and we knew it.

"Slide into the water easy, Bill. Get behind that raft and hang onto the tow rope," I instructed urgently, pointing to the second raft. "Keep your head down. When he gets closer, we can get under the rafts." By being under the rafts we might escape detection.

The approaching plane was getting closer but still far enough away that the Japanese pilot might not have spotted us in the raft. The fact that he appeared headed directly toward us, however, seemed to indicate he had at least seen something and was coming closer to check it out.

I slid over the back of the first raft and felt the water come quickly up to my neck before I could grab the tow rope that secured the spare raft. We each quickly reached an arm up over the sides of the rubber rafts, clinging precariously to the slippery fabric.

My flyer's boots began filling with water, becoming heavy and cumbersome. It was too late to remove them now without being spotted for sure. They would be a dragging weight when we tried to hide under the rafts with nothing to hold on to. Bill and I were strong swimmers, thanks to the YMCA's summer swim classes. Still, I felt panic swell in my chest.

The red dot on the plane's wing was now clearly visible, and it was banking toward us. I yelled at Bill to get under the center of his raft. "Maybe the Jap won't spot us!" I shouted, spitting out salt water as my head bobbed close to Bill's.

"You scared, Johnny?"

I could see fear flame in his eyes. "You bet," I admitted truthfully.

Even if the Japanese pilot had not spotted us, he probably would waste some machine gun shells in sinking the rafts. The life jackets would keep us afloat, but even if we survived the Zero's attack, fending off sharks would become the greatest danger with no rafts.

"Get under water now!" I shouted, as I raised my arms and pushed off the raft. I forced my body below the surface and immediately felt the sting of salt water on my scorched eyeballs. Bill was just feet from me, directly under the second raft, propelling himself lower by pushing upward with his bent arms. I began instantly mimicking my friend's movements, knowing the enemy pilot might spot us just below the glassy surface of the calm ocean.

Several seconds passed as we struggled to stay beneath the rafts without being dragged farther down. It was almost surreal, watching as a hole exploded in the bottom of the raft above me. The force of the machine gun bullets ripping into the rubber sides expelled the air with a loud whoosh. The sound rang in my ears just as I felt a hard jolt to my head and right shoulder. There was a burning sensation in my right side followed by a rush of coolness. I could see

Bill and tried to reach out to him, but my arms felt suddenly like iron weights I couldn't lift.

Then I felt Bill's arm wrapping around my shoulders to halt my descent. I felt no pain, only the cushion of his strong, supportive arm. My senses were engulfed in a blackening whirlpool as consciousness faded, pulling me away from Bill, away from Gadsden, away from Sylvia, whose face was there, smiling teasingly, her dancing eyes the color of the sea. She waved good-bye as I melted into the beckoning black abyss.

2

He could sense movement and could hear the whispered orders of the nurse to the orderly about what should be noted on the chart labeled Winstead, John H., Lieutenant, Second Class. She raised the limp hand at his side. Her fingers pressed against his wrist to monitor his pulse. Those same fingers began gently probing the bandage around his head.

"The swelling is down on the scalp laceration. No new bleeding. Pulse fifty-four, temperature 99.5," the nurse said matter-of-factly. "That's good," she added softly. The young orderly looked up from the chart and nodded in silent agreement as the nurse leaned closer to Winstead.

The patient's face was no longer flushed by the stubborn fever that had wracked his thin frame with chills for nearly a week after the young flyer was brought on board the hospital ship from the submarine. That was at Okinawa. The ship would stop again in Honolulu before the long voyage to its final destination, San Francisco.

He was improving but the coma persisted.

He could smell the nurse's salty breath, a reminder of the salt pork served for breakfast and even some evening meals aboard ship—so different from the nourishment coming from the heavy glass bottle suspended on a steel hook above the right side of his cot.

The nurse was just turning away from the young lieutenant when she froze. Had his eyelids fluttered? The movement was so slight she could not be sure. It could signal he was coming out of the coma. Should she call the doctor?

"Did you see that, Anglin?" she asked the orderly.

"See what?"

She had her answer. But there it was again. This time she was sure she saw the eyelids flutter. "Anglin, go get Major Drummond. Tell him Lieutenant Winstead may be coming out of his coma. Hurry, Anglin." She spoke those last words to the orderly's back.

As the nurse moved around to the other side of his cot, the patient tried to focus on the nurse's anxious words. He wanted to reach out and keep her from leaving his side. His arms remained still at his sides. Only his memory was moving, drifting back to Gadsden, to the big white clapboard house on Carpenter Street, to home. His mother was there now, her gentle smile soothing, brushing the hair back from his warm brow. His father was there also, bending over, worry traced in his deeply furrowed brow.

He felt a warm hand clasp his left hand and gently squeeze it reassuringly. "The doctor is on his way, Lieutenant," the nurse said. He wanted to let her know he knew she was there. He tried to open his eyes. The effort was exhausting and his mind drifted away, back to Gadsden, back to the far recesses of memory undisturbed by the trauma caused by the bullet.

* * * *

I said hello to Gadsden on a windy, biting-cold day in late October, much to my mother's delight and my father's chagrin. My birth was what was politely termed a "late in life" baby. My mother was nearly thirty-eight, my father well past that milestone.

To my two brothers and sister, I was somewhat of a curiosity and very much an intruder into their world, an interloper who demanded far too much of my mother's time. And I was noisy at all the wrong times.

My mother, Ada, would hold me close and smile fondly. My father, Edward, mostly would scowl when I came into his sight. The challenge of raising another high-spirited Winstead into and through the college years, when one should be contemplating retirement, no doubt permeated my father's thoughts as he gazed at me. He generally chose to ignore me, which was probably the best course for both of us in those early years. Mother afforded such abundant joy and affection that I seldom noticed or missed his seeming lack of those personality accoutrements in my formative years.

Gadsden's biggest industries in those days were steel and a burgeoning rubber plant that brought one or more of the famous Goodyear family to our city often enough for the hierarchy of Gadsden society to remain somewhat high-nosed year round.

Even during the Depression, we were relatively prosperous—not rich but certainly far better off than many of our neighbors. My father sold the steel that the Gadsden mill belched out of its furnaces. There seemed always to be a need for that basic product, even when the output of other industries went wanting for buyers.

We lived in middle-class comfort, surrounded by neighbors who also were weathering the Great Depression well.

There was the druggist, James Beauregard Stevens, who lived next door with his wife, Maudie. They were childless and that was to be, for me, a fortuitous situation throughout my young life.

In the spring and fall, and most especially on summer mornings when the air was still—so still and languid it invited everything and everyone to move in a slower fashion—the most tantalizing and delicious smells would waft from the open windows of the Stevens home. Even in a belly filled with oatmeal, toast, and sweet milk, there was still room for a fresh-from-the-oven sugar cookie.

A piece of warm apple pie always added a tartness to the cool lemonade Maudie poured in tall glasses to wash the pie down. No solid should linger long in one's stomach without liquid accompaniment, she would always say, filling my tall glass a second time.

The husband she called Beauregard—JB to everyone else who knew him—was a mammoth man, standing six foot four on a stocky frame, topped by a shock of thick, coal-black hair tamed with liberal amounts of Brylcreem applied daily. He spoke in a booming voice that matched his size and was known to everyone in Gadsden.

The drugstore he owned at the corner of Second and Broad, which had been passed to him from his father and grandfather, was a meeting place for discussion and gossip by just about everybody in town. It was one of the few places colored folks in our town would venture.

While working there briefly in my early teens, I learned the depth of JB's soul. The names of many of the poorest in our community could be found in his ledgers as a result of the medicines they needed but could not afford. They paid small amounts to the pharmacist over a long period of time; often, not even then.

There was always a peppermint stick awaiting me at Stevens Drugstore whenever I went downtown with my mother, and she would stop in for a cherry Coke. If my friend Bill Deems was along (our street was named for his great-grandpa Chandliss Carpenter, a Confederate colonel in the Civil War), he also shared in the peppermint bounty. My joy was short lived, however, as the candy often preceded a visit to the barber—a visit to hell for me.

Mr. Sam, as that fiend with sharp shears was fondly called by the adult males waiting patiently for his barbering brand of torture, managed always to snip a bit of my ear and had the audacity to blame it on my squirming. The older I got, the less need I had for Mr. Sam's unsteady hand where my ears were concerned. I wore my hair unfashionably longer, having the smiling approval of my mother and the unspoken disapproval of my father.

From my tenth year on, my trips to the barber shop were generally alone, unless I wanted to risk my older brother's unrelenting verbal harassment. The light brown curls of my pre-school days slowly gave way to the same black hair as my father, before his became infested with thickening slivers of gray. I had his dark blue eyes framed by thick lashes and a square jaw that gave my lean face—and his—a permanent look of sternness and strength.

Traces of his youthful handsomeness still made my mother's face light up when he came home from work. She adored him and looked diminutive as he bent to kiss her lightly on the lips each evening, the afternoon newspaper tucked under his arm. As was his custom, he would remove to the parlor across from the dining room to read it front page to last before being summoned to the dinner table.

By age fifteen, I stood a good inch above my father's six-foot frame and was well muscled from years of swimming, baseball, tennis, and football.

Just after having my hair cut one muggy summer day, soothing myself with a chocolate soda at Stevens Drugstore, I heard JB's booming voice announce we were going to Birmingham: he and I and JB's best friend, Dr. Harlan Cunningham—a soft-spoken, thoughtful man with a perpetually furrowed brow who was as reserved as JB was gregarious. The two men had been inseparable since childhood. Through grammar school, high school, and the University of Alabama, they seemed joined at the hip, Siamesed by a synergy of thought and action that won them legendary reputations early on for mischief.

As adults, one elected medicine, while the other chose pharmacy.

When the time came to marry, they took for their brides Gadsden's two most winsome beauties, the Templeton sisters, Maude and Laureen, raised in wealth and schooled in the soft graciousness of Southern manners. Marriage brought the two friends graceful homes and a prominent place in Gadsden society, which, I was soon to learn, did little to discourage their reprobate ways.

JB and Doc Cunningham had been making trips to Birmingham for years, and those trips were the source of unrelenting speculation by many in Gadsden, including my mother and her coffee klatch, which held court in our kitchen each morning after Father was off to work, and we children were off to school or out to play.

Any whispered speculation on the suspected behavior of the two friends would abruptly hush when Maudie arrived. The subject would quickly turn to the weather or how to rein in the wisteria.

With the imposition of wartime ration coupons, coffee was reduced to one cup per klatch member, with cream siphoned from the top of a bottle of milk delivered every other day, and without the treasured two teaspoons of sugar, a penitence paid grumpily by each member of the klatch. MariSue Rawlings, from across the street and two doors down, would proclaim nearly daily her certainty that Eleanor Roosevelt never lifted a cup to her lips that was not sweetened. It was almost enough to turn any yellow-dog Democrat like herself into a rock-ribbed Republican, she would declare with just the right measure of vehemence in a soft Southern dialect that clearly marked her a Gadsden native. But the affront of drinking unsweetened coffee could not sway her sworn loyalty to her long-traveled political path.

Prior to Christmas and for other heavy-cooking holidays, klatch members would hoard precious coupons and generously share them with other members, depending on the amount of sugar called for in prized family recipes. No holiday dinner went wanting for traditional cuisine.

Now I, John Hamilton Winstead, at the invitation of JB himself, would be joining the subjects of the klatch's frequent speculation for one of their fabled trips to Birmingham.

I felt very much a man at fifteen. Instinctively, I rubbed the thickening whiskers on my cheeks, the forerunner of a bristly black beard that, in another couple of years, would cast a shadow long before five o'clock. Concerns about having to shave a second time in the same day was not at the center of my thoughts at that fateful time.

The trip was planned with a fair amount of secrecy. My mother was, of course, kept mercifully in the dark. Only Father knew with whom I was traveling and the destination. Like most men of his time, my father accepted as a long-standing Southern tradition, a son having his first sexual experience in a brothel. Father's one admonishment to JB was that I was not to taste any "spirits."

Liquor never passed the lips of my parents, staunch Baptists both. They did dance, which no doubt deepened the frown on the perpetually crotchety features of their pastor, the Reverend Hillard

P. Coates of the First Baptist Church. His view of sin, and theirs, separated over the question of waltzing and two-stepping on Saturday nights at the Elks Club.

What lay ahead for me would no doubt have caused the good minister a mild case of apoplexy. But among the mass of middle- and upper-class Southern males of those days, it was what was done to introduce young men, with rising testosterone levels, to the pleasurable reason for that particular hormone.

We arrived in Birmingham after a bumpy ninety-minute ride in JB's 1939 Cadillac.

Birmingham, in 1942, was a large, smelly city, with smoke from the steel mill furnaces darkening the facades of downtown buildings. It was muggy and hot that June evening. Sweat dripped down my brow onto my eyelids and formed little rivulets of moisture through the crevices of the cheeks my mother often cooed over, declaring with maternal pride that such lovely dimples had to have come from her side of the family. It was a part of my face that I would gladly have swapped for more manly hereditary features.

"Come on, boy," boomed JB, as he pulled the big car to a stop. "Let's get this show on the road. Follow me, son." He clapped me on the shoulder, and I thought I spotted a conspiratorial wink aimed at Doc Cunningham.

The house we parked in front of had a spacious yet patchy lawn, its appearance as unkempt as the house, which needed fresh paint. The peeling remnants of the last paint job clung precariously to the aged wood underneath, with more wood showing than paint. Inside, there was a much different appearance. Nothing neglected there. My look of shock and gaping mouth evoked a roar of laughter from JB and Doc.

"Never been in a place like this, have you, son?" JB knew the answer before he uttered the words.

A petite woman, a little on the plump side, approached us, her face alight with recognition and welcome. "JB, honey, how are you? Doc, where have you been keepin' yourself? I missed you on JB's last visit."

"Press of business, Millie. You know how it is when you're a doctor. Babies pick the most inconvenient time to come," he jovially explained.

She hugged both men and kissed them square on the lips, without an iota of shyness. It was apparent that Millie, JB, and Doc were long-time acquaintances. The plump, well-rouged face now beamed at me. "And who is this you brought with you?"

"This is a young neighbor of mine, Millie," offered JB. "I'd like you to meet John Winstead."

Millie nodded and smiled. Her kindly eyes focused on me with a mirth I was not appreciating at that moment. "We must find just the right young lady for our Mr. Winstead." With that, she turned and hurried out of the foyer, where we were left standing. In moments she was back with a younger woman in tow, pretty in a gaudy sort of way, dressed in a red gingham dress with a white Puritan collar that was not living up to its namesake. The plunging collar exposed a good portion of the smiling girl's ample bosom.

"Mr. John, this is Jenny. This is Mr. John's first visit to our home, Jenny. Take him upstairs and make him feel right welcome."

With that, grins broke out on the faces of my two hosts as they waved me toward the stairway. It was carpeted in a burgundy red, floral wool that, on close inspection, showed signs of wear and frequent cigarette burns. My eyes stayed glued to that carpet all the way to the second floor. At the top of the stairs Jenny slipped her hand into mine and led me toward a door at the far end of the long hallway, past several other doors, all closed.

"This way, John." She smiled at me reassuringly. But it wasn't enough reassurance for my rebellious stomach, which was doing somersaults. I could feel sweat rising on my forehead, despite my best effort at appearing nonchalant. That attempt was betrayed by my hormones, which were beginning to assert themselves against my inherent shyness.

This was a whorehouse and what was expected of me had been described to me by my older brothers and their friends. Those clandestine conversations were proving a poor education, regarding what I saw as Jenny swung open the door to a room at the end of the hall.

There it was: the bed, a big one, draped with a canopy of a colorful floral-patterned satin. The bed was covered with a matching bedspread and slightly mussed. The colors were muted blues and greens, not the garish red I expected from the raunchy descriptions provided by my older siblings. The room was almost pretty in a quaint, feminine sort of way.

"Do you want to do something or just have something to brag about when you get home?" Jenny asked matter-of-factly.

"Let's do something," I answered, surprising even myself at my lack of hesitation.

The response stirred a ripple of laughter that brightened Jenny's face and made it even younger and prettier. Right then, she was about the prettiest thing I had ever seen, and as she unbuttoned her red gingham dress with the incongruous collar and let it fall to the floor, the pretty became down right beautiful.

She had large, firm breasts, now fully exposed, and a slim waistline just above that part of a woman I had never seen in the flesh, only in fuzzy pictures squirreled away beneath my older brothers' beds.

Jenny took my hands and placed them, one over each breast. While I stood cupping her breasts, hardly breathing, she began undressing me. I could feel my hardness press against my slacks and then, blessed freedom as the zipper parted and they slipped to the floor. She deftly pulled my boxer shorts down as I stepped out of my slacks.

We stood in the middle of the room, both naked, the only sound my breathing, which by now was pounding in my ears. Jenny glanced down at my hardness, and nodding approvingly, led me to the bed.

What happened in the next five minutes was and remains still a vivid memory. A man's first sexual experience is supposed to be remembered when future sexual encounters dim with time or are simply forgotten. Jenny, I can see today, her face cradled in the pillow, pretending ecstasy that I am reasonably sure she was not feeling. But I was. And that's what mattered to Jenny. She knew a well-pleased fifteen-year-old first-timer meant a generous tip from the two whorehouse veterans who brought him. She deserved the tip, whatever the amount. Sex was everything I expected and more.

"How was it, boy?" JB asked pointedly as we approached the big car an hour later.

"Good" was my short reply. He bellowed one of his laughs and clapped me on the back again as he steered me into the backseat. The two friends traded stories peppered with ribald language and laughed heartily at their raunchy recollections of past deeds. I sat silent in the backseat, enjoying the rapport between the two, laughing with them at some of the stories. I was shocked at the frequency of their faithlessness to their marriage vows. Yet somehow, with these two, moral judgment seemed out of place.

If, indeed, there is an afterglow to sex, it shown brightly on my face that night. But it would compare only as the flicker of a candle to what was ahead.

3

The eyes were open, staring blankly up at the doctor, who was still thick-mouthed and groggy from being awakened from a snatched nap, the only middle ground the physician could find between exhaustion and collapse. *Two wards full of mostly head wounds and amputees. It's too much*, he thought belligerently. Too many half-dead men like Lieutenant Winstead required his medical skills almost non-stop, skills he had come to question and doubt with so many dying, despite his best efforts.

This man had somehow lived. Major Drummond was not sure how or why. And the young lieutenant appeared to be emerging from a nearly two-week coma. The doctor pointed the penlight directly into Winstead's blue eyes to measure the rapid decrease of the pupil. The dark-rimmed eyes, sunken in a face hollowed by weight loss, stared back expressionless.

"Lieutenant, I'm Dr. Drummond. If you can hear me, nod your head."

The head remained still. Jack Drummond was not surprised by

the response. Head wounds were the most deviling. The trauma of a bullet to the head was often fatal. Barring that, the victim might or might not regain consciousness, might or might not suffer brain damage. In this case, the bullet had entered only a shallow depth along the side of the head and exited behind the ear. A nasty scar would result, but hair would cover most of that if the kid lived.

"Mark the chart and check him every hour or so for the next few hours to see if there's any response to verbal initiatives," Drummond ordered brusquely. "Let me know if there's any significant change," he added over his shoulder, ducking his tall frame under the low doorway that separated one ward from another.

The nurse noted the chart the doctor had so abruptly handed her and walked back to the side of the young airman. Winstead had closed his eyes again, perhaps returning to the oblivion of his coma. Instinctively, she took his limp hand in hers and brushed a strand of black hair off his forehead. His eyes opened and stared up at her. With an effort, the dry, crusted lips parted. The nurse leaned down, straining to hear his first word. "Sylvia," he whispered in her ear.

* * * *

Sylvia Ross Barnes was easily the most beautiful woman in Gadsden. Long, curly blonde hair framed an oval face. Light freckles were peppered across her nose and upper cheeks, almost unnoticeable, even without makeup, which she never wore or needed for her flawless complexion. It was her eyes you noticed first, two large, luminous blue pools shadowed by thick brown lashes.

I saw her nearly every day. She ran the dry cleaners her father had founded and in which he had worked every day until he took his first vacation—in a casket, put there by his own hand with the help of a sixteen-gauge shotgun, just three weeks short of Sylvia's twenty-first birthday. His passing was rumored to be a source of relief to his family, especially Sylvia. If it was, she kept it to herself. Sylvia never mentioned her father. I never saw her cry or appear sad, even when a customer occasionally offered an awkward word of condolence. She would answer with a polite thank-you that seemed to discourage further discussion.

Still, family relief or not, Bryce Ross had chosen a scandalous way to exit the world, a route illegal under Alabama law, leaving his family to fend for themselves. The fending fell squarely on Sylvia. She ran her father's business, expertly and efficiently, with a willingness to work long hours in the dull interior of the small, narrow downtown building that housed the dry cleaners. Her late father must have detected these qualities in Sylvia, because he left the dry cleaners to her, excluding her mother and brother.

The *Gadsden Times* carried details of the will in a front-page story, spawning widely whispered speculation as to why her mother and brother were left out of the business. The will did, however, award Mrs. Ross a weekly stipend to come from the profits of the business.

It was my summer job to pick up the source of that income— dirty clothes—each day and take them to the dry cleaners, for which I was paid the handsome sum of fifteen cents a bundle. I could carry as many as five bundles in the twin baskets on the back of my bicycle, which previously had carried the *Gadsden Times* for the five years I delivered the morning newspaper to about a hundred of our neighbors. I made almost a dollar from the dry cleaners for a couple hours' work—good money for a summer job.

Best of all, I grew to like Sylvia. She was generally quiet, even withdrawn, and often too busy to talk. Sometimes I lingered, watching her surreptitiously through the narrow doorway that led to the workroom, watching as she sorted each new bundle, sweat beading on her forehead and pasting the back of her dress to her flesh. A deep flush would color her milky complexion as she moved between the canvas carts of sorted clothes waiting their turn in the noisily rumbling dry-cleaning machine. It exuded enough heat to send temperatures in the work area soaring well above the steamy temperature outdoors. Sometimes she would catch me staring at her and simply would flash a quick smile and turn back to her work.

When we did converse, I found her to have an active intellect and ability to talk about a variety of subjects, from the war, to swing music, to cars, to football, to history. For a girl, she seemed to know a lot, and that knowledge was enhanced by a boundless sense of humor she underscored with a rich, throaty laugh that lighted her face and flashed in her eyes. In those moments, she was so much fun I found myself not wanting to leave.

Sylvia's husband, Bubba, came by the dry cleaners from time to time to help himself to a portion of the contents of the cash register. Bubba was not his given name, but it had been attached to him at such an early age that nobody, maybe not even Bubba himself, could remember the name on his birth certificate. He would watch for any movement of the white curtain separating the customer counter from the back of the dry cleaners before deftly extracting money from the cash drawer. Then he would saunter past me with a wink and a grin and head out the door, always smelling of beer.

Ross Dry Cleaners was the kingpin of such establishments in Gadsden. The war had severely crippled manpower at the city's two other dry cleaners, and with so many of the men away in the armed forces, it was difficult for the women who took over. Sylvia Ross Barnes was a clear exception. She did the work with an expertness that pleased the most demanding customer. She also was expert at something else. I learned that late one Saturday afternoon when I was dropping off my last bundles and collecting another thirty cents.

"Johnny, what's your hurry?" Her voice had a soft, kitten-like quality.

"Nothing special. Bill Deems and I are going to the movie tonight, and I promised my mom I'd help her with some stuff around the house before I go."

"Stay a little while, please." Her voice was pleasantly coaxing.

I was meeting Bill at the house. The cowboy double-feature at the Princess Theater downtown started at seven. The Princess was the lone movie theater in Gadsden, owned by Gadsden's only known homosexual, Frank Benson. A morals charge nearly forced Benson out of the closet years before. The charge was never proven but the damage of whispered accusations and ostracism continued to dog him. My father warned me to steer clear of Benson, and Bill was given the same admonishment. So, like most of Gadsden, when we patronized his theater we seldom gave Benson more than cursory acknowledgment.

I was still behind the front counter, unloading the last bundle into a large canvas bin, when I felt Sylvia's arms encircle my chest and grip me tightly.

"You've got plenty of time to get to the movies. Please stay," she whispered huskily, pressing her warm cheek against my back, warmth I felt through my thin T-shirt.

My breath caught in my throat. For what seemed an endless time, I didn't breathe. When I did, my lungs emptied with a rush. My lungs were working again but not my voice. I slowly turned in her grasp and slipped one arm around her waist and the other arm around her neck, and began kissing her soft, moist lips. Her mouth opened responsively, and I felt her tongue touch mine.

"I need you, Johnny." Her face was flushed as she bent her head back against my arm.

"Yes," was my whispered response, the best I could do under the circumstances.

She bolted the front door and led me to the back of the dry cleaners, past racks of multi-colored clothes, freshly cleaned and waiting to be reclaimed by their owners. Across from a small, dingy bathroom was a cot with a rough wool army-issue blanket—Bubba's blanket, no doubt, from his short stay in the military.

The strapping six-footer had been mustered out due to bad arches. His unceremonious return to Gadsden several months before had been greeted with quiet contempt by many of the townspeople with husbands and sons in the armed forces, some of whom—including my oldest brother, Addison—were now serving in the deadliest battle zones. Addison was overseas—we didn't know exactly where—and my other brother, Collier, was in advanced training at a base in California. Both had enlisted while still in college, doing what many young men were doing: putting their lives on hold until the end of the war, the winning of which was never in doubt in their minds, nor in the collective mind of the nation.

Bubba's penchant for hanging out in Whipples Pool Hall and getting drunk frequently only served to further outrage already angry acquaintances. Bubba Barnes had been a hell-raiser since his early teens. The only respectable act Bubba was ever given credit for was marrying Sylvia Ross, with the apparent consent of her parents. And it was the only time Bubba Barnes was ever seen in a suit, borrowed from his father-in-law for his wedding day. Sylvia's father walked her down the aisle of the First Presbyterian Church, tight-lipped and unsmiling, an expression he maintained throughout his eldest child's wedding day. If he objected to her marriage to Bubba Barnes, he kept it to himself. Many in Gadsden laid Bryce Ross' suicide a year later squarely at the feet of his heavy-drinking, hell-raising son-in-law.

Bubba managed to move through school by meeting only the minimum requirements placed on him by an assortment of teachers, all of whom seemed beguiled by his blond handsomeness and teasing charm. In high school he excelled at football, basketball, and skirt-raising. Except to help himself to the cash-register proceeds, Bubba seldom came to the dry cleaners. When he did, he seemed never to find much to do, leaving Sylvia to earn the money he squandered at the pool hall. He could be found there most days, hunkered over the pool table with a cool beer always within easy reach, challenging anyone who walked in to a game. His invitation drew few takers among the regulars, who were more interested in keeping their money in their pockets.

"No chance Bubba will walk in on us?" I tried to sound nonchalant as I sat on the side of the cot, peeling off my slacks.

"He doesn't have a key. The back door only opens from the inside."

With that reassurance, I felt her arms entwine around me again and the soft curves of her slim figure meld into my arms. Her nakedness was warm against my skin. It became apparent that Sylvia, my second sexual experience, was far more experienced than I at the art of lovemaking. I felt happily drained and temporarily exhausted as we lay silently relishing the passion and pleasure of the minutes before.

She raised up on her elbow and stroked the hair clumped in sweated mats on my forehead, then ran her slender fingers through it to force it back to its combed position. Strands of blonde hair clung in damp ringlets to her softly flushed face, giving added depth and brightness to her large blue eyes.

"This wasn't your first time." There was more statement than question in her soft voice.

"No."

"Was this better?"

"Yes," I said, sitting up on the cot and leaning back against the cool wall.

She nestled in the crook of my arm, her disheveled, damp hair covering part of my face. I began to kiss the nape of her neck. I could feel my readiness. Minutes later, Sylvia left me prone as the rush subsided, while she cleaned herself in the cramped bathroom. When she returned, her face was masked in an expressionless gaze.

"You better go. Bubba might come back soon, and I don't want him to find you here."

I shared her sentiments on that score. Bubba outweighed me by about thirty pounds. I quickly dressed, then pulled her to me for one last, lingering kiss before we walked to the front of the dry cleaners. She did not resist. Without a good-bye, she ushered me out the front door.

I glanced back as I was pushing the bicycle away from the front of the building. She was there still, a wan smile briefly parting her lips. I turned back toward her and waved before I pushed off. Sylvia stood silhouetted in the doorway, bathed in the late afternoon sun.

"It was really good, Johnny." With that, she turned and closed the door, disappearing into the dry cleaners.

I realized at that moment how very beautiful she was, damp hair clinging to her neck and shoulders, her azure eyes brightened by the sunlight reflecting off the white blouse she had only partially buttoned. As I peddled toward home, I reflected on what had just happened and knew that a friendship, which had bloomed over the summer, had just flowered into something deeper.

4

"Sylvia," the raspy voice repeated. It was the name the young airman lying in the narrow cot called out each time Cornelia Scruggs came by to check on him.

"No, I'm not Sylvia, Lieutenant. Is she your girl back home?" It was the same question she had asked several times. Each time, the same response: blue eyes staring blankly at her from their dark-rimmed, hollow sockets. After notating the chart and hanging it back on the hook, she walked back beside him and placed his hand in hers, trying by touch to reassure and comfort.

"You've been gone from us for sometime, Lieutenant. In a coma. I'm glad to see you're returning. How do you feel?"

The eyes only stared at her. No answer formed on the dry, cracked lips.

"I'll bet you would like a little water. Anglin, can you get me a cup of water and bring it over here?"

The nurse did not see the spark of irritation flash across the face of the white-clad orderly, who had just returned from rinsing out a bedpan in the narrow latrine in the gangway separating this ward from the next. He had been on his feet for more than twenty hours. Weariness pulled at his legs and arms like an attached iron weight and dulled his expressive brown eyes.

He had just turned twenty-one. Jerry Anglin had not joined the navy to shove ceramic bedpans under butts or to smell body waste as it emptied out of bowel tracks into the pans. He was long past the gagging stage, but there were times, like now, when he was dead tired, that it raised bile in his throat. Still, it was not as bad as the smell of gangrene. There was no smell worse than rotted flesh. He felt a moment of silent gratitude that he had been moved out of surgery to work the wards. The hours were longer, but the work was less gut-wrenching.

Anglin filled a tin cup with water from a pitcher on the nurses stand, just inside the door of the cramped ward, in silent obedience to Scruggs' order. At least she was generally polite, not like Major Drummond, who only barked orders. He did not take kindly to being yelled at all the time by some muckity-muck doctor from Harvard Medical School.

In two hours, the orderly would get sack time. In two more days, he would get leave in Honolulu. *He could stand just about anything until then*, he thought, as he walked toward Nurse Scruggs. He handed her the half-filled cup of water, and she smiled her thank-you as she looked into his face. "You look bushed, Anglin."

"Yes, ma'am, I am. A couple more hours and I'll be off duty."

The nurse nodded absently while directing her comments to the lieutenant. "I have some water for you. Anglin, help me lift his head."

Anglin reached his slender arm under Winstead's head and lifted it several inches above the pillow, as the nurse touched the cup to his slightly parted lips. More of the water dribbled down

Winstead's chin than into his mouth. Scruggs lifted the cup away. "Here, let's try some more," she urged patiently, placing the cup against the crusted lips. This time more of the water went down. "Good, Lieutenant." She handed the cup to Anglin. "Do you know where you are, Lieutenant?"

The sunken eyes closed as his head burrowed gently into the feather pillow. "I'm home, Sylvia."

* * * *

Gadsden in wartime was a boom city. Its steel mill and tire factory belched smoke twenty-four hours a day. The work was non-stop, and jobs were plentiful. The Great Depression's long years of hardship were quickly forgotten in the euphoria of a steady paycheck. Many of those paychecks were being drawn by women, who left the tradition of homemaking to replace men in the war-necessitated production of steel, rubber, and textiles, the main industries of Gadsden.

These changes did not find their way into the surrounding rural areas. For country folks, little changed. For Jeb Thomas, life held to a continuing sameness during the early war years. He labored in our yard and our neighbors' yards for fifty-cents or a dollar a week during the growing season. In a good week he would take home a paltry ten or fifteen dollars to feed his wife and seven children.

Jeb Thomas was poor, black, and living in a time that held little opportunity for a Negro. All of my outgrown clothes went to the Thomas family and were well worn before landing around Jeb's neck as rags, which he used in his yard and maintenance work. At Christmas, the Thomas children would awake to find the benevolence of their white neighbors under the small, prickly pine tree, scavenged from the woods along the Coosa River.

The Thomas children attended a two-room, ramshackle school

29

just two miles outside Gadsden on the Glenco Road. The oldest Thomas child, Robert, had just completed his freshman year at Tuskegee Institute when he enlisted in the army, later to become one of the Tuskegee Airmen who served under Lieutenant Colonel Benjamin O. Davis in the all-black 99th Pursuit Squadron, which distinguished itself in the skies above Germany. Despite spending their growing-up years in the suburban bowels of Gadsden—poverty, not opportunity, the companion of their youth—Jeb and his wife, Millie, seemed to have instilled a fierce pride and ambition in each of their brood.

As a youth, Jeb taught himself to read. He later taught Millie. On those few occasions when I took something out to the unpainted two-room sharecropper shack that housed the family, I nearly always would find both parents reading with their children around a rough oak table, the top of which was perched precariously on wobbly legs. Jeb Thomas was friendly, yet deferential, to the white families for whom he worked. And he was held in remarkably high esteem by those families—for a Negro. He had a keen wit and a lively storytelling ability that won me to him long before I started school.

When Jeb came to do his weekly chores in our yard—pruning the bushes, pulling weeds, and mowing the lawn with my father's well-oiled push mower—I would make myself a nuisance, enthralled by his recounting of past times in Gadsden and the happenings among a part of its population that I had little contact with in those days. Segregation was not only the law in Alabama; it also was a long-accepted social practice.

Jeb's face was the blackest I had ever seen. His teeth were stained brown by the constant wad of tobacco that made one cheek of his lean face jut out. And when he laughed, which was often, his eyes lit up like two burning coals, and his thin frame shook. His was an infectious laugh that provoked anyone within earshot to join in. Jeb was black, but he was still well liked, most of all by me.

It was Jeb who casually let me know that I was being observed when I stayed past closing time at Ross Dry Cleaners. His mild warning came one day as he raked grass and clippings from the huge magnolia tree that dominated the front of our wood-sided house— the tree provided shade aplenty for the entire house in the scorching summers.

By the time I learned from Jeb that my after-hour sorties with Sylvia were being speculated about, I was completely under her spell. She had only to beckon, and I willingly and enthusiastically succumbed. I was smitten.

It intrigued me that so much of the underbelly of the white community was known to the Negro community before it became grist for the gossip mill among whites. How, I never knew, but I heeded Jeb's gentle warning—the next few days I dropped off my dirty bundles and beat a hasty exit before Sylvia could lure me to the cot in the back of the cleaners.

Those nights were wracked with longing. I wanted her. My dreams were filled with Sylvia—the sheen of her nakedness and the smell of her next to me. But there was a larger reason that kept me from giving into my longing: my father. I feared his condemnation. He had taken a strap to me only once in my life, and I knew I could be facing a second time if he found out what was going on in the back room of Ross Dry Cleaners. But even my tangible fear of his retribution was not enough to alter my course when next I saw Sylvia.

She was in the back, pulling damp clothes from the large dry-cleaning machine. I stood watching the play of her arm muscles as she lifted the heavy clothing into a tub. She had not heard me approach.

and so she tensed as I wrapped my arms around her, cupping her breasts in my hands.

"I've missed you," I whispered, turning her head up to me.

She smiled softly. "Me, too." Sylvia's eyes pooled and a tear drifted down her left cheek. "Was it something I said or did?"

I brushed the tear aside and felt a deep pang of remorse. She was nearly six years my senior, yet at this moment I felt more her equal. It was the first display of caring she had shown.

Often, as I lay in my bed in the isolation of my dark bedroom, I would imagine her as infatuated with me as I was with her. For the first time, I felt she shared my deep feelings.

I confided to Sylvia that my after-hour stays had been observed. Those few days apart only increased her hunger—and mine—a driving passion that then forced us into elaborate efforts to mask our times together. Some days, I would ride my bicycle home, put it in the garage, then walk back to the dry cleaners, taking a circuitous route through back alleys. I'd slip in through the unlocked back door behind the shop, infrequently enough to allay prying concerns about my working late too often.

Bubba was never around, seldom leaving the murky confines of Whipples Pool Hall before staggering home to the small apartment he and Sylvia shared above the dry cleaners.

I had not, however, counted on JB Stevens finding out. I should have known there was little that happened in Gadsden that the affable druggist did not know or hear about. He confronted me one Saturday afternoon in early August, striding over to the counter where I was sipping a cherry Coke before bicycling out on my dry cleaning rounds.

"Are you screwing Sylvia Barnes, son?"

The soft drink hung half swallowed in my throat at the abrupt question. I was too stunned to speak.

"Answer me, boy, and I want the truth." His tone was demanding.

"Yes, sir." My answer was barely audible, my voice constricted by fear rising from the pit of my belly.

"That's mighty dangerous, son. I know she's fetching, but if Bubba finds out, he will lay you low and her along with you. He's a mean one, son. There is no piece of ass worth what Bubba will do to you."

"No, sir." I did not feel the conviction I tried to put in that reply.

"Advice, son: lay off. Stay away from her. There's a dark side to that girl that I've never been able to put a finger on. But it's there. Doc Cunningham says so, too. Stay away, boy, and don't let your zipper-down get you in a mess, ya hear?"

"Yes, sir." Again, I summoned a resolution into my answer I did not feel.

"Good! Anyway, we need to take us a trip down to Birmingham real soon. How about Saturday, if Doc can get away?"

"Yes, sir. I would like that. I better be going and get the dry cleaning picked up." I was hurrying to the door when I impulsively turned around and looked at the man who was proving such a kindly mentor. "Thank you, sir. I'll heed your advice."

JB Stevens was back behind the familiar pharmacy window. He stood there with a broad encouraging smile on his face, pleased with my agreement to celibacy—at least with Sylvia—his hands never still in the counting of pills for one of Doc Cunningham's patients. He would prove a good friend.

Sylvia's smile faded and the teasing sparkle in her eyes dulled when I begged off her invitation to the cot the next afternoon. My excuse was lame, and we both knew it.

I saw her most afternoons as I dropped off the bundles of soiled clothes and hurriedly departed. I feared my new resolve would melt if I lingered. She would smile and nod hello but offered little else as she counted out my wages in small change; she made no further overtures toward me. Whatever hurt she felt was hidden behind the veil of her restrained friendliness.

I kept my word to JB, a decision I would regret. I had not counted on being deeply in love.

5

The smiling face above his was not Sylvia's.

"You're not Sylvia," he said, his husky voice filled with dismay and incredulity. Hadn't Sylvia been here? Wasn't it Sylvia who'd held his hand and touched his head with cool, soothing hands?

"I'm Lieutenant Scruggs, your nurse." Noting the alarm that flickered in his eyes, she took the young airman's hand in hers and squeezed reassuringly. "You've been badly wounded and have been in a coma. You're on a hospital ship. We'll be pulling into Honolulu tomorrow. Welcome back," she told him, her voice softening as a smile deepened the dimples, adding luminance to an already pretty face. "The doctor will be making rounds shortly. He'll be glad to see you've come out of the coma."

Jack Drummond did not hear her words as he swept into the ward, unconsciously ducking his tall frame before heading toward the young nurse at the far end of the ward. "Any change?" he asked brusquely, lifting the chart from its hook at the foot of the bed.

"Lieutenant Winstead, this is Major Drummond, your doctor."

Winstead's sunken eyes fixed on the tall man in white, who now was peering down at him.

"Well, I'll be damned. You're back, Winstead. How do you feel? Do you know where you are?" The physician took the airman's wrist to check for his pulse. "Still slow, but stronger. Good sign." He watched his patient's eyes fix on the sagging springs of the bed above him. "This ward's a bit crowded, Lieutenant. A lot of you flyboys managed to get yourself banged up pretty good." He noted the chart with the improved pulse rate. "Anything hurting?"

"No, sir."

"That's good. Maybe now we can get you to eat some real chow. Hungry?"

"No, sir, not really. How long have I been out?"

"Almost three weeks. A helluva long time, kid. You're lucky." Drummond jammed the chart back on its hook. "Get this boy some food, Scruggs. Something soft, like Jell-O or pudding." The doctor started away from the nurse standing at the end of Winstead's bunk, then turned abruptly. "Winstead, you've been asking for a girl— Sylvia, isn't it, Scruggs?" She nodded. "Do you want someone to come in and write a letter for you? Or you want the chaplain?"

"No, sir. Sylvia used to be my girl." He turned his head away from the nurse and doctor. "Not anymore," he muttered, more to himself than the two people awaiting his reply.

* * * *

It would not be the infrequent trips to the whorehouse in Birmingham that took some of the edge off my longing for Sylvia Barnes but a classmate, Ann McClelland. Her father was general manager at the steel mill where my father worked. She was blonde and petite, a combination which turned most male heads at Gadsden High School.

I quarterbacked the Gadsden Rebels football team. That seemed to be her major attraction to me. She also drove one of the best-looking and only cars on campus, a 1940 yellow Ford convertible. When the top was down, as it often was anytime the temperature jumped above sixty degrees, you could count on all eyes being turned its way.

That was the way Ann liked it. She was gregarious and flirtatious, bought her clothes in Birmingham, and could kiss for an hour without coming up for air. But that was all. My exploring hand made it into her bra some nights, but that was where the exploration stopped. It was enough to keep me interested, but not enough to wipe Sylvia Barnes from my mind. Sylvia would be there at night and odd times during the day, always naked beside me, her skin shiny with sweet sweat, caressing, arousing, awakening my longing for her. Seeing Ann at school the next day would abate the longing only temporarily.

Like Sylvia, Ann was fun. She laughed and teased, caressing with her eyes as Sylvia had done with her hands. Between football, work, and Ann, my schoolwork suffered. It was during the third—or was it the fourth?—lecture on the need for completing homework that my father raised the issue of how my relationship with Ann was going. Had I progressed beyond hand holding and kissing with Ann? He accepted my assurance that Ann's virginity was unspoiled, at least by me.

My father was a somber, quiet man who never raised his voice to me or my siblings in all the years we lived at home. His manner displayed all the authority needed; I spent less time with Ann. By the Christmas break, my grades were markedly improved.

I saw little of Ann over the Christmas holidays. I missed her teasing laughter, her biting sense of humor often turned on herself in moments of unflinching self-deprecation.

It was just after we returned to school in early January that she began coming to my home in the early evenings to study in the dining room, where my mother knit quietly while Bill Deems and I poured over our assignments. Shortly after Ann arrived, mother would vacate the dining room and take her knitting basket across the hall to the living room. When my father finished reading the *Gadsden Times*, they both listened intently to the radio for news of the war.

It now raged on three fronts—in Europe, in Africa, and in the Pacific. My oldest brother, Addison, was in North Africa. He enlisted the day after the bombing of Pearl Harbor. A muscular six-footer who excelled at anything athletic, he was immediately accepted. Less than five months after enlisting, Addison won his commission. We had learned just before Christmas that he was with the first contingent of Americans who crossed the ocean to fight for their country on foreign soil. Their location was described in the evening radio reports as North Africa, in a small, remote nation called Morocco. Its capitol would be made famous, not by the battle fought there but by a movie that would be released just one week after the first Americans troops had landed. It was not until after Bill Deems and I took dates to see *Casablanca* that I learned my brother was there, leading a platoon of specially trained commandos who were among the first ashore under the command of General George Patton.

My parents listened intently to the progress of the faraway war, as described by the war correspondents on the nightly newscasts, and their concern deepened daily as they awaited a letter or any word that Addison was safe. The days of waiting stretched into weeks.

When a letter finally arrived—some of which was blacked out by a censor's pen—Addison revealed his loneliness, his homesickness, and his resolve to stay the fight, to win the war. There were references to buddies. In future letters, some remained his companions, while others were no longer mentioned.

Letters from Collier were more frequent. He'd joined the Marines in a one-upsmanship move over Addison and bragged about the tough, no-holds-barred training. Despite the bravado in his weekly epistles on the life and times of a "Bama" boy in jaded California, his loneliness was apparent. Then came a letter, shortly before the second anniversary of Pearl Harbor, saying he was shipping out, heading for Hawaii for more training.

My mother knitted socks, gloves, and a sweater vest, and lovingly wrapped and sent them to the sons she missed and feared she would never see again. After Collier shipped out, letters from both brothers came only at sporadic intervals, some full of excitement over where they were, and others revealing their loneliness at being so far from where they most wanted to be. Addison never referred to the battles in which he fought or the slow, costly progress to reclaim North Africa from the Germans. Even the slightest hint at his whereabouts was marked out by the censors.

Two gold stars embroidered on cloth hung in our front window, a reminder to passers-by that two of the rambunctious Winsteads were directing their energies in more dangerous escapades than the rowdy pranks that had made them legends, however dubious, to our unwitting but generally tolerant neighbors.

I would read any letters from Addison and Collier to Ann and Bill in those evenings we hovered over our homework. Ann giggled at Addison's calamitous outrage at stepping frequently in camel dung, and Collier's descriptions of glistening white beaches and tawny bellies swaying to the hula rhythms accented by native drums. I envied both my brothers for the adventure of being far from home, away from the drudgery of schoolwork and parental curfews.

It was our nightly homework sessions together that bridged my early infatuation for Ann to a deeper friendship. Ann's father was repressive, an overbearing man who exercised his authority loudly over his quaking wife and frightened children. Primarily for the community to observe, he lavished all the blessings his position and paycheck would allow on his family. They were the envy of most in Gadsden.

But Ann was miserable. My family and I became her refuge from that misery.

Studying hard could bring freedom from her despotic father. She intended to go away to college and knew that for a woman to be accepted, her grade point average had to be high. To that end, she spent almost every evening at our house, bent over the books she viewed as her passport to a new life, a life without her father.

My father was generally there to answer questions about our homework, questions answered with interested authority, not with the shouted rebuffs of Ann's father. Father would sometimes lay down his pipe and the newspaper or book he was hidden behind to cross over the front hallway to the dining room when we sat stumped by a math problem or English assignment. He would stand over our shoulders and patiently help us work through an equation or a particularly difficult passage of Shakespeare or Milton. He addressed each problem or passage with an easy, respectful familiarity.

When the homework was finished, Ann and Bill and I would talk, friend to friend, about those things that seem so important when you are young, so unimportant in later reflections. Ann's eyes would turn soft and misty when she talked about the family she would raise in the years ahead, the husband who would be at her side, and a lifestyle that would provide both comfort and a home filled with love and nurturing. We still spent some time kissing when Bill was not there, and my hand would still find the roundness of her breast, but the initial passion had cooled. It was replaced by the relationship of two people who enjoyed each other's company thoroughly.

I could feel a cold drizzle just beginning as I peddled hard along the final block to the dry cleaners. It was Saturday, the only day I could work since the beginning of school. A chilly wind rushed against my bare head, stinging my ears and eyes. Bill was waiting as I parked my bicycle against the side of the building, thumping his hands against the early March cold, anxiety written in his frown.

"Bubba's in there, and they're fightin' bad in the back of the shop. I could hear him yellin' at her when I walked in to meet you. You suppose we better go in, or wait 'til he leaves?" The reluctance Bill felt about intruding on the situation was clear in his voice.

"I'll just drop these on the counter, and we'll scat," I told him. I tucked the several bundles under my arm and pushed open the door with my foot. Inside, I could hear Bubba's voice, slurred with drink, screaming at his wife. Then the sharp crack of a slap. I knew then the cause of bruises I had seen on Sylvia's face and arms so often in the past. She always explained away the marks as her own awkwardness, bumping into machinery in the back of the cleaners or falling. Anger welled up in me instantly. "Bill, come here! Bubba's beating her!" I shouted.

I did not look to see if Bill was following me as I ran toward the rear of the building where I had known such forbidden pleasure. Angrily, I ripped aside the sheet shielding the back room from the cleaning area. Bubba was standing over Sylvia, who was crumpled by the side of the cot where I had lain with her. Her head, nose, and mouth dripped blood, and Bubba landed a hard kick into her shoulder just as I threw myself at him. My rage stripped away any fear I'd had of tackling the burly man.

He turned in surprise, just as I lunged against his shoulder, knocking him to the floor. I was on top of him, punching at the arms that now covered his face, trying to fend off my blows. Just as Bubba seemed to recover his strength and free his left arm to return my punishment, a foot sent his arm flying over his head. Bill showed no mercy, striking the startled Bubba with a blow full to the mouth. Blood spouted from between his lips. The big man slumped silent and unconscious on the floor beside the cot, where his wife now lay sprawled, motionless.

It was Bill who spoke first. "Should we call the police?"

"No!" I cried, holding my heaving sides as my breath came in gulps. "Call Doc Cunningham. Tell him Sylvia's hurt bad and come right away. Hurry!"

As Bill darted toward the telephone on the front counter, I slipped my arm under Sylvia's head and pulled her against me. The blood oozing from her head and nose stained my shirt red. She moaned softly and turned in my arms. Even in her semi-conscious condition she could feel pain. The areas around her eyes and cheeks were already swelling, and I wondered absently if Bubba's blows had broken any facial bones.

Bill was back, kneeling beside me, his worried eyes staring at the pale, blood-streaked face cradled in my arms.

"Doc says he'll be here right away and not to move her 'cause she could have a concussion or maybe something broken."

It made no difference now. I just held her close to me and wished remorsefully that I had come sooner. Maybe I could have saved her the pain evident in her anguished moans.

It seemed an eternity, those ten minutes before Doc Cunningham walked past the sheet to where I still held Sylvia. Bubba had not moved in that time. He lay breathing heavily, in a sleep I suspected was induced as much by alcohol as by Bill's foot.

Doc Cunningham lifted Sylvia out of my arms and laid her gently on the cot. The ammonia he waved under her nose forced her eyes to flutter open, eliciting soft groans. The physician gently talked to her as he doused a clean cotton ball with hydrogen peroxide and began cleaning blood from the abrasions on her face and neck. His fingers expertly felt around the high cheek and oval chin that so added to the beauty of the now disfigured face looking up trustingly at him.

"Nothing appears broken, young lady. You're lucky. He laid some nasty blows on your face. Can you stand up?" Doc and I helped support Sylvia as she struggled to her feet and stood woozily clinging to his arm until she steadied.

"I'm okay now. Thank you, Doctor Cunningham. Is Bubba all right?" It was the first notice anyone had taken of the slumbering drunk stretched out on the floor just a few feet from us.

"He's fine, Sylvia. He'll sleep his off. But you need to stay in bed a couple of days and not go out. Can that be arranged?" he inquired gently.

"Yes." She offered no explanation how that would be done, since she was the only person I ever saw working in the dry cleaners.

"Can I call your mother for you, Sylvia? You need someone with you."

"No, please," she replied, looking into the doctor's face with pleading eyes, "let's not bother her. I can take care of myself."

"I can look in on her, Doc. And my mother can fix some food to bring over," I volunteered.

"All right, son. But she'll need some help for the next two or three days. And I don't think her husband's going to be in any condition to help." He glanced disdainfully at the still-sleeping Bubba. "Bill, call the police chief. I want this sorry son-of-a-bitch in jail."

It took the police chief and two of his officers to get the muttering Bubba Barnes on his feet and into the backseat of a patrol car. Bill and I assisted Sylvia to the small, drab, sparsely furnished apartment above the dry cleaners. Doc Cunningham followed us up the stairs. We turned away awkwardly as he helped Sylvia out of her blood-stained clothing and into a long flannel nightgown. When she refused the sedative he proffered, the doctor injected her with what he described as a mild anesthetic. Sylvia's eyelids closed. She was quickly asleep.

"Sleep. It's the best thing for her," said Doc Cunningham, as he clamped his black medical bag shut. "I best be going. I'll call her mother and have her come over to stay with Sylvia. She'll be all right in a couple of days. No permanent harm done."

"She doesn't want you to call her mother, Doc. I'll stay here with her."

The physician looked at me intently. "I'm not sure that's a good idea, son. Your parents might not like it. And we don't know how long they'll hold Bubba in jail."

"She's my friend, Doc. I can take care of her. She would want that."

"You're sure, son?" When I nodded, he handed me a glass vile with several small pills. "Give her one of these about every four to six hours. They'll make her sleep, and that's what she needs most right now to get better."

"Bill, can you take my bike home?" I asked.

"Sure." Bill had been standing quietly across the small room, unsure what to say or do. He seemed glad to follow Doc Cunningham as he moved toward the door. I had not told Bill about Sylvia. She was my secret, shared with no one, not even my best friend. I stayed alone with Sylvia that night, sleeping only intermittently in a rickety wood rocker I had pulled close to her bed. Doc Cunningham came by early the next morning, accompanied by my parents, who carried two plates of food, along with kindly offers of help.

Sylvia winced as the physician gingerly swabbed the cuts he'd stitched the evening before—below her lower lip and above her eye—as my parents watched in silence.

After spreading out the food on the small linoleum-covered table in the tiny kitchen, Mother offered to move Sylvia to our house, where she could nurse her. Still groggy from the sedatives, Sylvia shook her head but whispered "Thank you," before laying her head back on the pillow and drifting back into a restless sleep. When my father appeared to be on the brink of insisting I come home, the expression on my face must have silenced whatever he was about to say. My mother stepped toward me and held me close.

"You're a good boy, John," she said, brushing back the hair that hung over my forehead.

"Call if you need me, John," Doc Cunningham said, picking up his worn hat. "It's Sunday. I've got rounds to make and two babies ready to pop out. I'd better be off."

After Father pulled the door closed behind them, I sat back down beside Sylvia in the protesting rocker, watching her bruised and puffy face, first with anger, then anguish. The red blotches on her face were turning a deep purple. Her eyes remained so swollen they would barely open. She tossed in the drug-induced sleep, moaning in pain, her eyes fluttering awake frequently only to close quickly back in sleep. Her hand rested in mine while she slept, as if she was afraid to let go. I would trace the lines in the soft palm of her left hand, lifting it frequently to hold to my lips or against my cheek. Sometimes, as I held her hand, I thought I saw a shadow of a smile trace across her lips when she momentarily awoke.

My mother returned alone that afternoon. Father's absence confirmed his disapproval of my staying with Sylvia, a married woman and my employer. I sat in the small kitchen adjacent to the bedroom, devouring the generous plate of roast beef and vegetables my mother brought, as she sat beside Sylvia. With gentle insistence she was able to coax several spoonfuls of a tasty soup past Sylvia's bruised lips. Eating seemed to revive Sylvia, and she and Mother talked softly while I finished my meal.

As I helped Mother into her heavy winter coat, she said, barely above a whisper, "We'll be by in the morning to take you home, John." I knew then, with those words, the compromise my mother had reached with Father, which allowed me to remain with Sylvia. I nodded and kissed her softly on the cheek, knowing at that moment how fortunate I was that this was the woman who had given me life.

Sylvia was sitting on the side of the bed when I returned to the bedroom. I knelt down beside the bed as she opened her arms and enclosed me against her breasts. The words were barely audible. "I love you."

How simple that term of endearment, how simple those words. How much they told, how much they said, how much they meant. I was sixteen. Only recently had I started shaving daily. Yet I knew, with certainty, how deeply I loved her.

Doc Cunningham came the next morning and declared Sylvia on the mend.

Bubba never came. He was in jail and would stay there until he agreed to move in with his parents and away from Sylvia, orders he would disobey.

Early Monday morning, when I answered the knock at the apartment door, my father stood before me, his hands holding the breakfast Mother had prepared.

"I've come to take you home, son. Bubba gets out of jail tomorrow." I did not argue. My sleep that night was restless. I alternately saw Sylvia's puffy, bloodied face before me or the bloodied face of Bubba, the result of my fists and Bill's foot.

I did not heed my father's admonition or Doc Cunningham's advice. There were many more secret, sensual meetings in the back room of the dry cleaners in the weeks that followed Sylvia's harsh beating. Both of us took care to keep our lovemaking away from prying eyes. I left her arms each time more in love than the last.

6

It was my mother who suspected more than an employee/employer relationship between Sylvia and me. She confronted me with her suspicions at the breakfast table one summer morning when my father was away on one of his increasingly frequent trips to Washington DC.

Mother seldom raised her voice. Her tone always was quiet and patient, regardless of the concern in her words. There was worry in her words that morning—concern for me, concern for Sylvia and the condemnation that would be heaped on Sylvia if our relationship became known in the community, and concern for the safety of both Sylvia and me if Bubba became aware of his wife's infidelity.

Mother's intuitive awareness of our relationship took me by surprise and silenced any denial. She always told the truth and countenanced no lies from her beloved offspring. Instead, she wrapped her gentle love around each of us every day, in so many ways, from her good-morning kiss to a good-night hug, whatever the time of our arrival home. Never was there a word of reprimand about late hours—and never a sound that interrupted our father's rhythmic snoring asleep beside her. He never knew.

I faced her that morning with no rebuttal for her reasoned warnings. She did not tell me to end my tryst with a married woman, only the reasons why I must. I knew she was right. And I knew as I left the table, kissing her good-bye that morning, that I must, for the second time, end the time with Sylvia that endangered us both.

Sylvia stood silent as I told her I would not be with her again, not as her lover. And I was quitting my job with the dry cleaners. Her stoic expression belied the pain inflicted by my words. I assuaged my own pain by silently promising that this separation would be temporary. I would find a way for us to be together, away from parents, prying eyes, and husbands. The naïveté of youth is seducing. It was for me that day.

Blonde curls clung to the nape of her neck, secured by sweat that ran from her face as she toiled among the lumbering, noisy machines that removed the soil from so many of Gadsden's garments. I did not hear her heaving sobs as the door closed behind me, muting my own guilt.

Only later, in the darkened quiet of my bedroom, would I feel the depth of my own pain, the wrenching morass of love and longing. It was Bill who sensed my emotional abyss. Soon after I parted from Sylvia, Bill came to live with us, at my mother's insistence, a decision I applauded. Bill spoke little of his parents, ever. I knew his father was away most of the year, working in the oil fields of south Louisiana.

His mother, a thin woman with dyed black hair that reflected a blue hue when exposed to sunlight, had a hardened face that was prematurely lined. I knew she drank. That much my mother revealed. I was not aware of the biting gossip surrounding the time she spent at Whipples Pool Hall. It was not a place for women, not women who cared a smidgen about their reputations, but reputation was the farthest thing from Ethel Deems' mind when she entered Whipples. She was an alcoholic who preferred to do most of her drinking in public. The alcohol and the men who frequented Whipples assuaged the loneliness that, she told anyone who would listen, justified her behavior.

When Carter Deems first left to work in Louisiana, Ethel Deems went to Whipples only after their son was fed and in bed. Then the once-a-week visits to Gadsden's most notorious bar became more frequent. Ethel Deems had been drinking on the sly since her marriage to Bill's father. If Carter Deems was aware of his wife's drinking, he kept it to himself.

The Deems were quiet neighbors in their low-rent neighborhood, shunning contact with those who lived near them, staying mostly to themselves and taking little interest in their son. From his earliest recollection, Bill never saw his parents converse beyond a few words. They said little to each other and nothing to those around them, even him. He could not remember his mother or father ever hugging or kissing him. My mother's embracing him was a welcome warmth in his otherwise unloved existence.

Bill began staying with us after school when we were in first grade. It was such a ritual that by the time we entered high school, we were close friends who treated each other as brothers; we shared a fierce loyalty never questioned by our classmates. John and Bill, Bill and John. We were inseparable.

Bill was the brighter one. I relied on him for help with homework, and he relied on me to help him find a girl. He was handsome in a tall-and-too-thin kind of way, with reddish-brown hair that framed a swarthy complexion and deep-set brown eyes. He was also the best athlete on the football team. It was a mystery to me why, with those attributes, he remained so shy. During the summers we played tennis daily. I was one of the five members of a tennis team that would capture the state championship in our junior year. Bill was a better tennis player but refused to join the team, preferring to cheer for me from the bleachers. Football was his game—his only game. He became my favored receiver. Gadsden posted a 10–0 season in the fall of 1943. We talked football incessantly and talked of playing together for the University of Alabama. Bill focused on that goal, a goal that would be possible for him only if he won a scholarship. Like Ann, he viewed college as the means to escape his parents.

But always in the background of our plans for the future was the war. Would it be over by the time we graduated from high school in the spring of 1945?

We read the morning papers, gleaning news of the Allies' progress in stemming the Nazi assault that had spread across Europe like a giant tidal wave. We were far removed from the war, safe in the South, and our only thoughts of survival involved recognizing Mr. Humphry's trick math questions and getting an A. Bill's scholarship to Alabama might depend on that A.

The telegram arrived in early June, late on one of those deceptive Alabama evenings that cloaks you in its temperate calm, making you feel the steamy discomfort of summer is still a ways off. Bill and I were lazily kicking back and forth on the back porch swing when we heard the front-door knocker and Mother cheerily tell the visitor she was coming.

After more swaying, curiosity impelled us off the swing, through the darkened kitchen, and down the hallway toward the front of the house, to find out who had come calling at this late hour. We saw only the caller's back, a man in a dark-green uniform, descending the wide front steps as the screen door snapped shut. Mother stood there, unmoving, her head bent, reading the telegram.

"Who was it, Ada?"

Father's question lingered unanswered in the heavy silence. He peered over the rims of the horned-rimmed reading glasses, which rested on the bridge of his prominent nose. He'd been reading in the comfort of his faded maroon leather, high-backed chair on the far side of the parlor. The newspaper slipped from his hands and wafted silently to the floor as time seemed to slow. He appeared fixed in his seat, unable to move for what seemed long moments, as if unsure what to do. Then he rose heavily from the chair, and for the first time in my young life, my father appeared suddenly old to me as he walked into the hallway toward my mother, who was still facing the opened front door. Her only movement was when the hand that held the telegram fell limply to her side.

Father must have sensed the cruel message it bore. He did not reach for the telegram but instead wrapped his large arms around Mother, pressing her head against his thick chest. He rocked her gently, his cheek resting gently on the top of her head.

"He's dead, Edward."

The sobs began so quietly, they were barely audible, like a spring rain that begins falling softly before it builds toward a torrential downpour. I went to stand beside them, sensing now what tragic message was written in clipped telegram verbiage. With mounting dread I took it from her unresisting hand.

"We regret to inform you that Lt. Addison Edward Winstead was killed in action in North Africa. Stop. Lt. Winstead has been awarded a silver star for valor in the line of duty. Stop. You will be contacted by the War Department about burial arrangements. Stop."

So few words, so blunt, so hurtful, so final.

Addison dead, on the forbidding sands of North Africa, his life shattered by a German bullet as American and British troops assaulted the rear guard of Rommel's retreating army. He died in the crosshairs of a sniper's bullet as he led his platoon's charge on a German artillery battery.

I did not know Addison well. He was a brother removed from me in age, a sixth-grader when I was born. My chest tightened and heaved involuntarily as I struggled to suppress the tears that sprang to my eyes. Now I would never get to know this reserved, studious brother, who'd written of attending law school when he came home from the war. There would now be one less lawyer to deride, one less lawyer to make the brunt of jokes, one less lawyer to stand before a jury and argue a client's innocence ... and one less Winstead to bring more Winsteads into a world so fraught with demagoguery, violence, and hate. These powers had reached out and taken my brother before I could know him.

I felt my father's strong arm pull me toward my mother and him. My tears were released in the comfort of Father's embrace. From the dark oak-framed entryway into the parlor, Bill watched, silent and saddened.

7

It was August before Addison came home to Gadsden, to the quiet of Mount Hope Cemetery. He would rest in the grassy plain with other Gadsden sons who left with high hopes, dreaming of glory and a mission to preserve a way of life each cherished. Each lost his life in that effort, veterans of the Civil War, the Indian wars, the Spanish-American conflict, World War I, and now this war.

Friends and neighbors, some we knew only slightly, were joined by many others in Gadsden who just wanted to tell my parents how appreciative they were of my brother's courage and how sad they were he was lost to them. As the casket holding the remains of their oldest child was lowered into the earth, my parents gripped each other tightly. I saw my father cry as he held my mother protectively. Tears cascaded down my own cheeks unchecked.

"The Lord is my shepherd, I shall not want. He maketh me to lie down in green pastures..." The minister's baritone voice slowly recited the familiar passage, resonantly audible above my mother's sobs, which wracked her small frame as she clung to my father.

"Yea, though I walk through the valley of the shadow of death, I will fear no evil …" The minister's voice trailed off for me again, dimmed by thoughts of my brother, so vivid in my mind, standing there, towering above me, the baseball bat firmly in his hands, showing me how to hold it, how to swing it, how to connect with a baseball being thrown by his best friend, Dalton Moore.

Dalton stood near my parents, his own grief restrained within, his head lowered to mask his sorrow. When the rifle volleys cracked in the distance, he saluted smartly, tears finally freed, sliding down the freckled cheeks that made him stand out as one of Dwight Elementary School's legendary playground warriors who meted out quick revenge for derisive teasing about his red hair.

He left that evening, returning to Fort Polk in Louisiana. When he came home again, it would be to this same cemetery, to lie close to the friend to whom he was saying good-bye this day—Dalton would be one of the early casualties of Utah Beach in a distant place called Normandy.

By summer's end I would suffer another loss, which for me was just as grievous. Sylvia Barnes left Gadsden. Bubba Barnes had died in a drunken brawl, stabbed by a soldier on leave, who took offense to Bubba's denigrating remarks about those in uniform. After police took statements from the soldier and other witnesses, no charges were filed. "Self-defense" determined the coroner's jury.

At the funeral, Sylvia's eye was still discolored from Bubba's latest assault just a week before his death. She had called me after that beating, her voice choking with sobs. I held her in my arms that afternoon, begging her to leave him. She answered with silence and kissed away my protestations, dismissing my concerns with a passion that enveloped us both, temporarily banishing my fears for her safety at the hands of her husband.

Sylvia's mother and Bubba's father were the only persons who saw him lowered to his final resting place. There were no tears shed for Bubba, even by those closest to him. The day after Bubba's funeral, I saw Sylvia talking to Ollie Greenwell, a man I knew was an attorney. My hands thrust in my pockets, I kept walking past the dry cleaners, where a wilting funeral wreath still hung on the door. I felt an irrational anger at not being able to see this person who caused my every waking hour to be filled with longing for her.

Two weeks later, I learned the reason for the visit with the attorney. Sylvia announced that she had sold the dry cleaners and would be leaving Gadsden. There was no emotion in her voice; it was flat. When I asked her where she was moving, she only said somewhere far from Gadsden. That was when I asked her to marry me. She did not reply. Sylvia's face remained immobile. Only her eyes replied—with tears. She put her arms around my neck, burying her face against my chest, the sobs tearing through her and me. I apologized for making her sad. I wanted only to make her happy, and I would. Brash words flooded out of me: my plans for the future—to leave school, get a job, go to college at night. I'd care for her, buy her a home, make her happy. It was several minutes before I felt her body stilled, the heaving sobs quieted.

"I love you, Johnny. More than you will ever know. But you're too young," she said softly, tears spilling down her cheeks again. "Your whole future is ahead of you. Finish high school now. Then go to college. If we were married, I would only encumber you." She clasped my face in her hands. "Find someone to love as much as I love you. Be happy, Johnny. You're the only happiness I've ever known." She withdrew her hands and turned away from my embrace. "Go, Johnny. Go now. I've got a lot to do."

"Not 'til you tell me where you are going," I demanded sharply. "I won't leave until you do." My voice was emphatic, angry. I resented her dismissing me like an intrusive schoolboy.

"I love you, Johnny. Good-bye." The last word was barely a whisper.

She turned and went behind the white curtain, disappearing into the darkened interior of the back room, leaving behind only the lingering whiff of the fragrance she always wore. It floated on my senses like a petal detached from its mother plant, teasing me for a moment and then evaporating. She was gone and so was the fragrance of her. I turned and walked out.

Sleep brought no solace that night, and I awoke feeling tired and troubled. Mother noticed but discreetly said nothing, lingering a little longer with her good-morning kiss as if to say, I'm here if you want to talk. I didn't.

I stopped in front of Ross Dry Cleaners and stood staring at the locked front door. The sign inside the door's window read, simply, "Closed." Sylvia had left without saying where she was going.

It was excessively hot that late August day, but I felt a cold wave of despair flood over me. I had lost her, lost her to an unknown place, maybe to some unknown man. Had she run off with someone else and not had the courage to tell me? Anger displaced my despair. That was it. She had run off with another man. *If she could cheat on her husband, she could cheat on me,* I thought scornfully. I wanted a reason for anger, to nullify my hurt.

Suddenly, I hated my age, my youth, the lack of control over my life. If I were eighteen, I could marry Sylvia without my parents' permission. She said she loved me. Why did she leave without me? There was no answer, only an emptiness that overwhelmed me and felt like a blow to the gut.

Football became my passion. It dominated my every waking

hour. I ran harder, threw longer, took tougher hits, and was never ready to quit when Coach Gordon called an end to practice. On Friday nights, a good count of Gadsden was in the stands, around the end zones and lining the fences, to watch a team that would march to a second consecutive state championship. Bill Deems was my target on almost every pass, and we passed a lot. That brought the Gadsden Rebels and me statewide attention.

On the final home game of the season, the evening was perfect—a clear fall sky glistening with stars, a slivered moon, and a temperature of fifty-five degrees. When we ran onto the field, the Gadsden faithful exploded in cheers. I looked to be sure my parents were in their usual seats in the stands. Next to them sat a man I recognized instantly from his picture in the *Gadsden Times*: Frank Thomas, the head football coach at the University of Alabama. Bill had already spotted Thomas when I gestured toward my parents. This could be his night, our night, to win a free ride to the University of Alabama. It was a heady feeling, being watched by the man who could determine our future.

We played it to the hilt. I hit Bill for four touchdowns and 230 yards in the air, not to mention the hundred-plus yards we picked up through the middle of the line with Jimmy Joe Jeffrey, our fullback, and end-around runs by halfback Billy Pierce.

The fall of 1943 was etched in the minds of Gadsden; it would be the year with which subsequent good seasons would be measured and compared over steaming cups of coffee at the Palace Cafe and Stevens Drugstore.

The cheers failed to penetrate the silence within. I shut out my pain by shutting out those around me—Bill, my mother, and even my father, when he made an awkward attempt to reach me beyond his usual hello, good-bye, and how-is-school inquiry.

It was Ann to whom I finally turned one tortured night, as we sat in her car with the top down, looking out on Noccalula Falls above Black Creek, the creek across which Gadsden's most famous resident, Emma Samson, led Confederate troops to escape pursuing Yankees.

It was the first Ann knew of my relationship with Sylvia. She listened in silence. When I finished, she pulled me to her, laying my head in her lap, and stroked my hair. It was enough. Telling her was cathartic but exhausting. I lay in her lap a long time, quiet, safe in her friendship, my pain swabbed by her silent empathy. At that moment in our young lives, I felt a love—a different kind of love—as deep for gentle, funny, teasing Ann as still burned in me for Sylvia.

The following spring, I took Ann to the prom—me in my father's hand-me-down suit, she in a blue taffeta gown that complemented her tiny waist and allowed a peek of cleavage above the gathered net on the bodice. The layers of scratchy net which made up the long shirt made dancing difficult, but Ann looked beautiful. That night we made love.

Ann knew I did not love her in the way I professed to love Sylvia, but she said that I should be her first, to be gentle, never to speak of it to anyone, especially Bill, and never to ask her again. She gave no reason, but it was a pact I made and a pact I would keep for many years.

The day school was dismissed for the summer vacation, I arrived home to find my mother dissolved in tears on the parlor couch, her arms wrapped around one of the overstuffed pillows. She shielded her face from me and braced her shoulders from the heavy sobs that shook the rest of her body.

The telegram lay on the coffee table. My brother, Collier, had been wounded somewhere in the South Pacific and was being sent home aboard a hospital ship that was to dock in San Francisco in about a week. There was no mention of his condition or the extent of his injuries. There was a telephone number to call and a contact person.

I held my sobbing mother tightly, trying by force of my love to quell the pain that heaved within her, when my sister, Sarah, arrived home unexpectedly early from her sophomore year at Auburn University. Her emerald eyes stared uncomprehendingly at the scene she'd rushed into so exuberantly, shouting, "Mama! I'm home!"

It took only a moment before a look of sheer horror spread across the milky beauty of her porcelain face. Her light brown hair cascaded, mostly untamed, to her shoulders in a mix of waves and curls. Her relief was visible on learning Collier was alive, and she joined her arms with mine around our mother. We held Mother for many minutes until the grief, the fear, the pain of possibly losing another of her precious offspring was spent.

My father arrived home by train two days later from Washington DC, haggard, his face aged. We were all there to meet him. Not a demonstrative man by nature, he welcomed each of us into his arms and held us longer than I could ever remember, as if by letting go, he would lose us as well.

That evening, as my mother and sister cleared the dishes from the dining room table, Father began making plans to travel to California to be with his second born. He spoke quietly yet firmly. He would go. Mother would stay in Gadsden. The trip, he said, would be too tiring for her. He, on the other hand, was used to traveling. And there was the possibility that he could pull strings and catch a ride on an army transport plane.

My mother listened, unresponsive, as he outlined plans for the trip to California, a trip made longer by the wartime restrictions on civilian travel. Then she spoke. There was no mistaking her tone. She was going with him. Better still, he could remain in Gadsden, continue his frequent and necessary trips to Washington, and I would accompany her.

Father always made major decisions in our family, sometimes consulting my mother but often not. His word was the authority and final. Not on this night in June. In the days and weeks ahead, I learned my mother's quiet demeanor masked a grit that even my father could not back down.

Six days later, our wartime priority tickets in hand, Mother and I were ready to board the L&N train that would take us on the first leg of the long journey to California.

8

It was June 30, but the radio still crackled with reports of the Allied invasion of France that had begun June 7. There was little detail in those reports, but somehow the voice of Edward R. Murrow brought assurance that the long-anticipated invasion was succeeding. His broadcasts were reinforced by Movietone newsreels visually attesting to the heroic effort being made to reclaim the heart of Europe.

Several Gadsden sons would be among the casualties on Omaha Beach, Utah Beach, and other stretches of French soil won back by their last measure of courage. Addison's best friend, Dalton Moore, was among them.

On that sultry June morning, we stood on the wood platform of the Gadsden train station. Mother was surrounded by her husband and children, her friends and neighbors, some of whom had known her throughout her life in Gadsden, where she had lived since birth. Most were members of First Baptist Church, where she had been the organist for as long as they could remember. My mother was an accomplished musician even before she was a teenager, and it was the church congregation each Sunday that heard the fruits of her long hours of practice. It was a talent tithed to her church throughout my growing up years and beyond.

The morning sun highlighted the gray sprinkled in her dark brown hair, pulled back in a familiar bun she had worn every day of her adult life and loosened only at night in the privacy of my parent's bedroom. Within months, the brown would all but disappear.

She was embraced by each church member who had come, as well as by friends and her closest neighbors, JB and Maudie Stevens, whom she would miss most.

Doc Cunningham and Laureen were there, the physician holding my mother in a long embrace, so long that I stole a glance at my father and then at Laureen. Both seemed unconcerned by the show of affection. Mother had known this man since her school days when, with the awkward stealth of a ten-year-old, the future physician had stolen a first kiss behind the two-story school from the comely girl on whom he'd fastened his attention. Several years later, he stood in the front parlor of her parents' home when Ada McPherson exchanged wedding vows with Edward Winstead. Later, the doctor would deliver Ada's five children and stand just behind her as she buried the tiny girl who lived only hours, cementing a friendship that endured and grew in respect and affection as both matured.

When he finally released my mother, Doc grasped my hand long and firmly, then pulled me his into his arms in a bear-like hold. "You take good care of this little woman, son. We'll miss you both. And bring that brother of yours back all healed. I've got enough to do, keeping the rest of Gadsden healthy."

His laugh was hearty, but the frown that narrowed his brow revealed a deep concern for us as we traveled across the country in wartime. Seats on passenger trains were subject to the whims of troop movements. He expected the hot, dusty cars of the swaying coaches to take their toll on Mother's energy and patience. She accepted the hardship of travel without complaint and with her normal quiet forbearance. Ada McPherson Winstead was a woman of strong resolve, who would see her second son safely back to his home in Alabama.

My father was the last to embrace her. Holding her against his chest, he lifted her chin with one hand and gently kissed her offered lips. He pushed a stray strand of hair back from the face that looked up adoringly at him. She seemed so small, so frail, clutched against my father, who stood a head taller. They were quiet people by nature and upbringing. I had never seen my father embrace Mother like this, lifting her off her feet to bring her level with his face, kissing her long and passionately. Children seldom ascribe romance or passion to their parents. I did on that day and knew that the love they displayed to all of us would last long after the physical passion cooled.

Back on her feet, my mother became aware again of her friends and neighbors and children. A scarlet blush flooded her face, which she lowered shyly. But the glance she shot my father as she stepped aboard the train telegraphed she had no regrets for this unaccustomed display. Father was still in view, waving to us as the huge train sluggishly gained speed and rounded the curve at Bentley Street, eclipsing him and the others. My mother's face remained pressed against the window for several minutes. When she turned to me again, tears shimmered in her crystal blue eyes.

Beside my father stood Ann McClelland, my friend and soul mate, waving to me, her eyes misted with tears. We had talked long into the night, mostly about Brent Houghton, the egghead football player she had started dating that summer. Houghton came from moneyed stock, an old-line Gadsden family that traced its pedigree to the antebellum plantation era. They had a social status Ann admitted she coveted, almost as much as Houghton coveted her. She wanted advice on how to fend off his persistent sexual advances without diminishing his interest.

Houghton was a dilettante, she explained, with whom she could share her love of literature and art. I saw his interest in her as solely libidinous. I kept that thought to myself and advised her to be candid with Houghton, to tell him how she felt and that he must respect her feelings if their relationship was to continue. That advice proved the undoing of the relationship, as I would learn on my return.

The Alabama landscape changed throughout the day as the train sped past cotton fields dotted with sharecropper shacks, the weathered roofs of which were draped with an almost ethereal glimmering hood of sunlight in the afternoon heat. That night we slept in cramped but welcome hanging cots, lulled to sleep by the rhythmic swaying of the Pullman coach.

By morning we were in Memphis. There we changed trains and had time for a hot meal in the station's only restaurant. It was crowded with military in an array of uniforms, most likely headed west, many to embark for the Pacific theater, where the fighting now raged, island by island. The soldiers, sailors, and Marines were carefree, chatting and laughing, the fears and strains of war not yet written on faces little older than mine.

I could hardly hear the harried waitress when she demanded our order. Ten minutes later, two eggs, swimming in grease beside two slices of bacon, were dropped unceremoniously in front of us, followed by a communal plate of burned toast that had been salvaged by scrapping off some of the black. It was our first full meal in nearly a day, and we were too hungry to complain.

When we boarded our train amid the clamor on the platform,

it was onto a Santa Fe, the line that would take us the rest of the long journey to San Francisco. We remained on the same train for the duration of the trip, stopping in Tulsa, Oklahoma City, and Albuquerque, and then northwest across the breathtakingly beautiful San Mateo Mountains.

I had only read about the fabled West. It raced by our window, a changing kaleidoscope of thickly forested mountains, deserts, and high plateaus, rising from the sparse grasslands like richly painted pottery. The next evening we walked as far as we could to the front of the train to watch a spectacular sunset, the sun so large in the sky, as it sank below the horizon we felt we could reach out and touch it.

On the fifth day, a distant view of the Golden Gate Bridge, still eerily draped in the remnants of thick morning fog that shrouded the Bay City earlier, confirmed our arrival in San Francisco at mid-morning.

Weary and sweaty, we descended into the din of sprawling Union Station, our ears assailed by the impatient hollering of porters directing passengers on and off the dozen or more trains. Our senses were assaulted with the smell of hundreds of human beings, mixed with diesel smoke from engines idling along the station's many platforms.

I held Mother's arm firmly as she descended the metal stairs placed at our train car. The distracted porter wished us an absent-minded good-bye as his sleeve was tugged by a woman wrapped in a vast fur coat, demanding to know if this was car number twelve. It was not.

At the earlier stops, we had seen soldiers and sailors, in small groups or individually, on the platforms. But here there were whole platoons of forty or more men moving to the directions of a barking officer. It was apparent from the numbers and haste of the troops that this was a major hub for military travel.

We waited more than an hour before being hustled aboard a sad-looking bus that was to ferry us to the army hospital between San Francisco and Palo Alto. Two hours later we were deposited at the barracks reserved for relatives of the wounded being cared for at the hospital. Neither my mother nor I had ever been beyond Birmingham. Now we were at the other end of the country, two-thousand miles from Gadsden, wanting nothing more than a hot bath, a hot meal, and for my brother to be well.

The showers were in restrooms marked for males or females at the end of the dingy hall. Our room was cramped; its only furnishings were two military cots with the mattresses rolled up, and a sheet, blanket, and pillow beside each. Our suitcases had to be stowed under the cots. There were wooden pegs on the wall above each cot to hang clothes. Primitive, yes, but it brought no complaint from Mother. She and I showered quickly in our appointed baths. Hers had been converted so hurriedly to accommodate women that urinals remained in the restroom.

The hospital was a half-mile walk from the family barracks along a lane lined with stately ponderosa pines that shaded our approach to the six-story hospital. Its wings reached out in four directions, like oblong wooden arms from the center building. The walk appeared to invigorate Mother, who spoke little as we traversed the wide, grassy mall from the street to the front entrance of the drab gray-painted military hospital. She was wearing a favorite floral chintz dress, which she had sewn herself especially for Easter. It still showed the wrinkles from being too long in a suitcase, but it slimmed her figure that was growing thicker in middle age, and it seemed to make her step sprightlier as she hurried me up the front steps of the hospital.

Inside, a receptionist, who apparently doubled as a telephone operator, directed us to ward five on the third floor, hollering a warming that visitors must take the stairs, as the lone elevator was reserved for staff and patients.

Mother was a little breathless from the steep flights of stairs and panted beside me as I inquired of a nurse in a stiffly starched white cap, "Which way to the bed of Lieutenant Collier Winstead?"

"I'm sorry," she said politely, "but Lieutenant Winstead cannot have visitors unless it's family."

"We are his family," Mother replied evenly. "I'm his mother and this is his brother, John."

The nurse seemed unsure for a moment. "Please wait here, and I'll get the doctor on duty. He'll have to give the approval for you to visit Lieutenant Winstead."

With that, she departed down the hallway and through a glassed double-doorway.

What she said had a disquieting effect on Mother, who stood staring at the double-doorway, her cheeks still flushed from the brisk walk and subsequent trek up three flights of stairs. As the minutes passed, the color slowly drained from her face. I felt a sudden wrench in my gut. Something was wrong. Something more than we had been informed in the telegram. It seemed an interminable ten minutes before the nurse returned with an older man, who clearly was in need of a haircut. He had a stethoscope wrapped scarf-like around his neck.

"I'm Dr. Wilson," he said, extending his hand to my mother and then to me. "I understand you're here to see Lieutenant Winstead."

"Yes, Doctor, he's my son." My mother's voice was steady, but the hand she placed in mine was trembling.

"Have you come far?" the doctor asked, his face kindly.

"Yes. From Gadsden, Alabama."

The doctor's face betrayed his surprise at the distance, but he replied simply, "Is your son expecting you?"

"No."

"Are you aware of his injuries?" the doctor asked as he eyed my mother intently.

"Only that they were very serious, and he was in critical condition at the time we left for San Francisco."

"You will be relieved to know, Mrs. Winstead, that your son is much improved. He still faces a long recuperation. I think you should know …" The doctors voice trailed off, and he looked down, uncertain how to continue. Then he looked again into my mother's face. What he saw appeared to reassure him and he said softly, "Come with me."

The long hallway led through glass doors labeled "Ward Five." The doctor walked silently ahead of us and through the double doors to a doorway halfway down the long wing. He paused to hold the door open while we stepped inside a spacious room with four beds.

"Your son is in the last bed, Mrs. Winstead. I'll be just down the hall if you need me."

"Thank you, Doctor," Mother answered hesitantly, turning toward the bed the physician had indicated. The bed was difficult to see in the dim light, the remnants of late afternoon sunlight coming through a west-facing window. Mother was still gripping my hand as we approached the bed.

"Collier, it's Mom. We've come to be with you, son, and take you home."

My brother turned his head toward us, and tears slowly formed two pools of agony in his stricken eyes. It was at that instant my mother gasped. She was seeing what I was now seeing—the white sheet covering the flat mattress where there should have been a leg.

9

It was a rare more temperate day when our Army Air Corps transport plane landed bumpily on the grassy lane that served as Gadsden's airport. A fine mist was falling, bringing welcome moderation to the normally sultry temperatures that marked late July in Alabama. The landing strip led to a Quonset hangar where a small group of people huddled under a steel awning awaiting our arrival. My father, his face pale and grim, began walking toward the plane, sheltered under an umbrella held by JB Stevens.

It was Father who arranged the flight from California, calling on his wartime connections—connections he seldom spoke of but which we learned in the coming months went to the highest offices in the War Department. While my father was too old to serve in uniform on the front lines of the war, at home his efforts were tireless in helping supply front-line troops with the hardware needed to win.

The Gadsden steel mill already had been lauded on several occasions for its output of steel, basic to building the munitions of war. The American industrialist recruited by President Roosevelt to head the War Resources Board, Edward R. Stettinius, Jr., came personally to thank the Gadsden workers—and was treated to one of my mother's best Southern culinary efforts. Her cooking was a manifestation of Southern hospitality at its finest.

Stettinius had been followed by the Secretary of War Henry L. Stimson, a rare Republican in the Democrat cabinet of Franklin Roosevelt but a patriot who put country well ahead of politics. He also tasted my mother's now famous Southern-fried cooking, and he left our home with a copy of her prized recipe for cheese grits to present to Mrs. Stimson. These were men with whom my father had frequent contact, which helped bring his wounded son home to Gadsden aboard the relative comfort of a plane. An army corpsman accompanied us to help care for Collier, who spent most of the long trip strapped to a cot in a drug-induced sleep. The pain in the remaining stump of his leg was still agonizing.

Mother looked pale and weary as she stepped down from the small plane into Father's outstretched arms. He wrapped her in a prolonged hug. I held JB's umbrella over both of them against the persistent misty rain that ran down my forehead, sending droplets lightly splashing onto my nose.

We stood in a small group as the corpsman gripped my brother under his armpits and lowered him into the uplifted arms of the pilot, who helped Collier position the wooden crutches under his arms. Collier stood still, leaning on the crutches, looking down at the grassy tarmac. This was not the homecoming he'd envisioned when he left Gadsden two years earlier in such high spirits, anticipating the adventure ahead.

"It's good to have you home, son." Father's voice betrayed the raw emotion he tried vainly to hold inside him. Collier looked up with anguished eyes as Father hugged him warmly. Long repressed tears spilled out, his first indication of the bitterness and hurt that he was returning home an amputee. Mother could only watch with her hands clutched to her mouth. She had spent every day at Collier's bedside during our stay in California, beginning that first afternoon, reluctantly leaving each evening at lights out and returning each morning before breakfast.

As I turned away before the scene evoked my own tears, I spotted Bill Deems standing beside Doc Cunningham under the canopy, his face mirroring the sadness of this homecoming.

Collier had always been the most outgoing of my siblings, his humor a hedge against his penchant for practical jokes that had been a constant source of irritation to my father. It was Collier who stretched curfews, sneaking in well after midnight by climbing the wood trellis that supported Father's pampered roses and wisteria. The trellis was conveniently located just below the window of the bedroom Collier shared with Addison. I could often hear my brothers whispering far into the early morning hours, sharing stories of adventures and sexual escapades. Both of them had many to recount. They reveled in the occasional discovery that they had shared the same girl.

High-spirited was the kindly term that friends used to describe my older brothers. Teachers and some neighbors, victimized by their fabled pranks, used terms not so endearing.

It was a different Collier who returned home this day, nodding unsmilingly to Bill's greeting and limply shaking Bill's outstretched hand. I was glad to see Bill, admitting to myself, somewhat guiltily, that I'd missed him more than I'd missed Father. A wide grin was etched across his face as we shook hands, and it was apparent he'd missed me as well.

The wide latticed porch of our home circled from the front to around the south side, and it was teeming with people who'd gathered to welcome Collier home. Some waved their greeting as he hobbled on the crutches up the front walk. Hands reached out to pat his shoulder, and several arms steadied him as he struggled up the four steps leading to the porch.

Former high school classmates, including the girl who had been his prom sweetheart and other girls he had dated, came up to shake hands. Some kissed him shyly on the cheek. Collier seemed briefly cheered by the warm greetings and the numbers of friends there to welcome him back to Gadsden.

Standing in the shadow of the big magnolia tree shading the porch was Jeb Thomas and his wife, Millie, who was as talkative as Jeb was quiet. She had also worked for my family for years, helping Mother with housecleaning and occasionally cooking. Collier spotted them and went to the side of the porch, a smile flickering for an instant across his face.

"Hey, Jeb, Millie, good to see you."

"Welcome home, Misser Collier," Jeb called from under the tree. Millie's plump face beamed a warm smile at Collier as she waved her greeting.

"Hey, Millie, I want more than a smile. You got to come up here and give this old broken warrior a hug."

For the first time that day, a smile lit up Collier's face as Millie came up on the porch to hug the "warrior" she had diapered as a baby. "I'm glad you're home, young'un. On the stove in the kitchen you'll find some of the best turnip greens you ever put 'tween those lips." Millie chuckled as she wrapped her plump arms around Collier, squeezing lovingly. She then ambled off the porch to stand by her husband, away from the swarm of white faces that again surrounded Collier, all seeming to want his attention at once.

The friendly mobbing was interrupted by a squeal of delight just as the front screen door burst open and Sarah came flying out, her curly hair askew, her pretty face a mirror of my mother at that age, alight with smiling welcome. Her outburst had been enough to part the crowd around Collier. Our sister took him in her slender arms and, while still holding onto him possessively, she waved a greeting to me as I stood beside Bill, watching the homecoming.

Collier was finally released from her imprisoning hug when she spotted Mother and rushed toward her. Sarah had passed up summer school and the chance to earn additional credits to stay home and take mother's place while we were in California. She fixed meals for Father, did the wash, and helped Millie clean house. Sarah wore her new responsibilities regally, no matter how menial the challenge.

By evening, Collier was too exhausted, physically and emotionally, to eat Millie's greens or any of the tasty foods she and Sarah had been preparing since early morning for the homecoming. He went to bed in a spare room just off the parlor that Sarah and Millie had refitted as a bedroom, so that Collier wouldn't have to climb the stairs to his old bedroom on the second floor. But the next evening, Collier insisted on returning to his own room, despite the painful climb, so that he could sleep surrounded by memories of Addison, their football-playing days, high school sweethearts, and a life he would never know again. That room became his retreat from his family and the reality he faced. A month after his return, Collier was taken by an army ambulance to a hospital in Birmingham to be fitted for a prosthetic leg and to learn how to walk without crutches during his convalescence there.

In the fall, Collier entered the University of Alabama–Birmingham to complete a degree in business administration. The optimism and exuberance that marked his personality from earliest childhood slowly began to triumph over the loss of his leg and to eclipse the scars of war.

Only the loss of Addison would continue to bring him pain. I loved Collier, but I knew I could never replace Addison, who seemed man-sized and remote to me from my earliest recollections of him. Bill Deems would be for me what Addison had been for Collier, both brother and best friend.

On the night of the homecoming, Bill and I lay awake talking, mostly about the trip to bring Collier back and what had happened in Gadsden during my absence. We promised to start making up for some of our lost time together by cruising McEwen's Drive-in the following evening.

It was only after Bill drifted off to sleep in the adjacent bed, and I lay on my back with my arms folded under my head, waiting for sleep to overtake me, that I thought of Ann. I wondered why she had not been at the airfield to meet me. It was my last thought before sleep erased her from my thoughts.

10

It was the weekend before Bill and I made it to McEwen's Drive-in. Between us we had just over a dollar, enough to buy ourselves and our dates a hamburger, fries, and a small Coke.

While I was in California, Bill had begun dating Lila Dillingham, the daughter of Gadsden's much feared police chief. Some of Bill's shyness in asking Lila out was overcome when his mother, who never learned to drive, gave him an old A-model Ford that had been gathering dust in the Deems' garage since Bill's father left to work in Louisiana. It was not the most stylish ride, but it beat walking and increased our visibility among the eligible females.

I lucked out when I called Betty Lou Jarvis on the telephone and found her with a rare Saturday night free. She was nestled comfortably in the crook of my arm as we swung into McEwen's. Betty Lou was one of those girls you could depend on having a good time with, just not the kind of good time you told your mother about and not the kind of girl you took home to meet your parents. She dyed her hair blonde, which was somewhat scandalous for a teenager.

Those dyed locks framed a pretty face with large brown eyes and a permanently provocative expression. Her white blouse was open just far enough to reveal a deep canyon between her buxom mounds. I was looking forward to more than a peek.

Bill circled the drive-in twice before we settled on a parking spot, waving to other teens we knew and acknowledging greetings from friends and schoolmates I had seen little of that summer. Betty Lou drew wolf whistles and knowing looks of approval from some of the boys, who no doubt had enjoyed her charms as well—or at least wished they could.

A homely waitress with a too-hurried, too-overworked frown on her face locked the food tray in place and took our money without comment, frowning deeper when she realized there was no tip.

I was kissing Betty Lou, and we were hunkered down in the backseat where I could feel the swell of her generous breasts against my chest. I was quickly losing my appetite for food. After the tray was latched to the driver's side door, Betty Lou whispered, "Let's come up for air," and she pushed me gently away in favor of her hamburger, fries, and Coke. She flashed another provocative grin that promised more and better things to come, after food.

Lila had moved closer to Bill during the time my attention was diverted from the front seat, and now she snuggled up next to him as they ate. This could indeed be a fortuitous night for both of us. Lila Dillingham, however, was not an easy mark like Betty Lou. She was pretty, petite, soft-spoken and obviously smitten with Bill. It was the first time Bill had had a steady girlfriend, and he appeared equally smitten with Lila.

I finished my food and was getting ready to satisfy my other appetites by pulling Betty Lou down in the backseat, while she giggled a mock struggle against my aggression, when I spotted Ann

McClelland in a car across from us. She was cuddled close to Brent Houghton, the progeny of a long line of Houghtons who traced their Alabama pedigree for anyone who would listen. Somehow, the Houghtons had maintained their land and their money through Reconstruction, when many of Gadsden's other patrician families were living in genteel poverty, stripped of their land and sources of income by greedy carpetbaggers.

My mother's grandparents suffered that fate and never financially recovered. Father's grandfather survived Reconstruction in the rural area around Gadsden, managing to eke out a living until prosperity returned to the landed gentry. Unfortunately, father would lose his share of the family wealth to a conniving stepfather, who lavished most of the proceeds of my grandmother's estate on his own three children, excluding my father entirely. Father never talked about it, at least to me, but he never forgave his mother for the loss of what he considered his birthright, despite Grandmother's establishing generous trust funds for me and my siblings.

Houghton's arms were wrapped possessively around Ann, who was sipping from a paper cup between kisses. She did not acknowledge my wave. I had not heard from Ann since my return. My calls to her home had not been returned.

Betty Lou nudged me impatiently. "What's so interesting over there?" she whined, taking my face in her hands and forcing my attention back to her.

"Nothing," I lied.

But at that moment I had to see Ann, to see what was wrong and learn why she was not returning my phone calls and why she hadn't contacted me.

"I'll be right back, okay?" I did not wait for her reply; I jumped out the back door, ignoring Betty Lou's petulant look.

Ann saw me first, then Houghton. I could smell the liquor even before I reached the open window of the chrome-plated Dodge coupe. Ann's head dropped slowly, her eyes avoiding mine. Houghton's arm remained tightly around her shoulders, the defiant look he leveled at me belying the off-handed greeting.

"Hey, Winstead, I heard you were back. Sorry about your brother." Houghton's eyes were glazed but steady. He could hide his drinking well, except for the telltale smell.

"Thanks." I looked past Houghton at Ann's downcast head. She refused to look at me, fixing her eyes on the paper cup she gripped, twirling the straw around absently with a finger. "Hi, Ann." There was no response. "Ann, you all right?" I asked imploringly. Still no response. "Ann." Something in my demanding tone must have struck a chord. It was apparent when she looked at me that she had been drinking. There was more than soft drink in the paper cup she held.

"She's fine, Winstead." My attention shifted to Houghton. "We're just having a good time. How about you? I see you're with Betty Lou. She's a great lay."

It was not Houghton's words that triggered my anger as much as his supercilious tone. I opened the front door of the car and pulled him out roughly. He was nearly my size, but the anger that tore through my gut made him no match for me, and he knew it. He played football, his only claim to school involvement, and he had a reputation as a bully. His money and casual good looks were the lightning rods that attracted girls. He seemed never to lack for dates. With little prodding, he would share his sexual exploits with any male who would listen.

While Houghton stood unsteadily against the car, I reached my hand in to Ann.

"Come on, Ann. I'm going to take you home."

"No, not like this." Her voice was little more than a whisper.

"Come on, Ann," I coaxed soothingly. "We'll go to my house. You can stay there tonight and your dad will never know. I'll have Mom call and tell him. Come on. Let's get you out of here."

"What about Betty Lou? And Bill?" Even if her words were slightly slurred, it was evident she had noticed us despite not acknowledging my wave.

"Bill can take Betty Lou home."

I reached out my hand to her across the front seat. Ann hesitated only a moment before I felt her small hand grip mine. Setting the paper cup on the dashboard, she slid toward me and out of the car, gripping the open door to steady herself. She was drunk. Nausea overcame her attempt to stand upright, and much of the liquor her unaccustomed system had taken in came wrenching out on the drive-in's pavement. All I could do was hold her by the shoulders until the shudders wracking her body had stilled. Houghton watched, expressionless, offering no help.

I took Ann's arm to steer her toward Bill's car, and Bill was there to support her other arm. Even Betty Lou offered a concerned hand to help Ann into the backseat of the car.

"I'll ride up front with Bill and Lila," Betty Lou offered.

"Thank you."

I held Ann in my arms as she sobbed and mumbled during the short ride to my home. I was wondering what I would say to my parents. On seeing Ann in the hallway as we walked into the house, Father sized up the situation immediately. "Take Ann upstairs to the spare room, son. I'll get your mother."

Ann was sobbing uncontrollably when my mother came into the bedroom with a wet towel. She waved Bill and me away from the bed as she sat beside Ann, speaking soothingly to the distraught girl and patting her face with the damp towel. The sobbing eased, and Ann even managed a mumbled apology, an apology shushed by my mother who told her to try to sleep and that she would remain with her. Bill and I followed my father out of the room.

"I'll call her father. He needs to know where she is," Father offered, as he headed toward the telephone in the rounded nook in the main hallway. Ann's reason for being here, Father silently conveyed with a knowing look to Bill and me, was something that he would not share with Ann's parents.

Later, after Lila and Betty Lou had been taken home, I lay awake, listening to Bill's measured breathing and thinking of Ann— my friend, my confidant. What was so hurtful inside Ann that she would get drunk and allow herself to become sexually vulnerable with a pompous ass like Houghton?

Why had she not returned my phone calls? Why had she not been at the airfield to meet me?

The house was still. Only my father's rhythmic snoring from the far bedroom interrupted the quiet as I slipped into the bedroom where Ann was sleeping. To my surprise, she was awake.

"I'm glad you came," she said softly. "I need to talk with someone, and you're the only person I can tell."

"Tell what?" I whispered, slipping into the bed beside her and pulling the sheet up to my chest. I slid my arm under her head to pull her close to me.

"Johnny, I can't go back home."

"Why? You think your dad will find out about your drinking tonight? My dad didn't tell your parents when he called. They won't find out."

"That's not it, Johnny. It's a lot worse." Tears formed and slid down her cheeks. "He's been coming to my bedroom late at night, when everyone's asleep."

"Who?"

"My father."

It was as if the words did not register. My father. That's what she had just said. The vile implication of that two-word answer refused to penetrate my consciousness. Fathers don't come to their daughters' beds. Such things don't happen in the real world, only in books like *Kings Row*. Not in Gadsden. Not to my friend. Not to this frail girl whose stricken body began shaking with sobs beside me.

"I can't go home, ever again. I can't stay there and let him touch me again." Ann turned her face up to mine, her tear-swollen eyes now sober. "I will kill myself before I'll go back there."

I knew from the fierce resolve in her tone that she meant it.

11

Ann never went home again. Her maternal grandmother's home near Anniston became her refuge. My parents never discussed Ann's father's abuse. Incest was a crime, but it was seldom reported to police and certainly not in Ann's case. Very likely, a girl of sixteen who was as physically mature and attractive as Ann would have been blamed as much as her father. She bore the shame in silence.

I would see little of Ann for some time after that dreadful night. When I did, there was a sadness about her that slowly snuffed out the carefree spunkiness of the girl I cherished as a friend. Her spirit diminished like a candle burning down to the end of its wick before finally flickering out.

It was my father who went to pick up Ann's clothes, and I went with him. He was distant but firm when Hubert McClelland answered our persistent ringing of the cheerfully chiming doorbell. McClelland offered no greeting. He looked at each of us coldly, then demanded, "Where's Ann?"

"We've come to get her things, Mr. McClelland," my father

announced in a tone that silenced any rejoinder. "She is going to Anniston to stay with her grandmother. My wife and I will drive her there tomorrow. Would you please get her things?" My father's voice had been steady and insistent. He stood stark still.

I expected the bulky McClelland, who stood as tall as my father but was many pounds heavier, to burst through the screen door and knock Father flat. McClelland's dark frown masked his thoughts. He had to realize Father must know of his sexual encroachments on his oldest daughter. He must also have realized as he silently glared at Father through the screen door, that he could go to jail, be kicked out of his church, maybe lose his job. Even worse for a man like Hubert McClelland would be losing the respect of his neighbors who thought of him as one of Gadsden's leading citizens. In the end, he turned without a word and gruffly ordered his cowering wife to pack Ann's clothes and give them to us. That was the last time I was to see Hubert McClelland.

Ann sat silent on the trip to Anniston the next day. Father took off from work to drive her to her grandmother's home. In the back seat, mother tried to distract Ann's thoughts with small talk, but when it did little to cheer the despondent girl, she fell silent. I hurt deeply for Ann but could find no words to tell her how I felt. I wasn't sure my words would make any difference anyway.

The grandmother's home was in a part of old mainline Anniston on a street lined with similar homes—all big and fronted by wide porches, with well-kept lawns that contrasted with the unkempt appearance of the chipping paint. Genteel but poor would describe this part of town, and those adjectives fit Maribelle Hopkins to a tee. She smothered her oldest granddaughter in a welcoming hug, holding her protectively close as Ann dissolved in tears.

"There, there, my darlin' girl, it's all right now. Granny won't let anything happen to you here. You're safe as you can be." Maribelle Hopkins gently held Ann at arm's length while reaching for a handkerchief buried in the voluminous pockets of her crisply starched apron. "There, wipe those tears away and blow your nose, child." Her kindly gaze focused on us for the first time as she asked, "Won't you folks come in and visit awhile?"

"Thank you, Mrs. Hopkins, but we better be getting back to Gadsden before dark. It's kind of you to offer," Father said politely. "I would like you to meet my wife and son. My wife, Ada," he said, nodding at Mother. "And this is my son John."

Ann's grandmother held out her weathered hand, its knuckles knotted by age and arthritis, to shake hands with my mother, then me. Her firm grip attested to her grit and resolve, qualities she would need in the next few months. I wondered silently how the cowering, frightened woman who handed us a shopping bag and small suitcase stuffed with Ann's clothes could have come from stock like Maribelle Hopkins.

"I'm pleased to meet you, Miz Winstead, and you, too, young John. Ann's told me so much about your family, and I'm very grateful to you for taking Ann in."

"It was our pleasure, Mrs. Hopkins," Mother answered graciously. "Ann has been a part of our family for a long while. She's a wonderful girl." Mother smiled affectionately at Ann.

Maribelle Hopkins lavished a broad smile on me, and I knew in that moment that I would be welcomed as a friend to visit Ann any time.

There was an awkward silence before Father stepped forward and held his hand out to the older woman, whose large arm still clutched her granddaughter firmly.

"Good-bye, Mrs. Hopkins."

"Good-bye, Mr. Winstead, and God bless you."

My father patted Ann affectionately on the shoulder. "If you ever need anything, Ann, just write or call us any time."

He stepped back as Mother drew Ann in her arms and held her there for some time, as Ann's tears flowed again. I can see Mother to this day as she was then, her hair pulled back in its usual bun, hugging the sobbing girl, transmitting a love and affection that seemed to solve so much in our family's lives. I still envy my mother her endless capacity for love.

As Mother released Ann from her embrace, Ann turned to me and stood shyly waiting for me to say good-bye. In those brief, awkward moments of silence, I realized how much I would miss her, how much her friendship meant to me, and, in the flash of those moments, how much I would like to inflict revenge on the man who had violated her. I pulled her into my arms. She wept softly as I held her to me tightly. In a voice choked by tears she looked up at me and said, "I will miss you, Johnny. Please, always be my friend."

"Course I will; you can count on it. Bill, too. And if you ever need anything, Ann, I'll be there for you. Don't you ever forget it."

I kissed her lightly on the cheek. "Bye, Ann."

"Bye, John."

Not long after Ann left to live with her grandmother, her younger sister joined her in Anniston, followed shortly by her mother, Irene, who moved out of the house on Cadet Street that had been her home for more than twenty years. Irene took up residence in Anniston to care for her daughters and her aging mother. Hubert McClelland died a year after his wife left. None of his family attended his funeral. His death finally quieted the rampant speculation that had followed the exodus of his daughters and wife.

Ann bade Gadsden good-bye when she was sixteen. It would be several years before she returned.

Ann's departure left me feeling lonely and adrift. At night, as I lay listening to the stirring of the attic fan, thoughts of Sylvia would come back to me. My longing for her had never ceased, despite her disappearance. I would hear talk of her from time to time, and once Doc Cunningham said he saw Sylvia at Ollie Greenwell's office across from Stevens Drugstore. He surmised she was probably finalizing some legal hitch involving the sale of the dry cleaners. A handsome girl, the doctor called Sylvia—a high compliment from a practiced eye like Doc Cunningham.

Where was she now? Who was she with? Those questions continued to torment me.

12

Football practice distracted me from thoughts of Ann and even from thoughts of Sylvia. The burning heat of late August drained all my energies, leaving me exhausted when I went to bed, well before my usual time, with no resources left to long for Sylvia, even in my dreams.

I drove myself hard in the days before school started, much harder than coach Gordon demanded—so much so that even Chuck Gordon became concerned. He cornered me in the locker room late one afternoon after practice to counsel me on the need to excel but not at any price. I listened politely, as I had been taught to listen to adults when they spoke to me. I promised to back off a bit—a promise I had no resolve to keep.

The physical exhaustion was therapeutic. Even on Sunday, when there were no two-per-day football practices, I went to the school track to run five miles. In the mornings, I was out of bed and on the floor doing a hundred push-ups. The exhaustion dulled the emptiness inside me. Even Bill could not appeal to my common sense, engaging only my temper when he tried. My heated responses finally discouraged any further efforts by him.

It was JB Stevens who rescued me from myself. He was sitting in the stadium stands near the locker room tunnel, and he motioned to me to come over as I was walking off the field following practice. The sun was on its evening slide toward the horizon in the humid, early September sky.

"Hi, JB." I waved, leaping over the low rail and bounding up the steps toward him. "What brings you to football practice?"

"You. And checking out what kind of a team we'll field against Emma Sansom next week. You're looking good out there."

"Thanks."

A long pause followed my reply as JB stared at the bleachers across the field. Gadsden High School had the largest football stadium in that part of Alabama. Despite few people owning vehicles and war-imposed gasoline rationing, it was filled to its nearly five-thousand-seat capacity every Friday night by either Gadsden High fans or Emma Sansom fans. The two schools shared the big stadium.

Football was an event. The wild cheering took our minds off the war, now waged on two continents, half a world apart and far from our shores. After the games, the women from the USO sold war bonds outside the stadium, bringing us back to the harsh reality of that fall of 1944.

JB suddenly seemed to remember his reason for coming to watch football practice. He turned his attention back to me. "Your mom tells Maudie you're having a tough time dealing with Ann's leaving."

"Yeah, a little. But I'm okay. I kinda miss her, that's all." I was not sure how much JB knew of the reason for Ann's sudden departure to live with her grandmother. My answer came almost immediately.

"You didn't get her in a family way, did you?"

"No, sir. Nothing like that. She was just unhappy living at home. Her dad was real hard on her." I hoped the lie did not show on my face.

"I'm glad to hear that's all it was, son. I could tell the two of you were good friends."

"Yes, sir, just good friends."

"Well, my boy, you need a little excitement in your life, and I've got just the thing." He held a key out to me. "Take it, John. It's a key to a house I own out on Attalla Highway. Get yourself a girl and go there. It will do you good to enjoy some female companionship of the distracting variety." JB chuckled and winked conspiratorially. "I'll cover with your folks if you want to spend the night. A night with a fetching female does wonders for you when you're feeling down and out. It's the best prescription any day." He chuckled at his own words and gave me the inevitable slap on my back, just short of being hard enough to knock the breath out of me.

"I will need that key back at some point. And don't rattle to too many folks about having that key and where it came from. Doc Cunningham and I've used that house for a long time, and I'd hate for Maudie or Laureen to find out about our little secret. Wouldn't do either one of us any good with our womenfolk. You get my meaning?"

I did indeed get his meaning. "Don't worry, JB. I won't talk out of turn. I appreciate your letting me use the house."

The tall, jocular druggist walked toward the exit ramp and headed out of the stadium, leaving with a nonchalant wave. I had heard about the house on Attalla Highway and the rumors that the house was used for more than a regular domicile. Now I knew. I twirled the key around in my hand and decided maybe the good druggist was right. Betty Lou Jarvis might just be the right "medicine" to mitigate my morass.

Bill cheered the idea of a double date to the house on Attalla Highway—with separate bedrooms, of course. By Saturday night, all was set. We picked up Betty Lou first, then Lila. It was to prove an eventful night.

I was driving Father's big Dodge. It had roomier seats than Bill's old coupe, but the extra room was superfluous. The two girls were snuggled as close as they could be to us as we drove down tree-lined Forrest Street, named for the hero of my youth, General Nathan Bedford Forrest, that most dashing of Confederate cavalrymen.

I turned to kiss Betty Lou, whose head rested on my shoulder with her face turned conveniently up toward mine. Even with one eye partially on the road ahead, I did not see Homer Steiner until it was too late. He was crossing the wide street at an angle, carrying a bag of groceries from the corner market. The left front part of the car struck him, sending the rotund man sailing several feet to land on the grassy edge of the street, the bag of groceries scattering helter-skelter around him.

My whole body froze, and only instinct pushed my foot down on the brake. Bill's shouted warning had come too late. Homer Steiner's round body lay prone on the grassy bed where he'd landed. Bill jumped out of the car and raced over to the dazed man.

The squeal of the brakes and the shouting roused several neighbors from their dinner tables and newspapers and out to their front porches. The two girls were both looking back in horror. Lila started sobbing loudly in the back seat.

I sat with my hands still gripping the steering wheel, paralyzed by the fear of what I had done. Then I heard what sounded like the roar of a giant bear—it was Homer Steiner, bellowing back to life amid the disarray on the lawn. It was not a pretty sound. What followed were some of the most colorful swear words I would ever hear, even in the sanctuary of a football huddle or later in the army.

Bill stood over the bellowing man, the words of concern that formed in his throat frozen there by the fury of the huge man now struggling to his feet. Bill stood stricken. He seemed to be awestruck by seeing what appeared to be a dead man rising back to obvious life without significant injury. It was Steiner's son Eric, running from his front porch toward his father, who finally penetrated Bill's immobilizing fear.

"Don't let him catch you. If he does, he'll kill you," shouted Eric, as he sprinted toward his father.

Bill darted back to the safety of the car as Steiner managed to stand with the help of his son. Two neighbors had arrived at his side, extending the angry man a helping hand, which he gruffly spurned as he began to take his first steps toward our car, the jowls of his plump face quivering with anger. From the sanctuary of the car, Bill shouted, "Get out of here!" as I started the engine. It was barely audible over the shouted threats of the huge man thundering toward us. The car pulled forward in the nick of time, leaving Homer Steiner standing in the middle of Forrest Avenue, shaking his fist at our squealing tires and gray exhaust.

Shaken but undeterred, we headed for McEwen's Drive-in for food, then on to the house on Attalla Highway. The house was a white clapboard structure with a fresh coat of paint and a black rubber mat by the front door that read "Welcome to Our Home," a somewhat incongruous touch, considering the purpose for which the house was used. Betty Lou's and Lila's tears had given way to giggling over the image of the huffing Homer Steiner rushing toward our car as it sped off, his shouts still audible a block away.

The night was a warm continuation of a particularly hot and humid day. Nighttime had lowered the temperature, but not the humidity. We opened windows to air out the house and settled down on the worn overstuffed sofa, the only piece of furniture keeping a lone rocker company in the front room.

Bill excused himself first, ostensibly to use the restroom. Instead, he went to check out the bedrooms. The sound of flushing water masked the real intent of his brief departure. A subtle nod told me he wanted the bedroom on the left, down the short hallway.

The living room light had a convenient dimmer. The work we had in mind that evening was best done in a darkened room. Sexually frustrated by the loss of Sylvia and my monk-like existence in recent weeks, I desperately craved the release of sex.

In Betty Lou, I found a willing partner. Her plump breasts were pressed so hard against the fabric of her blouse that I could see the taut outline of her nipples. I evoked small gasps of pleasure from her by stroking the firm heads of the nipples through the blouse with one hand as I released several buttons with the other hand. When I bent down to kiss each breast, she lifted my chin and kissed my lips, motioning me toward the bedroom. I held her hand as we walked down the hallway to the first bedroom. A double bed, covered with a drab blue chenille bedspread, and a battered chiffarobe were the only furniture in the cramped room.

Betty Lou was insatiable, welcoming me back again and again, until even I was spent. It was shortly after midnight when the light knock on the bedroom door brought both of us out of a short sleep. Betty Lou lay in the crook of my arm, with my free hand cupping one of her breasts. It was Bill, telling us he had to get Lila home, or she would be in big trouble. Breaking curfews seemed not to be a problem for Betty Lou. We dressed hastily and were greeted in the living room by an anxious Lila and Bill.

"We'll have you home in a jiffy," I assured her.

Lila's home was on the eastern edge of Gadsden on the Glencoe highway. Her house was dark, except for the porch light, which seemed to illuminate the entire neighborhood. Bill dutifully walked Lila to the door, and he kissed her long and close before releasing the fearful girl to slip inside the house. She told us her parents slept under a loud ceiling fan that would deafen the sound of her footsteps when she climbed the stairs to the second-story bedroom she shared with a younger sister. Bill seemed relieved.

I dropped Bill off next at my house, which also was dark except for a front porch light. It appeared like a spotlight at that hour of the morning. Bill's night, I later learned, had not been as eventful as mine; Lila was returned home with her virginity intact.

Betty Lou and I had no intention of going home. We were both having too much fun. We headed back out to the house on Attalla Highway. It was only as we pulled in the driveway that we saw the back reflectors of JB's big Cadillac. It was parked nearly at the end of the graveled drive, out of sight of passers-by. There would be no returning to the house on this night.

I would return to the Attalla Highway house several times in the next few weeks with Betty Lou, always marveling at how well this secret rendezvous spot was kept from the two women who would have most wanted to know about it, the wives of those two most respected Gadsden citizens, Dr. Harlan Cunningham and his best friend, J. Beauregard Stevens. That their wives never found out was a tribute to the discretion of those lovable old reprobates.

The use of the house for its pleasurable purposes continued for another year, until JB had the misfortune of meeting a younger woman, who steered his lust to love. Darcy Langston was a pharmacy clerk who worked closely with him every day, bolstering his fading manhood with a comfort men often seek as the years strip them of sexual prowess. His infatuation flamed in her presence and turned him away from any of the other tempting dalliances he had brought to the house on Attalla Highway over the years. It was nearly his undoing.

After more than twenty childless years with Maudie, JB learned during a hastily requested meeting at the house that he was going to be a father. It was not welcome news. JB offered to take care of Darcy and the child. He had the financial resources to keep them both in relative comfort. But Darcy, apparently panicked by fear of marriageless motherhood, demanded the stricken pharmacist do something to abort the baby.

He refused, turning instead to his old friend Doc Cunningham, who counseled the younger woman on the danger of abortion to her physical well-being, as well as the risk they would all run with the law, which looked upon abortion as murder.

When Darcy did not show up for work the next day, it was Doc Cunningham who found her in her small, one-room garage apartment, her vaginal track torn, her womb crudely ruptured by a metal clothes hanger. She had bled to death. There was no telephone in the apartment to summon help. I wondered later if she would have used it, even if one had been available.

After consulting with Doc Cunningham, the medical examiner ruled the death from natural causes, sparing her grieving parents and sisters the grim reality of her death. But enough people had seen Darcy Langston brought to the morgue at Gadsden General Hospital that ugly rumors of how she died were whispered in Gadsden for months. Darcy went to her grave without ever sharing her love for JB with anyone, thus sparing him the accusations he heaped upon himself.

Neither JB nor Doc Cunningham ever returned to the house on Attalla Highway.

Although Doc Cunningham was regularly in attendance at First Baptist Church, JB had not set foot in the church since he repeated his vows to Maudie there, many years before. Just what drew JB back to church set many a member to pondering. Not Maudie. She neither suspected nor questioned her husband's motive, telling herself it was an answer to long years of prayer. The sight of JB sitting beside Maudie, with her arm linked proprietarily in his, induced a profound change in the normally stern demeanor of the Reverend Hillard P. Coates. He never failed to smile an acknowledgement of JB's presence.

Only Doc Cunningham knew the need for contrition that impelled his friend back to the sanctuary of First Baptist Church.

13

A magnificent ball of orange hovering just above the western horizon grudgingly gave way to a cloudless Friday night for the opening game of the football season. It looked like most of Gadsden was in the stadium stands when we kicked off against Emma Sansom. Gadsden was the bigger of the two high schools and boasted a more affluent enrollment. Emma Sansom drew its students from the families of steel workers and textile workers. Many of those sons and daughters would follow their parents into Gadsden's big plants. Few would head to college, as did many of those attending Gadsden High School. It was a rivalry that played out not only on the football field but also in the politics and economy of Gadsden.

On this night my mind was not on Gadsden's economic strata or its political divisions. The play was over right guard. Our fullback, Runt Edwards, had the ball and barreled forward for about seven yards. Not enough for the first down. Runt was a good pass receiver but someone I called on sparingly in that capacity. Bill was my favorite and most frequent target and was what Emma Sansom expected. What they got was a short pass to Runt Edwards over the center and a six-to-nothing deficit, as Runt galloped across the goal line untouched, after shaking off two early tacklers.

He was a horse, weighing in at over two hundred pounds, even without pads or the usual six or eight bananas Bill and I would stuff ourselves with just before the Monday weigh-in to boost our weight and the coach's confidence in his quarterback and halfback.

I kicked the extra point and was trotting to the sidelines when I spotted him—Frank Thomas, the University of Alabama football coach. He had been sitting in the stands with my mother and father last season. He was now standing near coach Gordon, his arms folded across his chest, stoically watching the play on the field.

He nodded to me as I drew alongside Gordon, and despite whatever might go wrong later on that warm September evening, what had just gone right would be enough. When I glanced over at Frank Thomas, he nodded slightly, a silent approval of my deceptive pass that had fooled the entire Emma Sansom line. Coach Gordon also was pleased and patted my back before hunkering down to shout instructions to the defense. I wanted to play football for the University of Alabama more than anything. I dreamed about being part of the big red Bama offense, of quarterbacking one of the best teams in the South, coached by the likes of Frank Thomas. He was a legend.

I had to prove myself to this big man who stood, noncommittal, along the sidelines. Plus, Bill needed a scholarship. It would be his passport to an education that his parents seemed neither willing nor able to provide. Bill and I pledged to each other long ago that we would go to college together, a team of two. Tonight, I could help us both fulfill that pledge.

Runt Edward's touchdown that night was his last. Bill scored on the next three passes I threw from the twelve, the thirty-two, and the fifteen. Each time I returned to the sidelines, I got a nod from Frank Thomas. More important, so did Bill. It was a record shellacking of Emma Sansom which became the buzz in Gadsden barbershops and pool halls for a week.

By the middle of the following week, invitations to attend the Crimson Tide's home game a week from Saturday arrived in the mail for both Bill and me. We hastily accepted and made plans for the trip to Birmingham, where the game would be played at Legion Field. I had been there several times with my father and older brothers. In Alabama, there was nothing that evoked more state pride than the Crimson Tide. Football was what we excelled at in Alabama—steel-making was next but a distant second. And Legion Field was where it all came together, offering the pride of accomplishment that could be felt statewide. I thought there could be no more beautiful sight.

My father let us use his big Dodge but with two strict admonitions: drive the speed limit, and watch out for potholes on the pavement. During the war, road repairs were done, for the most part, by prison chain gangs. Asphalt was severly rationed and quality control was not a term in prison guards' vocabulary. Even major roadways suffered.

We invited my brother Collier to come along, but he declined. Collier had excelled at football, playing tight end at Alabama before he put his country ahead of his college career. It was still too painful for him to watch what he longed to do and would never do again.

Collier's new prosthesis worked well. Having shed his crutches, he was walking two miles a day. The pain still made him wince at times and exhaustion sent him to bed early many nights. From Collier, though, there was never any complaint.

Following his return from the hospital in Birmingham, with

the help of Mother's loving solicitations and good food, his shallow spirit and skeletal thinness gradually gave way to the Collier we'd known before he was felled in a hail of Japanese fire on Saipan. It took the American invaders three weeks of some of the bloodiest fighting of the war to secure Saipan. Much of that time my brother spent aboard a hospital ship heading first to Honolulu and then San Francisco.

Katie Shannon, a nurse he met at the Birmingham hospital, became the other salve for his spirit. A sprightly young woman with a lively sense of humor, her good looks and good manners won my parents over immediately. She would brighten our house any Sunday that Collier was home from school, coming by car when she could find a ride or by early morning bus. She was a year older than Collier and that brought endless teasing from him about her future as an "old maid." She fended off his dark humor and darker moods with a contagious laugh that infected all of us, as did her unfailing optimism and zest for living. She loved Collier and was determined that he would love her back. He did, eventually, but until that time, we would watch in awe of her unabashed wooing—and we'd cheer her on.

Birmingham was bustling on that game-day Saturday. Fearing slow traffic, we left Gadsden early, which proved a wise decision. Even in the hardship of wartime travel, the population of Birmingham would swell by 50 percent on football Saturdays. Hundreds of fans could be seen walking from the downtown bus depot and train station to Legion Field.

Bill and I had barely enough time to eat at a small diner before heading to the stadium for the one o'clock kick-off. Nighttime football was banned as part of the nationwide blackout after dusk. We had special passes, signed by Frank Thomas, that allowed us to sit in the section reserved for parents of players—right on the fifty-yard line, about ten rows up, giving us a great view of the field. The Tide was playing arch rival, Ole Miss.

Morning rain threatened a mud bath by game time, but the sun opportunely appeared, banished the clouds, and flooded the huge stadium with drying rays. By kick-off, field conditions were nearly perfect. Alabama's play, however, was anything but. Fumbles, a safety, and misdirected passes falling short or long but seldom in the hands of receivers combined to send the Ole Miss Rebels back to Oxford happy.

The ranks of college football teams throughout the country had been decimated by the draft. Walk-ons were more welcome now, and scholarships more plentiful, even for players whose abilities would have relegated them to back-up status on pre-war teams. Bill and I could make this team.

The locker room was musty and shrouded in gloom. Frank Thomas was in an office marked "Coach," a small cubicle cluttered with stacks of books and papers. The door was open, and he motioned us to chairs in front of his desk, a sorry wooden giant that looked more battered than his teams' defensive line that day.

"Too bad we couldn't welcome you with a win. Three of our best linebackers went into the armed forces at the end of the school year, and we just can't replace them. If you don't have a good defense, you can't mount much of an offense." Thomas looked downcast, more beaten by the lack of players than Ole Miss. It would be a long season for the Alabama coach.

"It's okay, Coach. It's still Alabama, and it's still where we want to play next year, if we can." I wanted to say something to soothe his dejection, but there was every sign my effort had fallen short.

"I hear you boys are best friends and want to go to the same school."

"That's right, Coach. Bill and I have been friends since grammar school, and we plan to room together at college. Do you think you could use us both?" I asked hopefully.

"I reckon we can, son. We sure as hell need something more than we had today. We could have used your passing arm and Bill's sure hands." We were in. My heart pounded. What Bill and I had talked about and planned for was going to happen. We would be playing football at the University of Alabama next fall.

"Does that mean we may get a scholarship, Coach?" Bill asked.

"Yes, son, it does."

"That's great, sir. I couldn't go to college without a job or a scholarship. My folks just can't afford it."

"I understand, son. A lot of folks can't send their kids to school. You won't have a regular job, but I can promise you this: after my practices, you'll wish you had a regular job. Believe me, it would be an easier way to get through school." Frank Thomas grinned for the first time. "You think you're up to the kind of work I have in mind for you?"

We answered in unison: "Yes, sir."

"How old are you boys?"

"We'll both turn eighteen next month," Bill offered. We knew Thomas was concerned about our draft status.

"Let's hope this damn war is over by this time next year. Well, boys, I've got to get back to Tuscaloosa shortly. I'll be in touch." He stood to shake hands. "How is Collier doing? I didn't get to see him when I was scouting here last week."

"He's doing better, sir. He's got a new mechanical leg that works great. He doesn't have to use crutches anymore."

"I'm glad to hear that, John. Your brother was a fine young man. We missed him today at tight end. Tell him I said hey!"

"Thank you, I will, sir."

Frank Thomas managed a smile as he walked us to the door. He was a large man in reality, and even bigger in our eyes. We walked back through the quiet locker room, past the players getting dressed, their faces still showing hangdog expressions. This is where we would be next fall, showering in the dank locker room under the bleachers. Both of us vowed, with the bravado of high school seniors, that next year we would be celebrating in this very locker room, not mourning what should have been.

It was shortly after four, and we were not expected home before midnight. That left plenty of time to get something to eat and look around. I promised to drive Bill past that palace of pleasure where a young woman named Jenny had introduced me to the pleasures of manhood.

We settled first on a drive-in eatery near Legion Field, crowded with cars, where a greasy hamburger and a root beer were served up as dinner. Our next stop was a quick look at the house on Porter Street. It looked even more drab in the late afternoon light, its gray wooden clapboard dotted with the last vestiges of stubbornly clinging paint that had probably been applied twenty years ago. It looked sadly neglected from the outside, but the lights illuminating the windows testified to the liveliness inside.

"This is it?" Bill's tone was filled with incongruity.

"Who cares what it looks like outside?" I countered defensively. "It's what goes on inside that counts." We did not have ten dollars between us—the price of a visit inside—so we drove off and pointed the car back downtown.

"How about a milkshake?" I suggested.

Bill liked that idea. It wasn't sex, but for two teenagers, it was the next best thing: food. The drugstore on Main Street was packed with clamoring football fans sporting red sweaters and shirts, some with red felt Alabama pennants laying across their laps or propped precariously against the counter. We found two empty seats at the far end of the counter. Watching the two young girls and the older man working behind the counter reminded me of my on-again, off-again soda-jerking days at Stevens Drugstore. We declined menus and within five minutes were sipping thick chocolate shakes.

I had just finished spooning the last of the thick shake into my mouth, the paper straw having given out, when I looked up into the long mirror that framed the length of the soda fountain—and there she was. I stared, stunned, my empty spoon still poised above the shake glass. Sylvia had not changed in the year since she left Gadsden. Her shoulder-length blonde hair fell around her face as she bent over the cosmetics she was rearranging in a display case.

Bill followed my eyes to the mirror, then looked to me. I never revealed to Bill—or anyone else—the depth of my love for Sylvia. He asked about her at times, but his questions often were posed with unaccustomed hesitancy—questions I sidestepped or outright rebuffed.

"I'm going over to say hello. Okay?"

"Sure. I'll stay here."

I stood looking at her bent head for several long moments before she felt my presence and looked up.

"Can I help—?" The "you" never made it past her lips. "Johnny!"

14

Sylvia eyes widened in alarm as my whispered words of accusation poured out—words that unleashed the pain long-festering within me at what I viewed as her spurning my love, a love she had claimed to share with me. I wanted her to know the depth of my hurt.

When I finished, there was a protracted silence between us before she spoke, her own voice hushed against the fear of being overheard by customers who lined the soda fountain counter just across the aisle.

"I've missed you terribly, too, Johnny." Her luminous eyes pleaded for understanding. "I never meant to hurt you when I left. It seemed the easiest way, for me and for you." She did not elaborate.

"You said you loved me," I retorted defensively. The hurt I'd buried these past months since Sylvia left Gadsden welled up in sudden, intense anger. I wanted to hurl viperous words at her, transfer my hurt, my loneliness, my longing for her.

"I did love you, Johnny. Very much." Her voice was gentle, pliant. She sensed my anger as instant and irrational and tried with gentleness to make peace between us. "But there can never be the two of us again," she said, keeping her voice low. "You're still in high school and you're six years younger than me. What would your parents do if they thought we were serious about each other? They would put a stop to everything, and you know that."

I could not disagree. My parents had been supportive without understanding when I stayed with Sylvia following her brutal beating at the hands of her husband. Whatever Doc Cunningham had told my parents appeased their concerns about us. I knew my mother thought it was an infatuation for an older woman, and at one point I think she may have suspected the sexual relationship. However, in all our time together during the long trip to California and back, she never brought it up in our conversations. If she knew the truth, it was something she kept to herself.

Sylvia looked around apprehensively, then began to busy her hands rearranging bottles of cologne on the glass-topped display case.

Sensing her discomfort, I asked, "When do you get off? I have my father's car. I could pick you up and we could go get something to eat."

"What about Bill?" she asked, for the first time meeting the eyes that furtively reflected back at her from the mirror behind the counter. I had completely forgotten Bill, still sitting at the counter, his milkshake glass now empty.

"I think Bill has an aunt living here. Maybe he could visit with her while we go out," I replied. "Or maybe he could take in a movie."

"I don't get off for another hour. I'm not sure ..." Her voice trailed off uncertainly.

"Sylvia, I just found you again. I won't just walk out of here like nothing's happened. I'll pick you up in an hour. I'll wait outside. I'm driving my dad's Dodge."

Sylvia still looked conflicted. "Sylvia, I am coming back for you." My tone was adamant. "Forget all those other things. They don't matter. What matters is I have found you, and I'm going to see you. Tonight," I said with all the firmness I could muster.

She offered no further objection. "All right, Johnny. I'll see you in an hour."

I crossed the aisle back to where Bill was watching us in the mirror, his curiosity winning out over his natural discretion.

"I'm going to pick Sylvia up when she gets off in an hour. Do you think you could go to a movie or something. Don't you still have an aunt living here?"

"Yeah. You want to drive over there and see if she's home?"

Bill was an intuitive person with an innate kindness that precluded him from questioning why it was important for me to have dinner with Sylvia and not include him. Despite our closeness, I never shared with Bill much about my relationship with Sylvia. And he never intruded by asking about our involvement or why she had left. It was Ann he thought I loved. He had even predicted Ann and I would one day marry.

He is right. I do love Ann, but on a different plane than Sylvia. Ann was my friend, my soul mate, the one person in whom I confided my love for Sylvia. If she had any concerns about the relationship, those concerns remained unspoken. She'd accepted it, as soul mates do, and never pried. I missed Ann. When she left Gadsden, I was enraged at the cruel pain inflicted on her by her father's incestuous acts. I was angrier still that Hubert McClelland's despicable concupiscence for his daughter had removed her from my life.

I was content to let Bill believe it was Ann, not Sylvia, I loved.

I drove Bill to his aunt's house in a neighborhood near downtown Birmingham. She was surprised and flustered by his visit, sheepishly apologizing for the messy condition of the front room of the bungalow. Her two boys were sprawled on an overstuffed couch and acknowledged us with sullen nods. Our presence hardly interrupted their attention to the radio and the detective story playing itself out in the small, dingy room.

Bill introduced me to his aunt, who wiped her hands on the soiled apron that camouflaged a thick waist before extending her hand to meet mine. She was shyly aware of her clumsy manners. Bill tactfully arranged to spend the night, explaining that I would be visiting family friends and would pick him up in the morning.

Bill's aunt had no telephone, so I excused myself and headed for the nearest pay phone to call my parents collect and let them know I would not be home until tomorrow. My excuse was an overheating radiator that a friend of Bill's was looking at and should have fixed by the next day. A stuck thermostat, I lied coolly, adding we would be staying with Bill's aunt that night—a half-truth there.

Forty-five minutes later I parked in front of the downtown drugstore in a spot easily seen from inside. Sylvia was there. I almost feared she wouldn't be. She spotted the car as she came out the door, wrapped in a long, blue wool coat against the chilly fall night. I leaned over and opened the door, and she slipped inside, pulling the coat up around her neck as if to protect herself against even cooler air inside the car. She looked ahead, rather than at me, and seemed ill at ease. I took her hand that was still gripping the collar of her coat, pulled it to my lips, and kissed it gently, then turned the hand up to kiss the softer inside of her palm. She leaned her head back against the seat, her eyes closed, but made no move to pull her hand away from me.

"Hungry? Let's get something to eat."

She nodded her head, eyes still closed. I kissed the inside of her hand again. Her breath drew in sharply as her head turned away toward the passenger door. I drove to a small, lonesome cafe on the edge of Birmingham. Even though it was a football day, we had our choice of tables, all covered with red checkered oil cloths. We selected one in the back, out of earshot and away from the curious eyes of the two other patrons—an elderly man sitting at the counter, sipping coffee and reading the evening newspaper, and another man at a table near the door. He was bent purposefully over his plate, shoveling the remaining morsels of food onto a piece of bread with a knife.

We ordered the blue-plate special: meatloaf, mashed potatoes and gravy, and canned green beans. The food was served almost immediately, piping hot, with a homemade roll. I was still hungry, and it tasted surprisingly good.

We ate without speaking. The observant waiter cleared away my empty plate and asked if everything was all right, noting that Sylvia had eaten only a few bites of her dinner. She smiled and assured him it was fine; she simply wasn't as hungry as she thought. He took my money, promising change, and disappeared into the kitchen.

"Where do you live?"

Sylvia had been staring after the waiter. My question brought her attention back to me.

"Not far from here. Is that where you want to go?"

"Yes."

Sylvia had spoken little during dinner. She seemed pensive, lost in her own thoughts. Her chin rested on her steepled arms and closed hands, her head turned away from me, seemingly unaware of my scrutiny. In the months since I last saw her she had lost weight. Her deep blue eyes appeared even larger, framed by high cheek bones made more prominent by the weight loss. She wore no makeup, and the freckles that dotted her nose and upper cheeks stood out, making her look much younger than her twenty-three years. As she turned back to look at me, I realized again how even more beautiful she had become.

The waiter returned shortly with the change from my five-dollar bill. The rest of the night lay ahead. It was only a short distance to Sylvia's apartment, which was over a former carriage house behind what had once been a gracious home with a wide portico. The house was located in an older neighborhood, which, like so many other parts of Birmingham, had been stripped of its handsomeness by the austerity imposed by the Great Depression.

I had parked the car a half-block away. Sylvia was not allowed male visitors by her elderly landlady. With darkness for cover and Sylvia's assurance the landlady would probably be asleep by her front parlor radio, we made our way quickly up the creaky stairs on the side of the carriage house to her apartment. Inside was a Spartan room, devoid of any extraneous color or décor. The only furnishings were a drab horsehair-filled couch, a single chair with a worn seat cover, and a small wooden table that held the room's only light, a lamp. The apartment was one large room with the small kitchen directly behind the front area; to the side of the kitchen was the bed and a large chiffonier absent a mirror.

Sylvia pulled down the blinds before turning on the lone lamp. It gave off minimal light, leaving the room in deep shadow.

I helped her shed her coat, laying it on the back of the chair, and pulled her into my arms. There was no resistance. My desire, so long pent up, was instant. She looked up at me and displayed the same

pent up, was instant. She looked up at me and displayed the same urgent need. I removed her clothes, which fell where we stood in the center of the room, and holding her at arm's length, I feasted on the beauty of her nakedness. Reaching out, I gently stroked one breast with my thumb while cupping the remaining area of the breast. Her breathing became more rapid as sensations rushed through her. Then I gently tasted the other breast with my tongue and heard the first soft moan as she pulled me closer to her. Her hand reached for my belt. I halted the motion.

"Later," I whispered. "Let me just make you feel what I have wanted to make you feel for so long. How long has it been for you, Sylvia? How long since you felt a man's hands on you?" It was a question I wanted answered, that I burned to know, that I demanded with gentle strokes that elicited deep moans of pleasure.

She put her hands over mine, stopping the pleasure. "There hasn't been anyone else, Johnny."

I hated myself for asking, for forcing her to tell, for causing pain where there had been only pleasure moments earlier. I folded her into my arms and cradled her next to me, feeling tears dampen my chest. "Damn it, I'm sorry, Sylvia. I had no right to ask. Don't cry. Please don't cry. I never want to hurt you." Lifting her chin with my finger, I kissed her lips, her cheeks, the tears clinging to those cheeks, and then found her lips again, this time parting them with my tongue. I felt her return the pressure. Her arms were around my neck, and I held her close and long before lifting her legs to wrap them around my waist.

I made love to her several times during the night, each time spending all of the passion within me, only to feel it revive as she lay in my arms. In between, we talked about the eventful year we were apart. She'd sold the dry cleaners and had given the money to her mother, who refused to operate the business founded by a husband she barely tolerated in life and despised in death.

Sylvia had taken the $2,500 from Bubba's military life insurance policy and used it to enroll in nursing school at Samford University. Despite the school's being coed, Sylvia was barred from living in the women's dormitory because she had been married. Rental housing proved difficult to find and came at a premium induced by the flood of workers into cities like Birmingham, where jobs in war factories were plentiful. Sylvia felt grateful to find the dingy garage apartment, despite an impecunious landlady who demanded the rent be paid weekly, in cash, and imposed severe restrictions on visitors to the apartment.

Sylvia spoke despairingly of the loneliness that engulfed her after leaving Gadsden. Letters to her mother were returned unopened. She finally quit writing. Despite her intense longing, she had not considered contacting me. Instead, she filled the emotional chasm in her life with a crowded schedule of classes, long duty hours at Birmingham General Hospital, and weekends working at the drugstore to help pay her rent.

With her loneliness had come a deep sadness. I could hear it in her voice as I drew from her the details of the last year. She had made no friends since moving to Birmingham. There was a sameness to each day that subdued her natural spirit and zest. Sylvia had changed.

We slept intermittently. Daylight appeared too soon. I had to leave before the landlady could notice my exit. As I dressed, Sylvia lay quietly with her head on the pillow, the white cotton sheet partly covering her.

"I want to marry you, Sylvia. Now! I can get a job in the steel mill. I've been promised a full football scholarship to Alabama next fall. We can save some money between now and then, enough to get you through school." She answered my proposal with silence, turning her head away. I leaned over and pulled her face toward me. Her eyes were deep blue pools of sadness.

"I love you, Sylvia. I don't give a damn about our age difference. I want you now. We could be married this weekend. My folks won't object if they know how much you mean to me." I wanted to address what I felt would be the biggest obstacle to our marriage before she could object.

"I love you, Johnny, but you're too young. You must finish high school and not work in a steel mill. You won't get a scholarship if you don't graduate."

That was something I had not considered—the need for a high school diploma to enter college. "Then I can work part-time at the mill and stay in school. There are other guys doing that right now. We can make it, Sylvia," I implored.

"No, Johnny. She began sobbing.

The tears did not deter me. "My grandmother set up a trust fund for me to go to college. I could probably get that money now, since I'm getting the scholarship next fall. It's worth several thousand dollars. I can talk to her and see if she'll let me use it now instead of later. She's a great old gal. She married my grandfather when he was still in med school, and she was five years older than him."

"Johnny, it won't work. I bring along too much baggage."

"Baggage! What the hell are you talking about?" Irritation singed my tone.

"I was pregnant when I married Bubba." Her voice faltered for a moment. "I lost the baby." She turned her head to face the far wall and sobs began to rack her body. "Johnny, it wasn't even his baby."

I was stunned by what she just told me, stunned to silence. Sylvia never told me why she married Bubba, a man she clearly didn't love and even despised. I assumed it was to get away from her parents. Now, there was someone else involved. "Who was the father, Sylvia?" I thrust the words at her bluntly, almost brutally.

"I can't tell you, Johnny. I can't tell anyone. It's long over. I miscarried early in the third month. No one knew I was pregnant, not even Bubba."

"Sylvia, I love you. There can't be secrets between us, not now, not ever. I want you for my wife. What happened in the past doesn't matter. But there can't be any secrets between us."

"No, Johnny, I can't tell. Please don't press me. The truth will only hurt more."

She turned away from me again, tears streaming down her face. I wanted the truth, even if it did hurt. My mind began feverishly reviewing possibilities. Whom had I seen Sylvia with? Whom had she dated? I realized the only man I ever saw her with was Bubba. Anger swept all reason aside.

"Who was it?" I demanded roughly, turning her toward me. "Tell me, Sylvia. I love you. I have a right to know who was screwing you before me." I did not intend to vent my anger so harshly, but her disclosure hurt deeply, knifing at my pride. I was demanding to know whom she'd been with without considering how I would deal with the consequences of the answer.

"Who was the father, Sylvia?" I pressed.

Her answer was muffled by the hands covering her face. I could detect the agony in her voice but not the words. I grabbed her shoulders and turned her back to face me. "Who was it?" My voice shouted the savage demand.

"My stepfather."

The revelation didn't register with me. Her father was dead.

There was no stepfather, only her father, Bryce Moss. Sylvia saw the confusion on my face and struggled out of my grip.

"Bryce Moss was my stepfather," she said as she attempted to control her sobbing. "He married my mother when I was two, and they moved to Gadsden." Her eyes lifted up into mine, pleading for understanding. "He started touching me when I was in first grade. It got much worse when I started to high school. I told my mother once, but she just yelled at me and said I was lying. Doctor Cunningham was the only one who knew about the pregnancy besides me. He arranged for Bubba to marry me. We dated once, in high school, but I didn't care for him. The doctor knew Bubba's folks and knew they wanted him to settle down. Doc Cunningham went to Bubba and told him I really liked him and we should get married."

Her tears dried as the words poured out, replaying the deaths of Bryce Moss, then Bubba, then her indifferent mother. In death, there had been some repentance on Moss' part. He had left her the dry cleaners.

I watched the burden of what she carried inside play out on her face, and hated the thought of Bryce Moss' hands fondling her slim body, stopping in forbidden places. Or Bubba Barnes' rough hands rubbing those places so soft and pleasurable.

Insistant anger churned inside me. There was no Bryce Moss or Bubba Barnes to lash out at, to aim my anger at; there was only Sylvia. I harbored an unspoken suspicion that only irritational anger gives vent to. "If you could screw me in the back room of the dry cleaners, what did you do to attract your stepfather's attention?" I hurled the insinuation without thinking and regretted the words even before they were fully spoken. But it was too late. I could see that in the stark disbelief on her face.

"Oh, God, Johnny! I was only six years old when he started.

How could you even think I would do something to encourage him? He raped me." Pain constricted her voice, and tears again filled her eyes.

My contrition was immediate. "I'm sorry, Sylvia, I didn't mean it." I knelt down beside the bed and reached over for her. "Please, Sylvia, I didn't mean what I said."

She slipped out the other side of the bed and wrapped the top sheet around her. She stood in the middle of the room, looking small and vulnerable, with her back to me. The sobs slowly subsided, and she stood quietly for some time before turning back to me. A mask had descended on her face. It was a face I had seen once before, in the recesses of the dry cleaners, when I told her I could not see her again after suspecting my mother was aware of our sexual liaison. More words of regret rushed to my lips, silenced by a foreboding that engulfed me before they were spoken.

"Good-bye, Johnny. I love you. But I never want to see you again."

15

Bill had been waiting for me for more than an hour when I finally arrived. I circled the block several times after leaving Sylvia. Her face had been inscrutable. I even stopped the car for a while in the same place it had been parked overnight. Why had life dealt such pain, such grief, to the two women I cared for the most? I had watched the vibrant joy fade in the Ann that I first knew, never to return. In Sylvia, there was none of Ann's carefree high spirits, only a burning need to be loved and accepted. She had my love, but I had cruelly refused my acceptance. I knew, in those silent moments in the car as I watched the sun rise more fully in the eastern sky, that I had lost her.

I drove to Gadsden in silence. Bill did not intrude on my sullen mood, content to watch the passing countryside.

Once again, football became my emotional purgative. It was a physical release for the anger, the hurt, the frustration I secreted inside on the return to Gadsden. My parents were reluctant to question my withdrawal. It was my brother, Collier, home for a weekend break from college, who came into my room two weeks later. Bill was still in the living room with my parents, pursuing their Saturday night tradition by listening to the Grand Ole Opry on the radio. I had retreated to my room on a lame excuse of doing math homework, not really caring if the assignment was ready to be handed in Monday.

When the door opened, I looked up sullenly, expecting it to be mother, there to coax me down to rejoin the family.

"What's eating you, brother?" Collier got right to the point.

"Nothing," I lied before relenting. "Nothing I want to talk about, okay?"

"You've got Mom really upset, or maybe you haven't noticed." My brother's typical impatience was showing. If he was trying to make me feel guilty, it wasn't working. "What happened in Birmingham?" he pressed on. "Bill won't say. He just says to talk to you. So, I'm talking."

"Nothing happened in Birmingham." I wished he would go away.

"If it wasn't something in Birmingham, then what's the withdrawal crap?" His tone became more cajoling. "If it's female problems, I could write a book, so talk to your old brother. Did someone 'Dear John' you?"

"Nah, it's nothing like that."

"Yeah, it is. And her name is Sylvia. That much I got out of Bill."

The mention of Sylvia startled me. "Goddamn him! Why doesn't he mind his own business?" I retorted hotly. I resented Bill's confiding anything personal about me to Collier. Whom I had lost and how I had lost her was something that I wanted to bury deep, so I could grieve alone and deal with my insensitivity, devoid of the more painful criticism I knew I deserved.

"You're hurting, little brother. Talking can help. I have big ears, all the better to listen with." Collier did have big ears, a part of his anatomy that had been the brunt of good-natured ribbing in the family since I could remember. He wore his hair unstylishly long for those days to help hide the size of his ears. The big-ear offer lightened the tension between us.

"I'd have to talk for a day non-stop, just to make those things seem like they were getting any workout at all."

Collier smiled at my limp effort at humor. "Then talk, brother. I've got all night and all day."

Maybe it was his persistence or simply his refusal to take offense at my anger. Maybe it was just my need to unload some of the hurt and guilt I harbored inside. He was a good listener. I told him about Sylvia's sexual abuse at the hands of her stepfather, making him swear to tell no one; I knew he would not.

"You still want to marry her?"

"Yes."

"Then do it. Mom and Dad will go along. They just want you to be happy. I've got some money saved from the army you can have, to get started. It's not much, but it will get you by until you get out of high school."

I had never ascribed generosity to my brother. He had always been closer to Addison. They shared a lot, including a two-wheeler when Addison was seven and Collier five, which they refused to let my sister, Sarah, use when she turned five. And I was threatened with death or at best, a sound beating, if I ventured into their bedroom.

"I appreciate the offer, but I don't think Sylvia would marry me now."

I could not tell even Collier of my dark accusation that she might have done something to lure her stepfather's shameful advances. That was something to remain unspoken, something I would deal with alone, without the cathartic release of telling someone else what I had said, even a well-meaning brother.

"How do you know if you don't call her or go see her and square things? It's the only way, little brother." Collier stepped closer and placed his hands on my shoulders. "Hey, just tell her how crazy you are about her and that you're gonna score the first big touchdown of the '45 season for Alabama. Women can't resist football heroes. How do you think I made it with Sissy Stanton?" Collier chuckled at the mention of the curvaceous Sissy.

"You made it with Sissy? Wow! She was a looker." I was impressed. Sissy Stanton had been in Collier's class but seemed to have a crush on Addison. She would occasionally come to the house, driving an old Ford with a rumble seat filled with giddy girlfriends. Those rather noisy visits were tolerated with disapproving resignation by my parents, who did not always use words to register that sentiment.

"Add and me made a dollar bet who could lay her first," he remembered, laughing. "Mom used to tell me that associating with 'that kind of girl' would get me in trouble. Well, it almost did." Collier laughed. "We had just beat Anniston that night. I scored a touchdown, so Add and Dalton let me come along to McEwen's. Sissy was there with her usual bunch. Dalton says, if I could pick her up, I could use his car, and he and Addison would get a ride back to our house. A buck on top of a good lay. That's a bet I couldn't pass up. So I talked Sissy into coming with me, and we headed out to the old Hadley place on Grider Road. You know that stand of trees with the tractor path? You can hide a tank in there. That's where I pulled into. It wasn't any time before I had her clothes off and mine, too. Boy, what a set of knockers on that girl!" He laughed again.

"I was just getting comfortable in the back seat, buck naked, when I hear this car pull up behind us. Next thing I know, there's a spotlight shining in the rear window. Sissy goes crazy, jumps out from underneath me, and starts reaching for her clothes in the front seat. The guy is a deputy, and he starts rapping on the side window. Sissy is trying to hide behind me. I'm trying to get my clothes, and then we hear this voice." Laughter bellowed forth from Collier. "It was a voice we both knew. That deputy was her brother, Henry."

"You're kidding. How'd you get out of it?" I asked, my curiosity now piqued.

"Well, Henry started yelling at me and banging his flashlight on the window. Luckily, the door was locked. I pulled my skivvies on and shot out the back door while he was trying to get in the front door. I nearly knocked Henry on his ass. He was yelling at Sissy at the top of his voice. She was giving him what-for back, just as loud, with words you won't hear in the navy, little brother. I was praying she would keep it up because my ass was still within shooting range."

"You were lucky he didn't kill you. So, how'd you get home? And how'd you get Dalton's car back to him?"

Collier laughed again, remembering that night. "When I got to the road, Addison and Dalton were there in Tommy Joe Lang's car. You remember Tommy Joe?" I nodded. "Well, they were parked on the side of the road just waiting for me to come running out of there."

"How'd they know you were there?"

"Because I had told Addison where I was going, and he and Dalton called Henry at the sheriff's office and told him he could find his sister getting screwed out at the old Hadley place. They got a big laugh out of it, especially when I told them I'd barely had enough time to stick it in."

"They could have at least waited a few minutes before calling Henry, to give you time to savor the moment."

"Yeah, you're right. Well, Henry took Sissy home in his patrol car. Dalton got his car back, and I got my dollar from Add, even if I could only say I barely made it with Sissy Stanton." Collier's tone smacked of satisfaction.

I still wanted to know about Henry, but that, said Collier, was another story. He ran into Henry Stanton several times after that. Henry never mentioned the night on Grider Road, but the fear lingered that he might whip out his gun and avenge his sister's lost virtue.

The smile faded from Collier's face. "I hear Henry went into the Marines and is in the Pacific somewhere."

Six months later, Henry Stanton would die on the beach of a remote pork-chop–shaped land mass in the Bonin Islands called Iwo Jima.

"Well, little brother, go propose to your Sylvia, and I'll give you some money to get married on. Don't worry about Mom and Dad. They'll be okay with it. Just give Mom lots of grandkids to fuss over." He stood up, a motion that forced a wince of pain because of the mechanical leg that still bothered him more than he would admit. "I sure as hell couldn't get out of that car and get away from Henry today," he mused wryly.

I stood for a moment, blocking his path to the door, feeling awkward about how to thank this brother I was just beginning to know. This was the first serious conversation in our young lives. For the first time, I knew that he was my friend as well as my brother. I held out my hand. "Thanks, Collier, for setting things straight in my mind. I've been pretty muddled since seeing Sylvia again."

He didn't take my hand. Instead, he wrapped his arms around me. "Be happy, little brother." He turned and limped out of the room.

I've never forgotten that night—the long talk, the closeness that evolved. Our lives have taken very different directions, but that night cemented our friendship, a friendship that remains an unwavering bond between us.

16

The following Saturday morning I drove to Birmingham alone. It rained overnight, a steady, light rain, soaking and warm—typical of fall in Alabama. Mother Nature spent her anger in spring; in fall, we were treated to her more gentle side. The moisture still glistened on the white cotton, brilliant against its supporting green foliage in the morning bath of sunlight. The harvest was late this year. Heavy spring rains had delayed the cotton planting, the staple crop of northeastern Alabama.

That dewy morning, Highway 11 had almost as many lumbering tractors as cars—tractors pulling huge wagons with wood-slatted sides and brimming with freshly picked cotton. In the fields on each side of the highway, small armies of Negro farm workers, old and young, bent over the rows of cotton plants, trailing long white canvas bags behind them. It was a ritual of harvest, repeated throughout the cotton belt in my generation and by generations past, with a sameness that belied the word progress.

Even in Alabama's largest city, farmers flocked to sell their goods and buy their groceries and other supplies on Saturday morning. The downtown was bustling with old farm pickups, distinctive with their faded paint, rusted beds, mismatched tires, and numerous dings marking their tough character as well as years of service. Many were filled with children riding in the back, along with Negro farmhands. The front seats of such vehicles always seemed reserved for adults.

I drove to the street where Sylvia lived and stopped in front of the old home with the wide portico. It looked smaller in full daylight, an unkempt, neglected reflection of its neighbors. I walked to the back and up the stairs to the apartment. I had been rehearsing what I would say to Sylvia all the way from Gadsden—how sorry I was that I'd hurt her so deeply; how the five hundred dollars offered by Collier would allow us to get married, get an apartment in Gadsden, purchase some furniture, and set up housekeeping while I finished high school.

Next fall, we would be in Tuscaloosa. I would work part-time, play football, and we could both go to college. We could make it and have each other. Forget the past. The future looked terrific. We would be together, and I would be there to insulate her from any further pain. To love her. To be loved.

There was no response to my knock. I turned the doorknob, and it opened. Few people locked their doors in those days. I went in. The apartment was unchanged, but a sudden panic prickled my neck. The bed was made. No dishes were drying in the drainer. I felt the knot in my stomach as I opened the small closet at the end of the kitchen. Empty. She was gone.

This was not the ending I'd planned. Sylvia would be here. She would cry softly and smile happily when I told her how sorry I was. She would quit her job at the drugstore. We would drive back to Gadsden. She would stay with my parents until we arranged for a marriage license on Monday. By next weekend, we would be married. I had planned everything on the way down. Why was she gone?

The thin, wizened landlady looked me over curiously from behind the partially opened front door and inquired if I was a policeman. Just a friend of Sylvia's, I assured her.

"She moved out Tuesday morning, even though the rent was paid up 'til the end of the week. Strange," she added. "Nice girl" was how she described Sylvia. Never gave her any trouble, unlike some other tenants. No, Sylvia had not said where she was going, just left, carrying two suitcases. Didn't even call a cab.

I thanked the woman and retreated to my car.

Downtown, the drugstore manager said Sylvia had given notice on Monday, saying she was moving, not saying where. He paid her at the end of her shift and she had left. Oh yes, she stored two suitcases in the back behind the pharmacy and came back for them Tuesday afternoon. He did not know of any friends who might know where she was. As I pressed, he became concerned and asked if I were family. Before I could answer, he suggested I check with the Birmingham police and file a missing persons report. That would not be necessary, I assured him.

As I was pushing the glass door open to leave, the manager came up behind me. "I didn't get your name. If she comes in again, you want me to mention you were looking for her?"

"Just tell her John Winstead was in. Tell her to give me a call when she gets a chance. She'll know where to reach me."

"Will do."

I thanked him again and left, knowing Sylvia would not get that message. She was gone—who knew where?—having left me for the second time. This time it was I who had driven her away.

The police sergeant behind the glassed enclosure was sipping coffee from a grimy cup stained with dripped coffee and dirt. He was an older man, his flabby middle straining the buttons that held his faded blue uniform shirt together. No, there was no missing persons report on a Sylvia Ann Moss Barnes. No, no one by that name had been involved in an auto accident. There wasn't even anyone by that name in the city jail.

I walked for blocks in the downtown, past elegant three-story antebellum homes on wide, tree-lined streets. Stubborn leaves still draped several trees in their colorful fall trappings—bright golds, blazing ambers, some light orange, and remaining touches of red. It did nothing to discourage the gray that shrouded my psyche.

Finding her would be nearly impossible. Sylvia had told me she had had no contact with her mother or brother since leaving Gadsden. It was unlikely she would contact them now. She probably still had some of the money from the insurance policy, so she could leave Birmingham and start over in another city or even move out of state. Despairingly, I realized I might never see her again.

I walked for more than an hour, leaving the car parked in front of the drugstore. I headed back toward downtown, not sure how far I had come. As I walked past the large stone building that was the Birmingham post office, with my hands deep in my pants pockets, I nearly bumped into a wood-framed sign set out on the edge of the sidewalk. Join the Army Air Corps; learn to fly; get the equivalent of a three-thousand-dollar college education. I stopped to read the sign again. The message was made to look as if it was spoken by a lieutenant in uniform, with his flying insignia prominently displayed. He was smiling back at me confidently. The appeal registered.

All the way back to Gadsden, the thought of joining the Army Air Corps began to take hold. Sylvia was gone, fleeing from me, leaving no clue about her destination. A sense of emptiness at losing her besieged my spirit and tore at my reserve. I wanted to cry, to feel the release from my pain that tears might bring. I had seldom cried in my life, even as a youngster. Tears were not manly; they were for girls, not boys. On those rare occasions when my mother took a switch from the backyard weeping willow tree and swatted me with it, I cried and loudly. Those tears brought a quick end to the discipline. Mother could not bear to see her children sad. We children learned that early on and used it to our advantage.

I withdrew once again, alone with both my loss and the reason for it. Even my brother did not intrude after I told him Sylvia had vanished. Concerned for me and for Sylvia, my brother called Sylvia's mother to ask how to get in touch with her. In a voice empty of any emotion, she admitted not knowing where Sylvia was, saying she had not heard from her daughter for some time. There was no concern in her voice, just a weary acceptance that it was so, and there was nothing she could or would do about the situation.

My withdrawal deepened. I mentioned the Army Air Corps poster to Bill, who was enthralled with flying. He would coax me many Saturdays to bicycle out to Gadsden's airfield, where the small blue-and-white twin-engine plane would drop off the canvas bags of airmail and pick up the bag of outgoing expedited mail.

At the Saturday matinees we attended when we weren't working, the newsreels played the latest air battles in Europe. We cheered when they showed B-17s blitzing German cities in daring daylight raids—raids that had begun in March 1944 to blunt Germany's ability to strike Allied forces after the invasion, which had begun on the beaches of Normandy.

It was the night before our championship game against Guntersville. I lay awake long after the century-old grandfather clock downstairs chimed midnight. Sylvia was always in my thoughts, the rounded fullness of her breasts taunting me, intensifying my longing and my sense of loss.

In the quiet of that early morning I decided my future. It would not be playing football next fall at Alabama. That could wait. I wanted to join the Air Corps, to fly, to join the fight my brothers had left—one in death, the other badly wounded. I was restless and bored with high school. I already had earned nearly enough credits to graduate, but a high school diploma was not necessary to join the Air Corps.

I looked over at Bill's sleeping form in the next bed. He was my best friend, the person I shared most things with, bad or good. I would be leaving him behind. The football scholarship to Alabama was, for him, the fulfillment of a long-held hope. Then I gave voice to the plan that had been forming but was as yet unspoken. Bill and I could join the Air Corps together. We could spend our two-year commitment together, learning to fly, earning our officer's wings, joining a combat air group.

I knew my mother and father would object vehemently. They had lost one son to the war and nearly lost a second. Would they be willing to risk their third son? I was confident I could convince them to sign my enlistment papers. They would not stand in my way, not if this was what I really wanted.

"Bill, you awake?" I whispered, knowing he wasn't. He did not respond. I called him again, a little louder this time, and he turned over toward me sleepily.

"Something wrong?"

"No. It's just … I've got a great idea. Let's join the Air Corps."

"What? Are you nuts? What time is it?" Bill was now fully awake, springing up in the bed, rubbing his eyes.

"It's about one. Look, we could join the Air Corps now. I'm tired of school, and I know you are, too. We could enlist, learn to fly, get our wings, and get assigned to a combat group. When we get out, then we could go to Alabama. We'll still be young. And even if we can't get a football scholarship, I read in the newspaper the other day that Congress is going to provide money to returning veterans to go to college. So we could still get our way paid through college. Anyway, that poster in Birmingham says the Air Corps training is like a three-thousand-dollar college education." I stopped to let that information sink in. "Whadda ya say?"

Bill stared at me for some time without speaking. Finally, he rested his chin on his drawn-up knees. "Okay, if that's what you really want to do."

"Great."

"What'll your parents say?" Bill raised the question that could pose the biggest obstacle to my plan.

"I don't know," I answered honestly, "but I think they'll go along if they know it's what I really want to do."

I waited until Saturday morning to tell them. They had been in the stands as we closed out our second consecutive undefeated season, and they chaperoned at the dance following the game. Bill and I were heroes to our high school classmates. The adulation of that Friday night also came from parents and teachers and from Doc Cunningham and JB Stevens. It was a heady night. My parents were not prepared for the plans I revealed the following day.

17

The day dawned damp and cool, with a misty fog shrouding the Gadsden train station. We stood on the platform outside the depot, our hands buried deep in our pockets, shivering in the chill morning air of early November. Mother looked small and sad standing by Father, his arm protectively around her shoulders, holding her close. In her right hand she held a tissue, ready to deal with the inevitable tears that marked her children's leave-takings. I was the last to leave, a milestone she made plain was decidedly unwelcome.

Father had said no when confronted with my decision. He was uncustomarily angry and firm. He would not lose another son to this war. Mother sat silent, her tightly gripped hands the only indicator of how she was receiving my announcement. In the end, it was my father who relented, coaxed by Collier, whose soft-spoken words brought reason to the family conference around the kitchen table. I think of that much-scarred oak table still today and wonder at how many major decisions in my life and the lives of my parents and my siblings were made around that piece of oval wood that dominated the airy kitchen.

Mother said nothing. When Father finally agreed I could leave high school and join the Air Corps, she quietly excused herself to the upstairs bedroom to grieve in private. She would accede to her husband's decision, but it would not diminish the sadness.

The big Louisville & Nashville engine lumbered noisily into the station on the tracks adjacent to the depot. The stop was brief, with only enough time allotted to pick up the few passengers ready to board for Atlanta.

Bill's parents were not there—he had not expected they would be, but their absence hung heavy for all of us. Mother hugged him to her, wishing him well and admonishing him to take care of himself and come back to her. Father shook his hand warmly, affection glowing in his eyes. For my father, Bill had become more Winstead than Deems.

Collier stepped forward to shake Bill's hand and glance a gentle blow off Bill's chin. "Take care of yourself. And take care of my baby brother. He needs someone to change his diaper and keep him in line." Bill smiled and nodded. Collier turned to me, extending his hand. "Take care of yourself, little brother. I won't be there to get you out of any scrapes. Be tough, and do what your sergeant tells you," he admonished, the last words catching in his throat.

"Sure, Collier. I'll be okay," I assured him, without real confidence that all would be well. Then, the hand that still gripped mine pulled me into a hug. It was a rare show of affection from this man who had been where I was going and had returned, his life forever changed by the tragic fortunes of war.

Along with Father, he was holding Mother, her shoulders shaking with emotion, as the train pulled out of view. The sobs started as she hugged me, whispering close to my ear that I must return to her safely. I promised I would, as I gently removed her arms from around my neck and kissed both of her gloved hands.

We love those who give us birth, who provide for our first years of life and growth, who nurture and care for us without ever really considering why. Love of parents, of siblings, is seldom profound, seldom something to which we give much thought. It is simply something we become conditioned to feeling. I realized at that moment, as my parents and brother grew smaller in my view, how much I would miss them, how much I loved them.

Mother promised to write weekly. Her letters, I knew, would be filled with Gadsden's happenings, its changes, its gossip. My father made no such promise. I knew he would leave this to Mother. Her letters would contain his greetings and greetings from Doc Cunningham and JB.

The train pulled into Atlanta that afternoon, stopping among several trains idling on parallel tracks. It was a huge station that reminded me of San Francisco. We had received instructions to meet the army bus in front of the station. It is where we headed, only to find no sign of a bus, which finally arrived an hour later. Bill and I were surprised to see several of the young men, who had been standing nonchalantly or sitting on their suitcases, scramble for a seat on the olive-drab school bus with "Army Air Corps" on its side.

The induction center was a large Quonset hut just outside Atlanta, sectioned off into several smaller rooms. We were ushered into an area filled with folding chairs that faced a battered desk flanked by the American flag and the Georgia state flag. The surly sergeant doing the steering ordered us to be seated and remain quiet. He then lectured briefly on army etiquette. When he said, "Ten-*shun!*"

we were to stand, and if that command preceded the appearance of an officer, we were to salute smartly.

I remembered Collier's advice to obey all sergeants, and I was not tempted to talk, even when Bill leaned over to say something. A finger to my lips discouraged any further conversation. It was an older colonel who led us in the oath to serve our country, followed by the Pledge of Allegiance.

"Welcome to the army of the United States of America, gentlemen," he concluded. "Ten-*shun*."

We were on our feet, saluting the back of the disappearing colonel.

Belongings in hand, we were ushered down the hall to another large room, partitioned into a dozen white-curtained cubicles. The moment for physicals was at hand. It is not an experience you write home to your parents about. I had been to a doctor only twice in my life—once due to bad tonsils that were soon surgically expurgated from my throat and another time when chiggers managed to infest my groin area with torturous, itchy bites that became the source of much merriment to Doc Cunningham and my parents. Neither instance compared to what I was now undergoing.

A hurried doctor in a white smock that covered his stocky frame declared me fit for the Air Corps and sent me down the hall to stand in line for a gauntlet of needles that were poked into our arms— protection against everything from tetanus to yellow fever. Bill was just ahead of me in the injection line. Before the first hypodermic needles were hardly through his skin layer, he was on the floor in a dead faint.

By early the next morning, Bill was awake but not well. The shots took their toll on many enlistees, and he was among that unlucky group. Aspirin helped. Sandwiches and donuts in the noncommissioned officers hut had almost as bracing an effect as the aspirin. Then it was off to another area of the induction center for a battery of tests we mastered quickly. By that evening, we were declared ready for Air Corps cadet training, and the barking sergeant sent us to bed with a welcome announcement. We would board a train for Miami, Florida, in the morning, to begin basic training.

Miami, city of sunshine, palm trees, fabled white-sand beaches, beautiful women in bathing suits. What a place for basic training. I was sitting on the side of the cot when the sergeant walked into the barracks and barked, "Winstead!"

"Yes, sir," I answered, jumping to my feet and saluting.

"Over here."

"Yes, sir."

"Got a problem, son," he announced officiously.

I was standing straight-backed in my newly issued army-olive shorts and undershirt, waiting for him to reveal the problem. He looked me over, then rubbed his hand over his raspy chin. A new growth of tough whiskers shadowed his chin and cheeks. He hesitated so long, I finally spoke. "Is something wrong, sir? Is it my family?"

"No, son, nothing like that. The fact is …" he hesitated again. "The fact is, you're color blind."

"Color blind? What's that mean, sir?"

"It means, son, you maybe can't fly." There was almost a hint of sympathy in his curt tone.

"But, sir, I've got to fly. That's why I joined the Air Corps. I got my folks to sign my papers, even though they didn't want to." I was pleading now, seeing my plans, my future, dashed by some idiot doctor who said yesterday I could not distinguish dark blue from black, yellow from orange. So what? What did that have to do with flying? I could tell a runway from grass. I would be able to spot the rising sun on the side of a Jap plane, or the German cross on the side of a Messerschmitt.

"I hear you lost one brother in North Africa and have another brother who was wounded in the Pacific." The sergeant's tone was kind. "Is that why you joined? To get even for your brothers?"

"No, sir, that's just part of the reason. I want to do my part. But most of all, I want to fly." I knew in my deepest core that was true. It was not just to escape the loss of Sylvia. There had been something compelling and luring about that poster in front of the Birmingham post office, the proud arch of the air cadet's chin lifted against the unfurling stars and stripes.

The sergeant rubbed his bristled face again, his eyes fixed on mine, his probing eyes looking for something. What? He apparently saw what he was looking for. The rough, leathery hand fell back to his side, and his shoulders seemed almost perceptively to straighten.

"All right, son. I'll fix these papers so you can stay in. I guess color blindness shouldn't keep a good recruit like you out. I'll drop it to 10 percent. And there won't be any more questions."

"Thank you, sir. Thank you very much." I wanted to hug him, this sergeant I would probably never see again, once I left Atlanta tomorrow. Instead, I saluted smartly.

"Good luck, son. And try to get home to your folks in one piece." His tone was kindly; then it shifted to its more familiar bark. "Dismissed." He turned on his heel, my health papers held tightly in his hand, and left the way he had come.

I stood for a moment, watching his khaki back disappear out the double door, relief sweeping over me. I vowed to myself that I would never do anything to dishonor the trust he placed in me by forging 10 percent where there should have been 50 percent color blindness.

The next morning we boarded a train for Miami, our new army-issue Air Corps cadet uniforms making us all feel a little cocky. The shepherding sergeant left us at the train platform, transferring his supervisory duties to a younger three-striper who boarded the train. He pulled rank on some cadets who boarded ahead of Bill and me and promptly fell asleep in the more comfortable seat he'd commandeered at the far end of the coach car, without acknowledging any of his new charges.

Miami's sunshine was in retreat when we arrived later the next day, vanquished by a wicked thunderstorm packing near hurricane-force winds that bent palm trees and people to its whim. Neither Bill nor I had witnessed nature's wrath unleashed with such ferocity. It was not the welcome we anticipated.

The olive-drab army bus—it looked like all the others by now—pulled up under the wide portico of the Palmetto Beach Hotel, a multi-story luxury resort I'd read about once in the *Gadsden Times* Sunday travel section. Just across Collins Avenue from the hotel was the ocean, waves pounding against the beach, spurred by the high winds. This was not the Miami touted in the article.

The bus door cranked open and a burly man in an olive rain parka leaped inside. He batted his billed cap against his thigh to shake off the water, and then fitted the cap back on his head with a practiced hand.

"Welcome to Miami, gentlemen. I'm Master Sergeant Paul Amesley," he stated in a deep voice with a thick northeastern accent. "You've been assigned to my care during your stay here. I'm sorry we don't have sunshine to welcome you, because this may be the only time you have to enjoy Miami's big draw. The only thing that competes with our sunshine for enjoyment are the whores down on lower Collins." There was cautious laughter from the two dozen cadets on the bus. "And that, gentlemen, may be the last time you laugh for a time. Now, if you would please get your gear and fall out by the bus."

A scramble ensued for the army-issue duffel bags given each of us in Atlanta. The suitcases Bill and I brought from Gadsden were being sent back to our homes with our civilian clothes still packed inside. Even our shaving items were army-issue. As we filed off the bus, the sergeant stood quietly, sizing up this latest hand the Atlanta center had dealt him. He hustled us into a single line, then ordered, "Ten-shun. Fall in two by two and get your baby-pink asses inside the hotel. It's time for a little growing up, gentlemen."

18

The army needed pilots. Waging war at two ends of the earth against stubborn, well-armed and well-trained enemies severely stretched even the United States' seemingly inexhaustible source of manpower and equipment.

Bill and I were placed with thirty other new cadets in an accelerated training program that could see us heading to a combat zone within six months. Our physical abilities, coupled with strong scores on the written exams, propelled us into the fast-paced training, a timetable that pleased us both. This made us the elite among our fellow cadets and added a little more swagger to our walk and demeanor, until the end of our first day of training—the first day of hell!

It began routinely. Reveille sounded at five, followed by a five-mile run along palm-lined Collins Avenue that began in the dark and finished as the sun was rising above the horizon of the blue Atlantic. Then there were thirty minutes of calisthenics on the beach.

By the time we sat down to breakfast, I was almost too tired to eat. Bill and I agreed that the two-per-day football practices in the searing Alabama heat of August could prove a godsend. The rest of the day, until seven in the evening, was divided between aeronautical classes at the army-commandeered movie theater, six blocks from the hotel, and practicing our marching skills several times daily between the hotel and the theater. It was a routine our wing of trainees settled into quickly.

We were also required to memorize the complete booklet of the Army Air Corps general orders. My laxness at this task was soon revealed to a burly sergeant who quizzed me. He found my knowledge lacking. So, I found myself scrubbing the third-floor marble stairway with a toothbrush for six hours. The punishment prompted me and the rest of the cadets in our wing to spend less time sleeping and more time memorizing.

Training was seven days a week. Our only break came on Sunday, when we were allowed to attend chapel service in the hotel lobby, conducted by a Catholic priest from a nearby parish. It was my first contact with a priest. He wore a black robe and starched white Roman collar. I marveled that he did not pull and tug at the stiff collar, which had to be uncomfortable in the humid heat of south Florida. The service was open to civilians as well, and a number of elderly tourists and seasonal residents of the hotel sat around quietly, some with rosary beads threading through their fingers.

Although we were unaware of it at the time, the cadet basic training in a posh hotel in Miami was the envy of the rest of the Air Corps. Housing trainees in a hotel that provided food service relieved the stress on other training centers that were bursting with fresh recruits being readied to take the place of weary veterans— veterans who had carried the harshest burden of fighting and dying in the months following Pearl Harbor. It took the American war machine a year to crank up to full capacity. By late 1944, the U. S. general command saw the end in sight.

As most people later learned, in the war room at the White House, an ultimate weapon—the atomic bomb—was under almost daily discussion as a means to shorten the war. It was finally agreed it should be used against Japan.

Under the direction of physicist J. Robert Oppenheimer, an American-born but Cambridge- and Gottingen University-educated scientist, the first of three atomic bombs was under construction at a secret facility in the desert near Los Alamos, New Mexico, just as our training as pilots was getting under way in Miami. The atomic bomb would be successfully tested at Alamogordo, New Mexico, the following July.

By the end of our four-week training, seven of those chosen for our accelerated wing had dropped out and were placed back with enlistees, who would spend an additional two to three weeks at the Miami facility. It was back-breaking and mentally defeating work that threatened each of us with failure every day. It made our final day in basic training all the more satisfying.

Early on the evening of our last day, we were dismissed by Sergeant Amesley with a gruff and short congratulatory speech and then handed overnight passes. We had our first precious eleven hours of freedom, and the announcement was greeted with a raucous cheer. It was almost enough to make me forgive this more affable Amesley for the grueling six hours I spent scrubbing those marble stairs.

Pooling our money, Bill and I hopped a cab to an area of Miami not highlighted in travel brochures—the bar and red-light district. It was a regular discussion topic in the mess hall, this seedy area that welcomed raw, young cadets from the more posh environs of Miami Beach. The swing music on the jukeboxes blaring out of dimly lit bars contrasted sharply with the more austere piano music offered in the elite drinking emporiums in the area where we trained.

Girls dressed in breast-baring blouses and skirts shorter than current fashions dictated stood around in twos and threes, puffing on cigarettes and throwing casual glances at the strolling men but turning away with bored expressions when a soldier came by with a girl on his arm.

We were given the usual warnings about venereal disease and advised to use condoms when having sex with a prostitute. Like most lustful teenagers with hope in their hearts, Bill and I always carried a condom in our billfolds, just in case an unexpected opportunity presented itself. We decided on the way into town this would be one of those just-in-case times. But first, a beer.

Florida had a drinking age of twenty-one in those days, a law strictly enforced, according to Sergeant Amesley. In our khaki uniforms, with the Air Corps Cadet insignia on our arms and with a swagger in our step because we had just passed a grueling four weeks that was sending us to the next plateau of combat pilot training, we viewed ourselves as adults and felt we should be treated accordingly. The first bartender with whom we came face to face disagreed.

"Sorry, boys. You ain't wet enough behind the ears for me to serve you a beer. I could lose my liquor license if the boys in blue catch me. I wish I could, but I just can't," he said, almost apologetically.

The scuttlebutt around the mess hall was that you could pass a bartender an extra buck or two and get your beer. It was worth a try. I fished in my pocket and slid a one-dollar bill slowly across the smooth surface of the heavily varnished bar top. The bartender noted the motion of my hand and deftly pulled the bill from my fingers and slipped it into his apron pocket.

Seconds later, two bottles of beer were placed in front of us. Two more followed those. After the third beer, we were set to go back to the street to negotiate the rest of our night's entertainment. By the time we were ready to vacate our stools at the bar, the tavern was crowded with military, mostly cadets, many with girls, and the din was deafening.

The street outside brought relief from the bar's noise and stuffiness. A soft tropical breeze enveloped us. The night sky was sprinkled with stars, the brightness of which was somewhat muted by the full moon. The beer left us feeling a little light on our feet and even more cocky. The garish neon lights of another bar a half-block away beckoned. It was a more upscale spot than our first stop. We paused just inside the doorway to scan the tables. Bill was the first to spot some prospects—two blondes sitting by themselves at a rear table with two half-full glasses of beer in front of them. "Wanna try them?" Bill suggested.

I was game. Three beers tends to make hormones somewhat unruly. The girls beamed welcoming smiles when we stopped at their table. "Mind if we join you?" I asked.

"Sit down, soldier boys, and buy us a beer," said an overly made-up blonde invitingly. "These are beginning to get warm." She was pretty in a not-very-wholesome way, with hair that got its color from a dye bottle.

"I'm John Winstead. This is my buddy, Bill Deems."

"Trudy Lewis." She smiled again and motioned to her friend. "This here's Jeannie Sullivan."

Jeannie seemed the more shy of the two. Her blue eyes were crowned by long, dark lashes, and she was by far the prettier of the two. "Hi." The greeting was said softly, accenting her shyness. If she was a hooker, she was new to the trade.

Bill sat down by Jeannie, and I pulled my chair closer to Trudy.

"Where are you boys from?" Trudy was the talker.

"Alabama."

Trudy noted the insignia on my shirt. "How long have you been in the Air Corps?"

"Four weeks. Let me get us a round of fresh beers." I caught the eye of a waitress and held up four fingers by the side of one of the girl's glasses and got a nod in response. The beers arrived a couple of minutes later. "What are you girls doing tonight?" I got right to the point.

"Not much. We were just looking for a couple of guys like you to show up so we could have a good time. You ready for a good time?" Trudy winked at me.

I had guessed right. They were hookers, but baiting their hooks from a different territory than outside on the street, a location choice that could cost us more money.

"How much is a good time?" JB and Doc Cunningham had instructed me that unless prostitutes worked out of a brothel, you negotiated price and place, usually a nearby hotel where the girl rented a room on work nights.

"Ten dollars for an hour of the best time you'll get in Miami."

Jeannie sat quietly next to Bill while Trudy and I arranged things.

"Sounds good to me. How about you, Bill?"

"Sure. I'm ready whenever you are." Jeannie nodded her agreement to the arrangement.

"Where to, Trudy?" I asked.

She motioned for Jeannie to follow her. Bill and I both emptied the remains of our beers and followed the two women out to the street, which was lined on both sides by bars and girlie shows with boisterous hawkers on the sidewalk. The hawkers shouted out to passing men, most of them in uniform, what was to be enjoyed inside their establishments.

Trudy took my arm, and we walked about a block to a revolving door fogged with fingerprints, which swung into the lobby of a seedy hotel. A balding man behind the desk nodded disinterestedly as the four of us crossed over to the narrow stairway that led to the rooms the girls rented on the second floor. The hallway was dimly lit with a bare bulb that cast shadows on the faded floral wallpaper.

Trudy stopped in front of a door with a number three painted on it. Jeannie took Bill by the hand to a room several doors down the hallway. They disappeared inside before Trudy could finesse the door to number three open with a bent key. I wondered how often that key had opened this door for an hour's pleasure. Although the wallpaper inside the room was painted over, it did not discipline the old wall covering to adhere to the surface underneath. The edges of the paper curled loose from the wall near the ceiling, adding a sad look of neglect to the dismal room.

"I need to get the ten dollars now ... if you don't mind." It was not an unusual request from a service provider, who had probably been cheated by other customers and was taking no chances with me. I pulled a ten-dollar bill from my billfold and laid it on the dusty dresser. Trudy nodded and began taking her clothes off, oblivious to me. She sat down on the edge of the creaky bed, naked, waiting for me to undress.

"Time's a-wasting, big boy. Can't do much with that uniform on. It's a lot more fun doing it bare-assed, like me." She grinned and reached her hands out to me. "Come on over and let mama help you out of those things." Her dark brown eyes were alight with a mischievous smile.

Somehow, the invitation did not seem that inviting. I pulled off my shirt and pants, then my briefs, and walked over to the bed. There would be no romance in this coupling, just lust spawned by raw carnal desire. I wanted a screw, and this was the first female available.

When it was over, I felt satisfied but strangely empty. I had tried to fantasize that she was Sylvia, and we were in the sweaty rear of the dry cleaners on the narrow cot. The picture of Sylvia was blurred by the reality of this woman's face beneath mine, her breath coming in well-practiced heaves, punctuated by an occasional groan. Sex was a living, not an enjoyment for Trudy, despite my brief attempt at foreplay. As I got back into my clothes, she reminded me that there was still time left of my hour.

"Didn't you enjoy it, honey?"

"It was good, Trudy, but once is enough." I tried to sound reassuring and grateful, knowing I could not.

That night in Miami was the last time I would seek sexual gratification from a prostitute. I had dutifully worn the rubber suggested by the army film on avoiding venereal disease. No danger there, I reasoned as I waited for Bill in the small lobby of the hotel. Bill took his full hour—and then some—before he appeared, smiling.

"Good?"

"Yeah! Jeannie was okay. She told me it was just her second time. First time was a fat-bellied salesman last night. I think she liked doing it better with me."

Many men fall for hookers. Having sex with a prostitute somehow evokes a man's sympathy, a sympathy that becomes a bond between the man and the woman he has hired. That bond transcends the customer/service-provider relationship between the prostitute and her john. Bill would seek out the company and pleasure of hookers often during his tenure in the Air Corps, as did many other men I met in the service.

My escape, however, was to memories. My comfort, my torment, was Sylvia.

19

Snow lay like a fallen white cloud over the tops of the Sierra Nevada mountains and was reflected in the turquoise waters of Lake Tahoe. It was well below freezing as we made our way to the classrooms in the large hangar, sheltered in the leeward side of towering pine trees, stretching in dark contrast toward the rocky, snow-covered higher ranges. This was no Miami.

Snow was rare in Alabama—it was something heartily welcomed and enjoyed like an unexpected visitor. You knew it would not last long, and that was all the more reason to build snowmen and slide down the hills of Gadsden on your mama's largest cookie sheet or in a large washtub. Snow was not as pleasurable an experience in the high country of Nevada.

It was December, nearing Christmas, and next week we would begin working on the flight simulator. In a month, I could be sitting in the cockpit of a trainer plane. I was ready, champing at the bit to get out of the confines of the classroom and get on with the reason I joined the Air Corps. A biting wind forced my hands deep into the pockets of my leather bomber jacket.

Inside the classroom, a coal stove provided heat and an oily aroma. A captain with combat ribbons pinned across his chest rapped the desk for silence. The voices of the cadets were instantly silenced.

"News from Europe, gentlemen. The Krauts are on the march and have the 101st Division pinned down near a place called Bastogne, in Belgium. It doesn't look good for our guys. The Germans went on the offensive a week ago. The weather is worse there than it is here. Lots of snow and fog are keeping our planes from getting help to our guys. The last thing I saw described a bad blizzard that's keeping ground troops from getting through to relieve them. A lot of our boys have been captured." The captain jammed his hands in his pockets and glared at the falling snow outside the classroom window. "A tough break for those guys over there. Prayers couldn't hurt, when you have time."

Impotent rage. It was what we all felt at that moment in the warm room, safe in the mountains of Nevada, far from the battle, the killing, the fear. It would be another three months before any of us would be ready to fly or navigate a plane on our own. In three months, the brave men fending off the German advance in the cold streets of Bastogne could be dead or in prison camps. It was a long, chilly day in the hangar classroom.

Not until after Christmas did we learn that elements of the Third Army under General Patton had marched for three days—through heavy snow in sub-freezing temperatures—to relieve the Americans at Bastogne and thwart the German advance, in what newsreels were dubbing the Battle of the Bulge. Prolonged cheers would ring out in the crowded classroom when our cadet wing later learned of the relief of the beleaguered American forces by old blood-and-guts Patton, who had the Germans in retreat.

All that was a world away and yet to come. It was Christmas morning. The sun glistened off the snow-covered branches of spruce and junipers around the training facility. We had a day off from the classroom and flight simulator training. At age eighteen, neither Bill nor I had ever been away from home at Christmas. It was a day when the Winstead clan gathered in the living room and, with the alacrity of childhood, opened gifts under the brightly decorated pine that was dwarfed by the high-ceilinged room. Then we would share a feast of ham and turkey and a plum pudding made from a treasured family recipe, passed down from mother to daughter through seven generations of my mother's family in America. Our home would harbor the delectable smells of cooking food. Neighbors dropped by to say hello and kiss my mother's cheek under the mistletoe that always hung from the chandelier in the foyer. JB Stevens exercised his proprietary right as our closest neighbor and friend by laughingly kissing my mother and sister full on the lips, under the tolerant eye of both my father and Maudie Stevens.

Far from our families, among strangers, Christmas now was a lonely day for Bill and me. There was, however, some taste of home. It had come in a package from my parents, full of homemade cookies, a fruit cake, nut bread—and letters. One of these letters, from my stern grandmother Winstead, expressed her affection, along with an admonishment to follow the precepts of my Baptist upbringing and stay away from loose women who, she warned, would prey on young soldiers.

My grandfather had been a country doctor who called on patients in a horse and buggy. During a vicious thunderstorm, his horse shied and bolted, overturning the carriage and crushing my grandfather beneath it. Grandmother later married the man who managed her sprawling farm, a mating her only son found disdainful and beneath her. She came to our house only at Christmas, and she came alone, knowing her husband was not welcome.

My father was a man of forbearance, admired by many in the Gadsden community for his charity, a quality of character never extended to his stepfather. It was to be a dislike that cost him his birthright. When Grandmother passed away the following spring, the two thousand acres of fertile corn and cotton growing land, farmed by Winsteads since their arrival in Alabama, were inherited first by my grandmother's second husband, and then by his three children, much to the chagrin of my parents.

There was also a long letter from my sister. Sarah was getting married to a boy she had dated briefly in high school who was now a captain in the army and stationed in Washington DC at the Pentagon. He had a three-day leave coming in late January, and she then would become Mrs. Robert Morgan. The Morgans were Gadsden's leading banking family. Social prominence was always one of Sarah's major aspirations. I grudgingly saluted her achievement.

The marriage would take place in Washington, and her letter was full of the preparations—the dress, the travel plans, and complaints about having no time for a regular honeymoon because the wedding was being squeezed into Robert's short furlough.

There was a brief mention of my brother. Collier was now engaged to Katie Shannon, wrote Sarah, but the formal announcement would not be shared with the family until Christmas Day. This, wrote Sarah, was a problem. She suspected Katie Shannon was Irish-Catholic, since she was one of eight children of an Indianapolis family. With an Irish name like Shannon, my sister sniffed in her letter, could she be anything but Catholic? So, that bastion of the Baptist faith, the Winsteads, might by joined by a Catholic. I could envision the horror of such a happening plainly revealed on Sarah's face. And how would a Catholic in the family sit with those staunch uptown Presbyterians, the Morgans?

My mother's letter was full of Sarah's upcoming marriage, but from a much different perspective. She was delighted at Sarah's choice of a husband, but saddened that she and Father could not attend the ceremony in Washington. Her letter also mentioned Collier's fiancée, how much more content he seemed these days, and how they were looking forward to welcoming Katie as a guest for the Christmas holidays. Mother wrote that Katie had put "sunshine" back into Collier.

She touched on most of our other friends and acquaintances. Jeb Thomas broke a leg in a tractor accident. He was unable to leave the house and work. The Thomas children were all helping with jobs until Jeb was able to resume his old routine. The Thomas' second-oldest son had followed his brother in joining the Negro brigade training at Tuskegee.

I felt badly for our handyman, knowing that he would have little money coming in to support his large family while his leg was mending. I later learned that Jeb's shattered leg had been improperly set by an inept young resident assigned to treat patients in the segregated wing for Negroes at Gadsden's main hospital. Sadly, mother wrote, Jeb might never walk again without crutches or a cane.

I had visited Jeb and Millie several times and always was welcomed warmly into the drafty wood shack that Millie kept spotless. It was the only home the Thomas family ever knew. I thought of Jeb lying in bed, unable to walk or work, the same bed in which he had fathered seven children with the kindly, gregarious Millie.

Doc Cunningham was down with pneumonia and laid up for two weeks in the midst of a flu epidemic. A young physician, who had recently moved to Gadsden from Birmingham after completing his residency at the University of Alabama hospital, took over the care of Doc's patients. Mother described the young doctor's efforts as tireless and heroic. So far, she added, she and Dad had escaped the flu.

There was a P.S. to mother's letter. The new doctor, Heddon Phelps, was Sylvia's cousin on her mother's side. I recalled Sylvia mentioning a cousin she saw occasionally in Birmingham. Phelps must be that cousin. He might know where she was. I felt some of the loneliness of this day fall away with this new hope of finding Sylvia.

Throughout Christmas Day, Bill remained quiet and withdrawn. Even at lunch, over a traditional turkey-and-dressing dinner, he said little. I did not intrude. No letter or card had come from his parents, only a letter from my mother, wrapped with a scarf she knitted for him to wear with his bomber jacket. He read her letter, then slipped it and the scarf inside his foot locker and lay back down on his cot, content to stare sullenly at the ceiling. Even my offer of cookies and fruit cake could not dent his shell of silence.

Later that afternoon, a young lieutenant appeared in the barracks to announce that buses would be available to take anyone who wanted to go into Reno. The USO club was hosting a Christmas party for all servicemen in the area, the lieutenant announced. A bus could already be heard pulling up in front of our barracks. There was an uproar as cadets swung out of their cots or dropped their card hands to grab uniform jackets, hats, and bomber jackets and sprint to the waiting bus.

"Come on, Bill! Let's go into town. It could be fun."

Bill was turned away from me on his cot and just shook his head.

"It's not going to get any better here," I reasoned. "Let's go have some fun. It'll take your mind off things."

"No, you go on. I don't want to go," he said, a sad belligerence in his voice.

"Ah, come on, Bill. It's Reno! It's got to be better than lying around here all Christmas Day."

"Goddamn it, I don't want to go." There was a fury and finality in his voice that stopped any further efforts to urge him to come. Bill still had his back to me as I left the barracks and boarded a converted school bus. I felt a tinge of guilt as the bus pulled away.

Bill had no say in who gave birth to him. He drew a bad lot— parents who had no love for each other and none for him. My mother must have known, or at least suspected, this dearth of affection. As a youngster, Bill bloomed in the fondness with which my mother enfolded him, giving him frequent hugs, kisses on the cheek, and holding his hand when he accompanied us downtown for trips to the grocery, the barber, or the drugstore. Bill learned to return affection openly, but only to my parents. He remained shy with girls, asking a girl on a date only when he could double with me, and often, only after I made a preliminary overture to the girl.

With prostitutes he seemed more at ease, more in control; he seemed drawn to them. He was the closest friend I had—would probably ever have—but however much we shared, I would never feel the pain he felt from his parents' rejection, the lifelong torment of not knowing why, and the concern—always—that it was somehow his fault.

A canvas banner that was draped across Reno's main downtown street welcomed us to "The biggest little city in the world." The snow-covered street was deserted. Even Harrah's Stateline Club was closed for Christmas, a disappointment to some of the cadets on the bus who anticipated being parted from some of their recent pay by a dealer or a slot machine. The small neon light on the front of the USO club was blinking erratically, and some of its letters were burned out.

Inside, a modest-sized floor covered in sawdust was filled with servicemen dancing with partners. As our group moved inside the door, we were greeted by one of the USO hostesses, a pretty brunette with brown eyes and a warm smile. "Hi, fellows. Welcome to the Reno USO club. Make yourself at home. There are donuts and coffee and sodas on the table against the wall." She pointed to a long cloth-covered table, behind which two women were serving cups of steaming coffee to cadets.

From the left side of the dance floor came a shout. It was the same lieutenant who had announced the bus for Reno. Beside him was a young blonde wearing a dress that showed far more worldliness and sophistication than her years. "I've been saving the table for you guys," he yelled from across the room.

A dozen folding chairs were quickly occupied by a rush of cadets to the table. I reached it first and sat down next to the blonde. Despite the ruby lipstick and too much rouge, she appeared to be about my age. She smiled a hello and held out her hand. "I'm Mary Ellen Helms."

"John Winstead. Glad to meet you." She was pretty in a saucy kind of way. "Wanna dance?"

"Sure."

The music of Benny Goodman boomed out of a jukebox, and the dance floor was jumping with jitter-buggers. We were both a little breathless when the music ended, still panting when we returned to the table, where the lieutenant pulled a bottle of bourbon from underneath. Signs at the front of the club warned against bringing liquor on the premises. "It's fine," the lieutenant said reassuringly. "There aren't any MPs here tonight."

He topped off my half-empty glass of Coke with bourbon and filled Mary Ellen's empty glass. I had smelled liquor on her breath while we were dancing. By the time I put away the fourth glass of bourbon and Coke, Mary Ellen was clearly drunk, and the lieutenant was stumbling to the head with a case of "too much, too soon."

I pulled Mary Ellen onto the dance floor. It was a slow number from Margaret Whiting. Mary Ellen put her arms around my neck, more for support than romance. I could feel her ample breasts against my chest and moving one hand subtly up from her waist, I brushed my thumb over one nipple. She involuntarily sucked in her breath. The nipple became hard with my gentle prodding.

"You want to kiss me?" she asked, a tipsy smile spreading across her lips as she stared tauntingly at me, large blue eyes glazed over by liquor.

"Yeah, but not here. Where can we go?"

"My car's outside. We could drive around."

"What about Lieutenant Mertz?"

"What about him?" she countered defensively. "He's too drunk to even know I'm gone. Let's go."

The lieutenant had not returned from the restroom. I was becoming a little unsteady myself as the drinks took stronger hold, betraying my lack of experience with hard liquor. Beer was the drink Bill and I preferred. By the time we got to Mary Ellen's car, my head was reeling. She pushed the keys into my hand. "You drive."

"Where to?" I asked.

"Down to the park at the end of this street."

The small park was dark, with only a narrow road through its center. I pulled over to the curb and then pulled Mary Ellen against me, turning her face up to mine to kiss her full lips with their smudged lipstick. The heater was finally pumping out warmer air against the near-freezing temperatures outside the car.

She let me remove her coat, and I fumbled drunkenly with the buttons on her blouse, finally releasing her breasts from the constraints of the bra. God, how round and firm. I buried my head in the cleavage, kissing my way to the nipples, which I covered with my mouth and sucked gently. She moaned softly and pressed my head against her. The front seat was too confining for what I wanted next, so I slid over the front seat into the backseat and coaxed her to follow me. As I tugged at her panties, she took my face in both hands and whispered something so softly that I wasn't sure what she said.

"What, Mary Ellen?" I asked, in a tone that hinted impatience.

"This is my first time." She looked at me with soft eyes, eyes that begged me to make the decision to have sex or not. The drinks, the feel of her, stripped me of any control. I wanted her badly and pulled her panties the rest of the way down her legs.

"It may hurt a little at first. I'll be gentle, and you'll enjoy it." I tried to sound reassuring.

"It's okay," she whispered. As my thrust tore through her membrane she let out a sharp yell, and I could feel the warm stickiness of blood. I pulled out to soothe her with foreplay. When I pushed inside her again, she was wet with desire and welcome. The promise she would enjoy it was kept.

When we returned to the USO club, the sex, the cold, and the elapsed hour since we'd left had a sobering effect on me. Not so for Mary Ellen, who may have been as new to drinking as she was to sex. Lieutenant Mertz gave us a stormy look as we approached the table, demanding angrily to know where we had been. "Mary Ellen needed some fresh air so we took a walk," I casually lied.

He was not appeased, but he was too drunk to challenge my excuse for our absence. Mary Ellen sank unsteadily into her chair, noting in a slurry voice that it was cold outside.

I was saved from any further questioning by a female voice over the loud speaker, announcing that the club was closing and that buses were now waiting to take us back to camp. I beat a hasty retreat back to the bus with only a quick good-bye to Mary Ellen.

Christmas 1944 ended on a less lonely note than it had started. Bill was asleep when I got back to the barracks, bringing a brief end to his loneliness as well. For me, the next morning would bring an end to sleep, a return to training routine, and the revenge of Lieutenant Mertz.

20

William Mertz was the scion of a wealthy Los Angeles family and a West Point dropout who landed, with the help of his politically connected father, a commission in the Army Air Corps, a safe harbor for an only son who had been a lifelong disappointment to his parents. His assignment to a training unit in Reno ensured that he would spend his time in the military in the safety of the States, to return at war's end to take up an assignment dictated by his birth as the only heir to the Mertz Shipping conglomerate.

Lieutenant Mertz was not a man who took kindly to an upstart cadet slipping away with his date. I learned the following day just how much his challenged ego was smarting. At the end of early morning drill and calisthenics, I was called out of the drill line and upbraided for failing to report with freshly polished boots. I glanced down at my smudged boots as a red-faced Lieutenant Mertz ordered me to remain behind and stand four hours of guard duty. This meant missing breakfast, but more important, missing flight classes.

Guard duty was cold, boring work, requiring marching up and

down the assigned area with a rifle at the ready, to ensure that no one entered the perimeter of the training camp. I had been patrolling my area for about two hours when Lieutenant Mertz approached. I ordered him to halt and identify himself. When he appeared before me, he demanded my gun. I refused. The regulations were clear. A guard must not turn over his weapon to anyone, not even a commanding officer. Lieutenant Mertz shouted his demand with his face just inches from mine. Those same regulations also warned an enlistee that you could be court-martialed for refusing a direct order.

The lieutenant stood before me, his hands outstretched, his breath coming hard. I reluctantly handed my rifle to him, still uncertain about why he was demanding the weapon.

"That was a mistake, cadet. You never hand over your rifle when you're on guard duty. Do you understand, Winstead?" There was a perverse glint in his steely blue eyes as he shouted the admonishment.

"Yes, sir."

"You will remain on guard duty, four hours on, four hours off, for the next four weeks, and you are confined to barracks for a month. Is that understood?"

"Yes, sir."

The severity of my punishment was immediately apparent. There would be no time to attend classes mandatory to taking my first actual flight instruction. I could appeal his punishment to the wing commander or even the base commander, but I quickly scrubbed that thought. No commander was going to take the word of a cadet over that of an officer. When that was the case, the officer won. Appealing would be futile.

Lieutenant Mertz shoved the rifle back into my hands. I snapped the rifle across my chest and brought it down to my left side and saluted at attention. He returned the salute and stalked off toward the barracks, shouting his identity to another guard several yards away near the camp gate.

That night, cold and exhausted, I determined a way to continue the studies necessary to take flight training. Bill agreed to take copious notes during the classes, notes I could study during one of my off-duty shifts. Four hours to study, four hours to sleep. I could make it for a month and not delay my pilot training by any more than two weeks. I also determined, while lying in my cot that night before drifting off to sleep, that no one-night stand, even with a virgin, was worth what I now faced.

The cold of that January was the worst in forty years in Nevada. Snow fell in copious amounts. Even with army-issue snow boots, the bitter cold penetrated and stayed, numbing my toes. My feet—my hands, too—would still be red when the alarm wrestled me out of sleep to stand another four-hour guard watch.

Staying awake to study Bill's notes from each day's classes was my biggest struggle. I would study during my morning break, when there was light in the barracks, and catch sleep during the four-hour break at night. Lieutenant Mertz came often to my guard station, checking my uniform and guard demeanor, but he could find no fault. Of that I made certain.

Week three. I was walking guard duty when Bill took his first flight in a Piper Cub. We had talked incessantly about our first time in an airplane, an experience we would share in the Air Corps. It was now to be his experience alone. Bitterness boiled up in me like rising bile, but it was an anger I could not regurgitate for fear someone would tell Lieutenant Mertz. The anger seethed silently inside. I complained to no one, not even Bill.

The lieutenant was proving a popular wing officer, buying rounds of drinks during weekend leave nights in Reno's several bars frequented by cadets. For young men far from home, with monthly paychecks well below a hundred dollars, free drinks were an appreciated bonus. I had other plans for Lieutenant Mertz on one of those weekend bar sojourns, plans I confided only to Bill in hushed whispers after lights out. The opportunity came sooner that I expected.

A blizzard had blown in off the mountains during the final hours of my guard duty. Temperatures dropped slowly throughout the day. My regular guard stint was from midnight until four, but a sergeant ordered me to cover an early shift from nine until midnight. The regular guard was on sick call. Despite wearing an extra pair of socks and long underwear, and with the scarf my mother knitted for Bill wound snugly around my neck, the howling wind penetrated my clothing and permeated every pore. Even with the insulation of hot coffee provided by the sergeant, I was chilled to the bone.

I walked faster, moving my rifle from side to side in an effort to ward off some of the cold. It was shortly before ten when I heard the first noise, subtle and momentary. I dismissed it as the wind howling through the pines around me and kept walking. The sound was getting closer, and it was no wind making the noise; it was a pair of boots.

I shouted halt and demanded the approaching person identify himself. Whoever it was halted but did not respond. I shouted again for the intruder to come forward. My heart was pounding in my chest so hard that I wasn't sure I could hear the response if one was given.

"Calloway, it's me, Mertz. Quit shouting. You'll wake the dead."

Lieutenant Mertz was just a few yards away from me, emerging from the shadows of two tall pine trees along a path that led back to the training field in front of the barracks. Walking several steps behind Mertz was a cadet I had seen often with the lieutenant. Don Shaunessey was a Hollywood actor who had appeared in several musicals during the past four years, and he made no bones to any of us about wanting out of this man's war. I watched him one morning slapping his face hard to make his eyes puffy and red. It worked. He was placed on sick call. That same ruse worked on several occasions. Both men were in civilian clothes and stopped short as I leveled my rifle at them.

"Halt and identify yourselves."

"Where's Calloway?" the lieutenant demanded, aware of an unfamiliar voice.

"He's on sick call, sir."

As the lieutenant came closer, he recognized me. "Put that rifle down, Winstead. Who the hell do you think you are? Shaunessey and I are just going into town for a little while. We'll be back before you go off duty. And for God's sake, don't shout like that. Hell, you could be heard in Reno."

His arrogant tone stirred my latent anger. He had been responsible for putting me out here for nearly a month in sub-freezing weather, while he was sneaking into town, obviously without a pass, to have a good time.

"May I see your passes, Lieutenant Mertz and Cadet Shaunessey?" I kept my tone even as both men stared hard at me.

"Don't be a pissant, Winstead. We're just going into town, and you're going to let us pass. Got it?"

"No, sir, I can't let you pass without a signed pass."

Lieutenant Mertz, his breath now coming hard, took a step toward me, his look menacing.

"Stay where you are, sir, or I will be obliged to shoot you." I brought my gun to my shoulder and aimed at his head. Shaunessey was standing stark still behind the lieutenant.

"Hey, Mertz, let's go back to camp. This guy means business." A slow smile chased the frown from the actor's face. "Look, Winstead, we'll just get back to the barracks. No harm done, okay?"

"No, sir, I have to call for the sergeant. He'll determine what to do." There was a rustle of pine needles to my left.

"Halt and identify yourself."

"It's me, Strickland. I heard voices and thought something was wrong. You okay?" Strickland was the guard patrolling the adjacent perimeter area.

"Can you get the sergeant for me?"

Strickland looked uncertainly at the lieutenant and Shaunessey, then back at me.

"These men are trying to leave camp without a pass. Get the sergeant, Strickland. Now!"

Strickland, who was no older than I, flinched at the barked urgency in my voice. "Sure Winstead, I … I'll be right back." He darted off toward the base office in the center of the camp, just in front of the barracks.

In five minutes, Strickland was back with Sergeant Major Hendricks. Hendricks saluted the lieutenant smartly.

"Lower your rifle, cadet. You've done the right thing," he said, without taking his eyes off the two men standing silently before him, both shivering in the cold. "May I see your pass, sir?" the sergeant asked in a cold, matter-of-fact tone. The sergeant knew the answer before asking the question. He approved all passes to leave the base before submitting them to the captain. There was no answer from either man. "Let's go back to my office, gentlemen, and see the captain. Consider yourselves under arrest."

For the first time, Sergeant Major Hendricks turned to me. "Good work, son. Resume your post. You, too, Strickland. I'll see you both in the morning after chow for a full report."

The soft-spoken sergeant turned back to the two men standing before him. "Gentlemen, follow me." Mertz and Shaunessey fell in step behind the sergeant, and the three disappeared, enveloped in the dark awning of the towering pines.

At midnight, my relief guard arrived five minutes late, muttering apologies. My joints were stiff with cold, and I felt strangely stiff inside, my emotions frozen in a kind of icy stagnation. There was no feeling of exuberance that the man who sentenced me to these weeks of a cold, dreary hell and delayed my flight training might be facing a court-martial. I felt only numb. It was two hours before I drifted into a fitful sleep, only to be shaken awake by Bill.

"You were hollering out in your sleep, John. You must have been having a helluva nightmare."

"Yeah, I guess so. Thanks."

I lay awake the rest of my sleep shift, troubled about Calloway, the cadet on sick-call I had replaced. He was a red-haired, freckled-faced teenager from Texas, even shyer than Bill. Calloway apparently had been letting Mertz through his perimeter to go into Reno. That could mean charges against Calloway and a possible court-martial and at best, a dishonorable discharge. Calloway was the type of guy easily cowed by people like Mertz. Should he be held equally guilty? He would be, if I was forced to tell all that happened. I could only hope the sergeant and the captain, or whoever questioned me later that day, would not ask.

Captain Jeffers did not ask, nor did Sergeant Hendricks.

Calloway was safe. I had seen him at morning formation. His eyes shifted quickly away from mine. Had he already heard about Lieutenant Mertz and Shaunessey? There was no way to know. I had said nothing to Bill about the events of the night before. Scuttlebutt traveled fast at any post and especially fast at a camp as small as ours. Strickland must have told Calloway. They were in the same barracks. That had to be it.

Captain Eugene Jeffers was a tall, thin man with a permanent scowl on a long face that already was showing the creases of time. He asked pointed questions and wrote down what I told him about stopping the lieutenant and Shaunessey. Sitting in a chair next to mine, Sergeant Hendricks listened without commenting. When the questioning ended, the captain sat staring at his notes, tapping a pencil absently on the wood desk. He finally looked up, his eyes locked on me, his expression bland. "You did the right thing, son. And it took courage. We know from what Lieutenant Mertz and Cadet Shaunessey told us that last night was not the first time they went into Reno without passes."

He paused, waiting for me to say something, but I did not know how to respond, so I sat quietly. The captain looked down at his desk for some time and then looked at me again. "They'll be dealt with." The captain did not say how. He crossed his long legs and sat back in the chair, looking at me thoughtfully. "I understand you have been on guard punishment for nearly a month and couldn't go to classes. Your friends in the barracks say you've been studying from a buddy's notes. Is that correct?"

"Yes, sir."

"Have you studied enough to pass the courses?"

"I think so, sir."

"You'll have to pass a written test, son. If you do, and you can take it today if you want to, I'm going to sign an order allowing you to get into flight school immediately."

"You mean it, sir?"

"Yeah, I mean it, son." A slight smile softened his face, deepening its lines.

"Thank you, sir. I came to fly. Thanks for the chance."

"Pass that test, and happy landings. Make it for your brother, son, the one who didn't come back. He's given you some big shoes to fill. He'll be watching out for you."

I wondered how he knew about Addison and if he knew about Collier's losing his leg in the Pacific. "Yes, sir. Thank you, Captain." I saluted, and he answered with a touch to his head, his attention already turning to the notes he had taken on what transpired the night before.

I never saw Lieutenant Mertz again. He escaped a court-martial, and I later learned he was surreptitiously and unceremoniously mustered out of the Air Corps, no doubt saved by his wealth and political connections.

Shaunessey also left the Reno base, busted back to his Hollywood habitat through the protective influence of his studio, to resume his status as one of Hollywood's luminaries. I pointedly avoided seeing any of his movies.

Two days after my reprieve from guard duty I slid into the cockpit of a Piper Cub with a trainer pilot, and knew it was where I wanted to be. Seth Williams must have sensed my enthusiasm for what he loved most in the world—flying. A World War I ace who returned from the war to build a successful air cargo and airmail company in the early twenties, Williams volunteered to train American pilots who joined the Canadian Air Force before the United States became involved in the war. After Pearl Harbor, Williams came back to the States to train pilots at the Reno airport, where the army had established a small-plane training school in early 1942 for primary flight instruction. There were several civilian pilots training cadets, freeing more military pilots for the war.

I knew my first time up with Williams I had drawn the best of the lot. He had a short fuse for mistakes, and as I quickly learned, I had better catch his explanation the first time. Repeating instructions was not within his patience-tolerance zone.

By the second week, I was at the controls throughout the daily flights. By the end of that week, Williams—moving the large chaw of tobacco from his left cheek to the other side and spitting—declared me ready to advance to primary flight training.

It was past eight, past dinner, when I got back to the barracks. On my cot was my first letter from Collier. He was well and enrolled again at the University of Alabama. His fiancée, whom he referred to as the feisty colleen from Indy, worked second shift at the army hospital in Birmingham. He complained that the only time he saw her for more than an hour was when he went to Birmingham for his weekly appointment for physical therapy. They planned to be married in May. Could I get leave to attend? That, I knew, was unlikely.

Mom and Dad were doing fine. He saw them every two weeks. He was driving now and had a car specially fitted for a man with one operable leg. The transmission automatically shifted so there was no need for a clutch pedal. The gas pedal was fitted on the left side of the floorboard to be used with his good left leg.

And he had seen Sylvia.

That revelation was in the short final paragraph. She was a student in Tuscaloosa and enrolled in one of his advanced literature classes. "Quiet and pretty" was how Collier described her. She had asked about me, and he gave her my address. He had not seen her since.

There was a post-script. Sylvia called the house in November, right after I joined the Air Corps, and Mother promised to send her my address as soon as they knew where I would be stationed for basic training. Sylvia had not called back. Collier wrote that Sylvia had not enrolled for the spring semester.

Even though Mother had provided my address to Sylvia as promised no letter arrived. I looked forward to every mail call with eager anticipation, only to suffer torturous disappointment. It was at night that she was with me, dominating my dreams, circling and teasing with a smile that lured me to her embrace, and then she would disappear. On my final day at the Reno base, the only letter handed me during mail call was the weekly epistle from my mother. There was no mention of Sylvia.

21

The rolling pasture lands of central California were patch-worked with enclaves of grape vineyards and fruit orchards. It was a fertile area and beautiful, a kaleidoscope of green hues and shapes formed by the variety of crops in the fields.

The army bus was headed to Tulare, a small air base just outside the rural, agriculture town from which it took its name. The base boasted new barracks and an airfield that would accommodate some of the army's larger planes, including the new B-29 Superfortress, the bomber we would learn later had been chosen to drop the highly secret atom bomb on the Japanese heartland.

Although it was early February, the air was balmy. The warm breeze blowing through the open window of the bus was a welcome change from the snow and penetrating cold of the High Sierras. The warmth gave little comfort to my torpid spirit.

There was never a guarantee of being assigned to further pilot training once you left Reno. For Bill, the dream of piloting a fighter or a bomber was over. He was assigned to navigation school and was headed north to a base in Washington state. It seemed unlikely we would see each other for the duration of the war, with our Air Corps careers now on different tracks. Bill and I had not contemplated being separated when we dropped out of high school and joined the Army Air Corps. We would stay together, fly together, celebrate together when the war ended. We had been together almost every day for eleven years. The war was now doing to us what it had done to so many millions of others—forced us to deal with separation.

But orders were orders, and there was no appealing an assignment. I was grateful to be heading to a base in Tulare, California, and wondered how much Captain Jeffers may have influenced my going there.

Our time at the base near Reno had been a glum period for Bill. Now he would not fulfill his dream to be a pilot. His outward rage was against the army. But I suspected he harbored as deep a resentment toward me, somehow blaming me for his not continuing flight training. He wrapped himself in an armor of melancholy that my commiseration and best efforts at humor could not penetrate. As he stepped aboard the bus for Washington state, he promised to write. I knew he wouldn't.

Sylvia was also lost to me. In the past, I never accepted fully that she would not be mine someday. I would find her, win her back. In the past, there was always family, there was always Bill or Ann or other friends to cushion my loss, to fill the void left by Sylvia's absence. Now I was alone. Listlessness cruelly supplanted my initial excitement at being assigned to advanced pilot training.

I rebuffed attempts at being included in conversations by cadets seated around me. It was night when we arrived at Tulare. I had spoken to no one.

The instructors at Tulare were hard-bitten veterans, some sent back to the States after being wounded. Others had flown their required number of missions and were rotated back home. They tolerated no excuses. The temperate weather made flying possible nearly every day, even in winter.

The planes were twin-engine trainers, smaller than the bombers and fighters we would eventually pilot, but bigger and a lot harder to handle than the "babies" we'd flown in Reno.

When we weren't flying, we were exercising or in class. Two hours a day were spent running the usual five miles, followed by calisthenics on the parade ground. It was a grueling program. By the end of the first month, nearly half of the cadets who arrived on the bus with me had dropped out and left Tulare, having been reassigned to navigation school or—worse—assigned to an infantry company. They were always replaced by another group of eager young cadets wanting the pride of wings on their shoulders and caps.

It was a Sunday morning when I witnessed the first crash of one of the bigger trainers. The plane was coming in for a landing, a cadet at the controls on his first solo flight. The plane appeared to be going too fast. A brisk wind lifted its nose momentarily, stalling the engine before it plummeted to the ground in a nose-dive. It was over in minutes, the life of the cadet engulfed in the fuel-fed flames that obviated any rescue attempt and mercifully silenced his screams.

All training flights were canceled for the remainder of the day, and the mess hall was uncomfortably quiet, each cadet sobered by what some, like myself, had seen or by what others just heard about. Flying was a skill that had to be acquired quickly and not under the most opportune conditions during wartime. It also depended on luck.

I lay in my cot that night, my mind a projector that kept replaying the plane coming in too fast, stalling and crashing in a ball of flames.

For the first time in months, I prayed. There was no room for errors. It was what the instructor preached each time we took off, each time we landed. Now I knew why.

By early March, I was ready to solo. My instructor, Captain Ned Bateman, had flown to Oregon and was fogbound. Another instructor, a cynical pilot cashiered out of a crack bomber wing because of his age and a past penchant for liquor, was assigned to supervise my first solo flight. His only words for me as I strapped myself in the cockpit, were "Try not to kill yourself." And he added ominously, "I wouldn't be surprised if you do."

I didn't. The take-off was letter perfect, the landing a little less by the book, but the plane came safely to a stop, despite hanging a little too long in the face of a stiff westerly wind.

Later that month, a new B-29 landed at our airfield. It was the bomber of choice, now that bases had been secured in the Mariana Islands, from which air raids could be launched against the Japanese heartland. The surrender of the Nazis was just weeks away. Russian troops would link up with General Patton's advancing army at the river Elbe, and that would bring an end to the European war and a redeployment of manpower and airpower to the Pacific Theater.

On the day that Germany surrendered, a major pinned wings on the pocket of my uniform and handed me the bars that marked my commission as a lieutenant. Orders arrived the following day, assigning me to a newly formed bomber wing at Hickam Field in Hawaii. I had seventy-two hours to report to a deployment center in San Francisco. After six months of intensive training—and still a teenager—I was an officer headed to battle.

Mother sobbed softly at the news. Her voice seemed so distant. Father was silent for some time before he told me to take care of myself, and in a voice choked with tears told me for the first time I could remember, "I love you, son. Come home safe to us." He was still sobbing as he handed the telephone to Collier, who wished me good luck, just as the operator's voice broke in with, "You're three minutes are up."

"John, Katie and I got married early. She's expecting. If it's a boy, we plan to name him John Addison—" Collier's voice was gone. The line was dead for several seconds before the dial tone returned.

I had waited in line for nearly an hour at one of the few pay telephones on base for these three short minutes to say good-bye. No time to say how much I loved them, how much I missed them, but long enough to know how much I was missed and loved.

An army moves on its stomach only if it is not aboard a ship in the turbulent Pacific in springtime. Seasickness is an insidious disorder that picks its victims at random, renders them helpless within hours, and disengages the entire food processing system of the body—at least, it seems that way as I repeatedly puked over the side of the rolling ship. By the time we reached Honolulu aboard the navy transport ship, I was gaunt from weight loss, weak from not eating, and convinced I was correct in never even considering the navy when I joined the armed forces of the United States.

With my feet finally on terra firma, my lack of seaworthiness aboard ship subsided. On my third day in Hawaii, I was assigned as a co-pilot on a new B-29 ferried over from the States. And for the first time since leaving Nevada, the gloom that had pervaded my spirits lifted. The B-29 was sleek and huge, the biggest plane in the American air arsenal, with a slender ninety-nine–foot body supporting a 140-foot wing span.

The pilot was a slow-talking major from Georgia, a good ol' boy who planted a wad of Juicy Fruit chewing gum in his granite jaw and chewed on that instead of chewing the fat with other crew members. He looked me up and down without comment when we were introduced, then stuck out the biggest hand I have ever seen on a man. His handshake left my much smaller paw aching.

"Welcome aboard, Rookie." The name stuck. I was called Rookie or Lieutenant Rookie from that time on by the rest of the crew.

My stomach churned with excitement an hour later as I climbed into the cockpit of the big plane. With eight fifty-caliber remote machine gun turrets and a twenty-millimeter cannon in the tail turret, a B-29 could be defended against just about anything the Japs sent against us. The instrumentation panels that lighted the cramped cockpit allowed night bombing and even getting back to base in the event of fog.

On that first flight out, we went to nearly twenty thousand feet, something we could do in a B-29 because the cabin was pressurized. That cut down the risk of air sickness, a lingering fear for someone who had succumbed to seasickness. It handled beautifully, like driving a Cadillac after owning a Ford for years.

Major Jimmy Bob Martin was a perfectionist pilot and expected the same standard of his co-pilot. He was also a patient trainer. The major, who preferred to be called Jimmy Bob while we shared the plane's cockpit, had been flying combat missions for two years in Europe. He had a veteran's savvy appreciation of a plane's assets and liabilities and the good sense to know how far to push the Superfortress. This was his first B-29. He declared it the best bunch of steel and copper he had ever flown. I agreed.

Within a week, I was exhausted but ready. The remaining war was waiting. Part of the exuberance of youth is the unwillingness to acknowledge one's own mortality. Perhaps that is why wars are declared by older men and fought by younger men. Still eighteen, I was ready to join the battle. At twenty-five, Major Martin shared my enthusiasm to engage the enemy.

"Get some sleep, Rookie. You'll need it." He grinned and punched my shoulder. "It's a long hop to Saipan."

"Yes, sir. Good night."

Major Martin and I were standing outside the officers barracks at Hickam Field as the top of the sun's round head was disappearing over the horizon. Before the sun appeared again, I would be boarding the B-29 that we had christened the *Lydia Sue* after Martin's wife, to head the plane's shiny, silver nose toward the Marshall Islands, then on to Saipan, in the center of the Mariana Islands.

Saipan had been secured by American forces a year earlier in fierce fighting and with high casualty counts, both for the Marines and the army infantry divisions spearheading the invasion. It was where my brother had been severely wounded.

As we approached Saipan from our high vantage point, there was no visible sign of the harsh reality that had played out here only a year before. The brilliant sun dazzled on the coruscating beaches, softly lapped by white-tipped waves. Above the sea, forests spread like lush, green carpeting over the mountainous terrain. Major Martin alerted the crew to a high cliff at the narrowest tip of the island: Marpi Point. He recalled the horrific tragedy that had unfolded from the 220-foot cliff, where hundreds of Japanese civilians leaped to their deaths at the urging of their military leaders, who warned of brutal treatment by the Americans if they were captured. Battle-hardened Marines witnessed the needless carnage, horrified but unable to stop it.

We arrived on June 13. My war was about to begin.

22

We landed in silence, our lips fused by our first view of Saipan—the rolling, foaming waves below us, flailing against the starkly chiseled cliff from which hundreds had blindly leaped to their deaths.

The airfield was a giant parking lot for B-29s and machines from bulldozers to tanks. Tanks were stationed around the perimeter of the airfield as a security measure, although Japanese resistance had been long quelled by the time we arrived.

Noisy bulldozers were cutting seams for another airstrip, and Navy Seabees in blue denim trousers and shirts were doing the work under the close eye of several khaki-clad officers.

Saipan was now the largest launch sight for air strikes aimed at the industrial heart of Japan. Our arriving wing of B-29s added another dozen planes to the growing arsenal already pummeling strategic targets on a round-the-clock schedule, anytime the weather permitted.

There were still a few craters on the far sides of the main runways, craters left by Japanese explosives triggered to render the airfield unusable by the invading Americans. The smooth airstrip on which we brought down the *Lydia Sue* was a tribute to American courage and efficiency.

Above the main hangar were large letters proclaiming "Welcome to Saipan—Home of the Seventh Air Force." We were part of that Air Force division and most of it, like our wing, was now concentrated in the Marianas, at air bases on Saipan and Guam, with another, smaller, more secretive base on Tinian.

After parking our planes in spaces designated by a flag-waving signalman, we gathered around Major Martin. "Stay here, boys. Let me check in with command," he drawled, "and I'll find out where bed and grub are."

The mention of food stirred affirmative responses. We had not eaten, except for cold C-ration beans and crackers, during the long flight to Saipan. The prospect of hot, fresh food was enough to keep us lounging beside our parked plane for more than an hour. When the major returned, he announced that hot food was ready in the mess hall and that cots were set up for us in a Quonset hut that served as a temporary barracks for airmen. That brought cheers from his crew.

The base was a makeshift affair, a mix of tents, Quonset huts, and other prefabricated buildings, all set behind the several large hangars where planes were housed during repairs. Bulldozers rumbled in the distance, a sound interspersed with the low roar of trees being felled on the far perimeter of the airport. This removed possible cover for a chance enemy sniper. There were persistant fears among the American commanders that Japanese soldiers were still hiding in the dense forests and numerous caves despite several sweeps of the island by Marines since capturing Saipan.

As we were moving double-time in the direction of the mess hall, we heard the distant drone of plane engines. They were approaching from the west, and we turned, shielding our eyes, to search the sky in the fading light. Finally, the planes were there, small outlines against the pink-streaked horizon, growing larger as we watched intently.

There was suddenly a scurrying of men and roar of motors coming to life along the edge of the airstrip. Fire trucks and water tankers took up positions along the edge of the runway. Hoses were loosened from their hitches on the sides of the fire engines by men in asbestos suits with helmets that covered their faces.

"There must be some boys in trouble up there," Major Martin said soberly. "More than a hundred bombers, with a fighter escort, headed out this morning on a run to Tokyo."

At least two of the lead planes had smoke billowing from their wings. The wing of the closest plane approaching the landing strip tilted sharply to the left, pulling the plane slightly off its landing course. It was apparently coming in with only one engine. As the plane dropped to within fifty feet of the runway, its nose lifted precariously, then dropped again as the plane skidded onto the runway, its four tires flattened by the hard landing. The plane then veered out of control, swerving off the remaining runway onto the cratered sidelines, still unable to stop, until it rammed into an earthen mound built to stop aircraft off the runway.

We watched, awestruck, as the crew members scrambled out of the cockpit and the side door of the big bomber. Fire had ignited the far engine. Yellow flames licked skyward, fed by remaining fuel now leaking from the engine's ruptured tank.

A fire engine and tanker arrived quickly at the side of the distressed plane, and several of the firefighters pulled the co-pilot out of the plane's side door and onto the tarmac, while other firefighters hooked up hoses to the water tanker's valves. The co-pilot was placed on a stretcher by medical corpsmen. The rescue took less than a minute.

Just as the stretcher-bearers arrived at the ambulance on the far side of the tarmac, the burning side of the B-29 exploded, spraying the rest of the plane with flames and sending jagged metal in every direction; some of that shrapnel hit human targets. The screams of several crew members and firefighters penetrated the mayhem of men, hoses, and machines that were circled around the burning plane.

More corpsmen arrived with stretchers, and we could hear shouted warnings to others near the bomber to get clear.

"Major, can't we go do something to help?" I asked anxiously.

There was a long hesitation, and when he answered, his response seemed blunt and cold. "No." His voice dropped to a whisper as he added, "We'd only be in the way of the guys trying to help."

I looked closely at the major and saw anguish on his face that I had not heard in his words, and I suspected that what we were watching for the first time was a scene he previously had witnessed.

Those around the major stared with growing horror and rising despair, feeling helpless and impotent, at the frightening tragedy unfolding on the wide runway some distance across from us. Two of the injured were facedown on the tarmac. One had a burning piece of metal protruding from his shoulder and back. The other was reaching out pleadingly to an approaching corpsman who hooked his arms under the wounded crewman's shoulders and began pulling him away from the burning plane. The corpsman was joined by other willing hands.

Then we observed the everyday kind of courage that one sees in war when men react instinctively to do their designated job, without regard for their own safety. The corpsman left the man he had just helped pull clear of the flaming bomber and ran back to a second man. Once again, he hooked his arms under the wounded man's upper arms and began pulling him away from the burning plane. Two more corpsmen picked up the wounded man's legs to carry him to a stretcher near a fire engine.

The first victim now lay still. Even from our distance, above the shouts of the rescuers, we could hear hissing as a wet blanket was thrown on the steaming metal in the man's back. For long minutes, three medics worked on the victim. When they stood up slowly, one by one, we knew their efforts had been in vain.

While the drama of dying in war played out before us, the returning planes continued to land. A second plane, with smoke trailing from its left engine, rolled safely to a stop, followed by one after another of the bombers and a single small fighter, which an officer standing near us explained had to follow the bigger bombers because of malfunctioning navigation equipment.

Because the B-29 could fly higher and faster than any other American bomber, there was not as much need for the spunky, smaller fighters. Most of those escorts, when needed, came from the navy carriers in the Pacific off the shores of Okinawa, the hard-won American base that was even closer to the Japanese mainland. The big bomber-bay payloads being delivered by the B-29s—up to twenty-thousand pounds per plane—were beginning to silence the network of anti-aircraft guns the Japanese had located around war plants and major population centers. More and more American planes were returning safely from these round-the-clock bombing sorties.

Knowing that did little to comfort the silent airmen around me. We had witnessed death. Some of us, like Major Martin, had seen it before. What I never got over was how quickly death happened.

The distance in time between life and death in war is counted in seconds—short seconds that seldom gave a man time even to mutter good-bye, to offer a final prayer, to feel regret. We had just witnessed that. It left us silent and shaken in the evening heat.

"Excitement's over, boys. Let's get some grub." Major Martin's voice refocused our attention on our empty stomachs.

The mess hall was empty. The only sounds as we ate were the forks and knives hitting against the tin plates.

The operations briefing room was our next stop. It was in a Quonset hut between the barracks and the aircraft parking area. A dapper colonel with the insignia of the Seventh Air Force on his arm waited patiently as the forty-eight members of our bomber wing were joined by more than a hundred other airmen who also had just arrived on Saipan. I scanned the room surreptitiously, noting most of these new arrivals were not much older than I. Only the two wing commanders appeared older than Major Martin.

"This is the Seventh Air Force, gentlemen, and I hope you came prepared to do lots of flying on little sleep and to eat only when you aren't bombing Japs, which is what you'll be doing most of the time." The colonel paused, looking around the rows of faces and noting affirmation on the faces looking back at him. "I see you're ready to bust a few Jap butts, gentlemen."

"Yes, sir," the hundred-plus voices shouted nearly in unison.

"I'm not sure about that, gentlemen. Are you ready to bust some Jap butts or not?"

The prefabricated building shook with the response: "Yes, sir!"

"I think you are, gentlemen. I think you damn sure are. And you get your first chance to do a little butt-kicking tomorrow morning. Report here at oh-four-hundred."

Someone in the room yelled, "Ten-*shun*," and we jumped to our feet and saluted as the tall, angular colonel walked briskly out of the room, ducking his lanky frame through the low doorway.

"It's shut-eye time, guys. Follow me, and I will tuck you in," said Major Martin, laughing.

"Major, you ain't exactly got the right assets to tuck me in properly."

The retort, from one of the *Lydia Sue*'s crew, Jim Harper, brought hearty laughter from the other wing members as they scrambled out of their chairs.

"Quiet, Harper. You'll give Rookie, here, the wrong impression of my intentions. He's still in a pre-stud state of innocence," the Major drawled, prompting more laughter, this time at my expense.

Jim Harper clapped me on the back as he walked past, still laughing. A gunner, Harper had a fierce independence that allowed only the most cursory formality toward officers, even the fellow Georgian who was his commander. Freckled and redheaded, Harper quickly ingratiated himself to the entire wing with his raunchy humor and common sense—a quality instilled in him by a long line of Harpers who had tilled the rich clay earth of his family's Georgia farm since the late seventeen hundreds. When Major Martin was assigned to the Seventh Air Force, third bomber wing, Harper was one of the few men he brought with him from Europe. Even without words, it was clear the major wanted this wise-cracking farmer guarding his rear.

There was no reveille to wake us, just the shatteringly loud voice of Sergeant Seth Barrett, a Utah Mormon who prayed almost as loudly and fervently as he bellowed good morning. Barrett was older, in his late thirties, and another of Major Martin's chosen few brought from Europe. Barrett was an untrained, shade-tree plane mechanic, who could analyze trouble on a B-29 quicker than anyone, according to his boss. The B-29s had been plagued with mechanical problems from the onset, delaying their introduction into the front line of air warfare. Barrett had been on one of the early B-29s when the engines still tended to overheat. He nearly lost his life when a malfunctioning B-29 crash-landed in England.

Boeing engineers eventually corrected the engine problems and made the plane a little lighter to land. Barrett remained skeptical. His ear was always trained on engine noises, and he listened intently for any hint of problems as other planes in the wing checked in on the intercom.

Barrett quickly became the nemesis of the regular mechanics, many of them mechanical and electrical engineers in civilian life who were barred from flying because of their age and were willing to accept a more menial job to stay close to the airplanes they loved.

By oh-five-hundred, the members of four bomber wings were assembled in the operations briefing room. Only pilots of one of those wings had flown over the Japanese mainland.

The briefing officer was a major with a distracting lisp that provoked frequent but politely soft laughter from his audience. Only once did he acknowledge the rudeness by reminding the offending airmen that if they screwed up his instructions and directions, they would pay the price to him when they returned, or they could pay the ultimate price and not return at all. The words had a sobering effect. Fifteen minutes later we were streaming out of the briefing room toward our planes. Our destination: Osaka.

Today would mark a high point in the devastation being heaped on Japan from the air. Nighttime incendiary bombing raids had destroyed or crippled much of Japan's vaulted industry and left thousands homeless. This would be a daylight raid, giving navigators and bombardiers an even better view of their targets.

For most of us aboard the *Lydia Sue*, it would be our first bombing flight. We had honed our individual skills. Now those skills would be blended into a team effort under the direction of the wing commander, Major Martin. He rolled the wad of Juicy Fruit packed in his cheek and called the shots.

As I pulled the leather flight helmet down on my head, my insides lurched. There was a small knot in the pit of my stomach that grew until it became a clenched fist striking at my chest, my legs, my arms, my hands. My breathing was rapid. My knees knocked against the controls. Speech became impossible, impeded by the taste of dry cotton choking my mouth and throat. It was the color draining from my face that gave me away.

"Hey, Rookie, don't sweat it. Everyone goes through this on his first time. Just do your job, and let me do the worrying for all of us."

The major's measured tone, not harsh or angry, belittling or condemning, had a calming effect. He began barking the checklist, distracting me from the acute embarrassment of letting fear show. Did he think me a coward? Would he trust me not to fall apart when we were over the target?

No time to pursue my self-questioning, as the propellers began turning. The major pulled the control toward him, and the big bomber eased forward, falling in behind another bomber, while the last member of another wing took off just ahead of us.

The *Lydia Sue* was now lined up at the far end of the long runway, ready for take-off. A signalman dropped his flag, and the B-29 lurched forward at the urging of Major Martin. Behind us, the other members of our wing were lined up for the round trip to Osaka. They followed our assent like long-necked geese, streaking down the runway, lifting quickly into the cloudless early morning sky.

Within minutes the twelve bombers assigned to our wing were

in formation, following the *Lydia Sue* as tightly as wing span and air speed would allow. We were cruising at about 220 miles an hour, which would put us over target in just over three hours. Then we could deliver our "brunch punch," as Jim Harper called this first daylight raid from inside his revolving gun turret at the rear of the plane, where he manned a twenty-millimeter cannon.

Up front, there was only the drone of the big engines as we glided over the calm Pacific, its endless blue rippled by the frothy whitecaps of the swells. By nine o'clock, we had our target in sight. My war now began.

23

"Bombs away." It was the bombardier, Les Akers, signaling that our payload of incendiary bombs was headed toward the target area picked at random by operations officers, who'd spent hours poring over maps of Japan's industrial centers.

There was one below us—huge buildings, where hundreds of Japanese workers were assembling bullets and bombs in one of the enemy's biggest munitions factories. It was diabolically located in the center of a residential neighborhood of neat row apartments. The operations officers knew many of the fire bombs they ordered heaped on the munitions plant would miss their mark and hit those surrounding homes, where mothers and their children would be playing, eating an early lunch, or napping. But this was war. Civilian casualties were one of the tragic costs of saturation bombing.

The bombs screamed earthward, hitting with a flashpoint of fire followed by a burst of smoke. In less than ten minutes, the several dozen planes around us unloaded tens of thousands of pounds of bombs on the targets below. The evidence of the devastation could be seen in the black smoke rising from the flames of dozens of fires. The bombs had found their marks with great precision.

Flak sent skyward by Japanese anti-aircraft guns split the air around the *Lydia Sue* with reverberating bursts. The enemy guns appeared to be concentrated on the north side of Osaka, where the briefing officer warned us that our smaller tactical bombers had not been able to neutralize all of the enemy batteries.

The bombers quickly ascended to eighteen thousand feet, unscathed and out of range of the flak, and began the turn south to Saipan. It was a short stay for such a long round trip.

"A good day's work, boys. The beer's on me tonight." The major's offer was greeted with cheers from all the crews in the planes around the *Lydia Sue* that comprised our wing. The major pushed a big wad of gum from one side of his mouth to the other and seemed to ease back in the hard seat for the long trip back to the base.

It went well—so easy, this first bombing raid. I had heard about the fierce flak that greeted American planes in earlier raids on Japanese cities, deadly flak that claimed lives and aircraft. Those airmen had paid the price for this piece-of-cake raid today.

The camera mounted on the *Lydia Sue*'s nose would tell the debriefing officers, better than we could, how on-the-mark our bombs had hit and how much damage had been inflicted on an enemy whose resistance appeared diminished. The B-29s could fly higher than the smaller Japanese fighters, minimizing fear of reprisal attacks. All of the bombers that left on the mission to Osaka that day returned to Saipan.

The makeshift club where we gathered that evening after chow was in a dilapidated wood hut left by the Japanese, the only thing standing when the Americans stormed onto the airfield. Its drafty, dry-rotting walls served first as a primitive hospital for wounded GIs, later as a radio command post, and now, as an alcoholic watering hole, providing a brief respite from the tensions of war. It served officers and enlisted men alike—there was neither inclination nor accommodations for separate clubs on Saipan.

"You did good, Rookie" Major Martin raised his bottle of beer in a brief salute.

"Thank you, sir." I tipped my bottle toward him in kind.

"We were lucky this first time out. It probably won't be as quiet and congenial the next time we fly over the Nips," the major mused somewhat sardonically.

"Did you ever get hit by the Krauts, Major?" asked Derrick Lawrence. He was one of the *Lydia Sue*'s gunners, near my age, from the meaner streets of south Chicago.

"Just once, but it didn't do much damage. Hit a hydraulic line, but we made it back okay."

Lawrence lifted his bottle to his mouth and took a long draw on the brew. "A lot of guys cashed in over Germany—at least, that's the scuttlebutt we heard during basic."

"A few I flew with over there didn't come back. It happens, Derrick. We were flying B-17s, and they don't go as fast or as high as B-29s. The flak was thicker, too. The skies are safer over Japan—at least, that's what I heard in operations just before they sent us out." Major Martin laughed and clapped Lawrence good-naturedly on the back. "It's time for lights out, boys. After all, tomorrow is another day." The major drained the last of his beer and headed toward the entrance, pausing to look at Lawrence. "Hell, Lawrence, that Jap flak won't come near your Yankee ass if you just start whistling Dixie when it gets too close."

The room erupted in laughter. Lawrence stood red-faced, smiling sheepishly, uneasy at the attention being directed toward him.

One of the vicious squalls common to the Marianas in summer

kept our planes grounded the next day. The torrential rain turned the base grounds into a river of mud, restricting any activity outside. I whiled away the morning playing solitaire and writing overdue letters to my parents, Collier, and Bill.

I had not heard from Bill since we were parted. Navigator school was considered as tough as flight training, so maybe he didn't have time to write. Or maybe his letters just hadn't caught up with me. A deep melancholy had settled over Bill after Christmas. He remained so withdrawn that I worried he would not write when we parted in February, and I feared it would be a long time before we saw each other again. The separation orders were devastating for both of us, most especially for him.

I was ordered out a day after Bill. There was nothing I could think to say to console him in his disappointment over not going to advanced flight school. We entered the Air Corps together to become pilots. It was his early fascination with flying that prompted my interest in the Birmingham poster, and his agreement to join up with me solidified my decision to enlist. I wondered sadly, lying on the hard cot, if we would still be friends in the future or fall into a politely cooled friendship, more like acquaintances. Bill's face was in front of me again, reaching his hand out to say good-bye.

"Take it easy, okay," I remembered him saying. "I'll write. Just let me know where you are after Tulare."

"Sure," I promised. "I'll keep you posted from sunny California. Don't do anything in Walla Walla I wouldn't do."

He had smiled wanly at my awkward attempt at humor. "See ya, Johnny." Bill raised his hand as if to wave, then let it drop to his side before turning to walk away, even before he stepped up onto the bus. He never looked back.

I enclosed a letter to Sylvia in my letter to Collier, with instructions to give it to her the next time he ran into her.

Dear Sylvia,

My brother told me he ran into you on campus, and I have asked him to get this letter to you. I am in the Pacific with a bomber wing, as a co-pilot on a B-29. It is a great plane. We are giving the Japs a little of what they gave us in the early days of the war.

Everyone here says the war will be over soon. I hope so. I will be coming home, and I want to come home to you. I love you and want us to be married as soon as I get stateside. Don't try to hide again. I will find you. We were meant to be together. My pay has been going into a savings account so we can have money to get started.

We have been told that Congress is going to give soldiers money to go to college. And we will have my grandmother's trust money to help out. I can work part-time and go to school, and you can stay home and keep house. Maybe I can still play football and even get a scholarship. Who knows? I do know it is going to work out for us this time.

I regret every day what I said to you. I hurt you deeply, and I'm sorry. My love for you will smooth over that hurt. And I will never hurt you again or let anyone else hurt you.

Please write and let me know you got this letter. My address is on the envelope.

Whatever has kept us apart in the past must remain in the past. In the future, we will be together. I will make you happy because we both deserve happiness and each other.

I love you and want you.

John

The humid rain that had been falling so heavily since before dawn ended abruptly, replaced by a sun-scorched sky. Searing heat quickly evaporated the pools of standing water and dried the mud left behind. I left the barracks before lunch to take my letters to the quartermaster's office for posting to the States. It would be weeks before I could expect a return letter from Sylvia, weeks of uncertainty, of waiting to know if she would be there when I got home.

Sylvia was pushed quickly from my thoughts when I stepped back inside the barracks. Major Martin was issuing orders for a bombing mission tonight. Get some sleep now, he said, and report to briefing at eighteen hundred hours. He ducked under the low door frame and was gone.

A night raid. My first. It's what the B-29 was designed for—to fly high, undetected, with the help of instruments that made take-offs and landings safer.

I tried sleeping, but thoughts of Sylvia and the mission ahead made sleep impossible. It was just as well, because a headquarters clerk stuck his head in the doorway and shouted, "Officers meeting in the operations room at sixteen hundred! Y'all come!" The announcement was greeted with a mix of groans and cursing from those who were sleeping or playing cards. The poker hands played out quickly, the money was divvied up, and the cards were put away for another time by men who hoped they would not be dealt a worse hand by fate.

Fifteen minutes later, the briefing room was filled with all ranks of officers up to colonels. The major with the lisp was at the podium. His stern look around the room brought quiet.

"Gentlemen, we have received information that the Japs are mounting a major kamikaze offensive against our ships parked outside Okinawa. We know the Japs are short on pilots but can muster about three hundred or more for this final win-one-for-the-emperor effort. Our information says the Japs will strike just before dawn. We have to hit those planes on the ground at Kyushu tonight, before they can take off." He paused and looked around at the solemn faces. "They won't be expecting us. It will involve B-29s and B-25s flying in low—real low. We'll load you up with incendiary greetings from Uncle Sam. The Japs can scramble Zeros off their ships in the neighborhood, so we're sending an escort to keep things more even and interesting." The major paused again, letting the importance of the mission sink in around the room. Flying a big bomber in low over a relatively small target was dangerous, especially a target like airplanes under camouflage tarpaulins.

"Another consideration, gentlemen. The Japs have two big ships just outside Kyushu. Expect some salutations from his high-ass, Hirohito. Those ships have a couple of fifteen-inch guns they can point your way. That's some heavy duty fire power that we'd like to neutralize. So, while you're in the neighborhood, how about dropping any leftover bombs on the decks of those ships? Mr. Truman and the Marines would be mighty appreciative. Any questions?"

There were none.

"You'll depart these shores at nineteen hundred. The weather looks good all the way."

The major gave us the latest pertinent meteorology update. Along with partly cloudy skies, we would be helped by a nearly full moon. Mother Nature was being very accommodating for this mission.

There was not even a hint of the usual carping when we got back to the barracks. Hitting kamikazes before they hit us was a welcome assignment. The Japanese had unleashed this heathenish offensive against American ships in the Philippines in 1944, but never were kamikazes employed more than at the battle for Okinawa, when suicide pilots sank thirty-six ships, damaged 368, and inflicted heavy casualties on seamen.

Revenge would be sweet.

24

Revenge that night came at a bitter and costly price. Our wing was out front, not by honor designation but simply because it was our turn in the rotation to lead the way for our group. It was the tail gunner, Jim Harper, who spotted the plane at five o'clock, a single-engine reconnaissance plane on routine patrol, well below us, but able to spot the waves of bombers accompanied by twice the usual number of fighter escorts. We were less than twenty miles from Kyushu, the giant naval and air base on the southern tip of Japan. We were flying lower than normal, and that gave us away.

Four fighters broke off and quickly ripped the small plane from the air, sending it flaming into the Pacific below.

Knowing the pilot had time to radio the base at Kyushu, Major Martin ordered top speed. We were over the target in minutes but not before half the kamikaze squadrons were in the air. The two hundred planes still on the field were easy targets for us, even at night. Wave after wave of bombers hurled tons of fire bombs at those planes. Our fighters, although sharply outnumbered, broke off to keep the

Japanese Zeros occupied while our big planes delivered their deadly loads with uncanny precision.

The Kyushu airfield, already heavily damaged by earlier bombings, was a smoking inferno, its hangars ablaze and severed parts of planes strewn across the bomb-pitted runways. The destruction on the ground was complete, but the battle was only beginning.

Japanese pilots who had scrambled so swiftly into action were now attacking the American bombers, flanked by our outnumbered fighters. The sky was filled with exploding flak from the still-active batteries ringing the vital naval and air facility below.

B-29s could ascend above the reach of the Zeros, but that would leave the fighters still vulnerable. The bomber formations sustained their hold, tight and protective, giving the Zeros little room to maneuver between planes. The B-29s and B-25s had eight gun turrets that could take down an enemy plane from almost any angle.

"Zero at twelve o'clock." It was Harper from inside the rear turrets bubble. The steady crack of his machine gun indicated he had the enemy plane in his sights.

"Maintain formation! Maintain formation!" Major Martin shouted to the planes following his lead.

"Major, I'm hit." It was Harper.

"Can you keep firing, Harper?" The steady crack of his cannon was the only answer.

"Rookie, can you handle a machine gun?"

"No, sir, they never trained us on that."

"Shit! Take over the controls, Rookie, and keep her headed home. I'm going back and check on Harper." He looked back at me sharply. "You can fly this goddamn bird, can't you?"

"Yes, sir. I'll get her home in one piece." I tried to sound confident.

If my fear was betrayed in that response, he took no heed as he darted through the door to the dark, tubular interior of the plane.

"Major, the Zeros are all around us. Can we go higher upstairs?" It was Major Hemphill of C-group.

"This is Lieutenant Winstead. Hold formation. The major's checking on our rear gun turret." I had never given an order before to a higher-ranking officer. Hemphill could countermand my order. But he did not.

"Roger, Lieutenant. Tell Martin to get the hell back to that cockpit."

The skies around us were blistered with machine gun shells streaking through the crowded night sky. Then I saw it: a Zero dead ahead of us at two o'clock.

"Zero! Zero! In front at two o'clock!" I shouted.

"Got him in my sights, Lieutenant." Seth Barrett said, his voice calm. His mechanical skills were matched only by his accuracy with his front turret machine gun. A puff of smoke, small at first, was the first indication Barrett hit his mark. A fighter came up from underneath and sprayed the soft underbelly of the wounded Japanese plane—a fatal blow. It went into a tailspin as smoke poured from the engine mounted underneath its cockpit.

"You do okay under fire, Rookie." Major Martin slid back into the seat beside me and fastened himself back in. "I'll take over now."

"Okay, groups," the major ordered, "let's go upstairs for some peace and quiet. Take them to twenty-thousand."

Major Martin pulled back on the control, lifting the *Lydia Sue*'s nose upward. We were now well out to sea, and the Zeros were breaking off the fight to save pilots and equipment for another day.

"Harper's dead." The major's voice was flat, emotionless. Paying quiet tribute to the fellow Georgian who had come with him from Europe, he added, "He took a Zero with him."

I was too stunned to speak. Jim Harper—the man who made us laugh, who could out-poker-face the best in the wing, who had a wife and child waiting back home, who talked of planting more tobacco and of leasing an elderly neighbor's acreage to plant pecan and peach trees when he mustered out. He would never again see his beloved Georgia farm again.

"This is Big Bear. All group leaders report on damage and casualties," Major Martin barked into his mouthpiece, his voice steady, his face grim.

The brief air battle had been costly. Four bombers and seven fighters downed, and twenty enemy kills confirmed. The major notified the base at Okinawa to dispatch ships to pick up survivors in the dark waters below us. Okinawa had been captured only weeks before and was the nearest American base from which to send help. Only a handful of the downed airmen would be there when the rescue ships arrived late that morning.

As we cruised closer to base, it was reported more than a hundred kamikaze planes had made it past us to hit the carriers, battleships, and destroyers off the Okinawa coast, the largest attack on American ships since the early days of the battle for that island. Once again, the navy was made to bleed by the sayonaras of misguided men bent on giving their last full measure for the emperor in return for a better life after death.

But this time, the navy was better prepared. Smaller, more agile gunboats proved their mettle, pumping flak at the incoming kamikazes, at times confusing the Japanese suicide pilots by diverting their attention away from the bigger targets. Of the 102 Japanese planes that attacked the American ships, all were downed.

The Japanese claimed one major victory that night, the disabling of the carrier *Williamsburg*. Listing dangerously, it had seen its last battle and was sent back to the Philippines for repairs. Other, smaller ships were also sunk or disabled with heavy casualties.

As we taxied to the parking area assigned our wing, a drab green hearse drove slowly toward the *Lydia Sue*, one of several such vehicles sent to collect the victims of this latest battle. The shutting down of the engines only intensified the silence. I slipped out of my harness and removed my leather helmet, hoping the routine activity would stir some reaction in Major Martin, who sat gripping the small wheel that guided the big bird. As if sensing my concern, he muttered, "Get on out, Rookie. I'll be there in a minute." He never turned his head as he spoke; his gaze was fixed straight ahead. He appeared beside us shortly as we stood silent, waiting for the body of our fallen crew member to be brought out of the *Lydia Sue*. Across the grassy tarmac, other flight crews were paying similar homage to their crew members lost in battle.

Jim Harper's lanky frame was covered with a white sheet as it was lifted down by those sent to collect his remains. As the stretcher carrying Harper was taken to the ambulance, we stood saluting, silent and unmoving, following the lead of our wing commander. One of the hearse crew returned with Harper's dog tags, wallet, wedding ring, and the small locket he wore around his neck with the face of his pretty young wife—now widow—locked inside. His good-luck charm, Harper said, explaining the feminine style jewelry. Sadly, it had failed him in the bloody skies over Japan. It was only when we turned to leave that I saw tears glistening in Major Martin's eyes.

There was little time to mourn. The next night our bomber group was back over the dark skies of Japan. The target: the center of Tokyo. The discipline imposed by the Japanese government on its people was never more evident than from the sky. Looking down, I could detect no lights. The blackout was strict and universally obeyed. The only light came from the flash of flak bursting around us. It was a heavier-than-usual greeting from the Japanese batteries.

On these night raids, the navigator's maps and coordinates became our eyes. Lieutenant Kevin McDougal had the challenge of guiding us to Tokyo, to the targets, and then back to Saipan. He mapped out the coordinates for a suspected airplane parts factory detected on reconnaissance cameras. It was a small, tough target, almost impossible to spot visually from our height in the blackness of night, but a three-quarter moon helped by spreading its sheer, sparing light over Tokyo and its suburbs.

Deploying bombs was as much a matter of guesswork as science at night. Tonight, McDougal would call the shots. That worried Major Martin, who never fully trusted any navigator but was wise enough not to let the navigator know it. His concern was evidenced by the number of times he shifted his usual wad of chewing gum from one side of his cheek to the other.

"Approaching target, Major."

"Roger, McDougal. Just say when."

"You can open the bomb bay doors, sir."

"Bomb bay doors open. Just say when, McDougal."

"It's when time, sir."

"Roger, McDougal. Bombardiers, please lighten our load." Before the words even drawled across the intercom, we heard the whoosh of the incendiary bombs hitting the night air.

"Bombs away, sir" crackled in our headsets.

Throughout the formations of B-29s behind us and on our flanks, we could hear the bomb loads heading downward. Then came the familiar flash of the hit, followed by the explosion and fire.

There seemed to be hundreds of flashpoints at once. By the time we climbed and turned for the trip back to Saipan, part of Tokyo was a hell of flames and explosions. Some of our bombs had hit with deadly precision.

The bombing continued around the clock, incessantly. By the following week, our group was back on the day shift, pounding Tokyo, Osaka, Kyushu, and Nagasaki. Resistance from the Japanese was now minimal. The enemy was using its anti-aircraft guns and its defensive planes sparingly.

By mid-July, we began hearing word of a super-bomb that could wipe out the center of a city. Scuttlebutt in the mess hall hinted that Tinian was to be the launching sight for delivering this new firepower against Japan's industrial centers. So far, headquarters had not ordered the knockout punch. The only order we heard from the brass was to strap ourselves back into the *Lydia Sue* and pack another twenty thousand pounds of explosive punch for Tokyo.

We rolled onto the runway at oh-three-hundred. This was to be a dawn raid against the heavily industrialized area north of Tokyo's center, the same area we'd pulverized the day before. We'd be back by dinnertime; the weekend to rest loomed invitingly before us. The *Lydia Sue* was scheduled to undergo some mechanical overhauling. The left engine was running hot, near the top of the tolerance level.

"Take her up, Rookie." The major lifted his hands off the controls to let me guide the sleek aircraft into take-off position. The signalman's flag fell, and the plane bolted forward. Major Martin had let me fly the *Lydia Sue* solo twice before to hone my pilot skills. He demonstrated his respect for my growing proficiency by occasionally calling me by my first name. Fresh pilots were sorely needed in the Pacific at the time I finished pilot training. There were not enough B-29s available for use as trainers. Co-pilots had to learn at the knees of seasoned pilots and in the line of fire. I was learning from one of the best.

The sky was cloudless, promising a hot, dry summer day. Below us, Japanese workers would be exiting trains into downtown Tokyo office buildings—those still standing. In the war factories just to the north, the day was well underway for many workers. Twelve-hour shifts had become a normal workday in those factories. Women, in growing numbers, labored side by side with the war-shortened male work force. The expediency of war had little regard for the centuries-old traditions of Japanese life—and American bombs had no regard for gender.

The flak was unusually heavy, the major observed as he banked the plane steeply toward the south. "The Japs have apparently moved more batteries in around the city."

Just as he finished speaking, the *Lydia Sue* shook savagely as flak shells exploded just off her wing. It deadened the sound of the metal smashing through the window in back of the pilot's seat but not Lieutenant McDougal's scream. When I turned in my seat, his head had already slumped over the navigator's console. A large shell fragment penetrated his helmet and apparently his skull. Blood oozed from the jagged wound, forming tiny rivulets of red down the side of his face.

I unsnapped my seat harness and stepped back to the navigator desk. My hand on his neck confirmed what I instinctively knew: Kevin McDougal was dead, a chance casualty of war, killed by a shell fragment that could have had any of our names on it. Fate targeted him.

"Is he alive?" the major demanded, turning to see for himself.

I shook my head. There was a dingy towel on the map shelf above the console. I covered McDougal's head to absorb the blood flow that was seeping onto the maps between his head and arms.

"Can you pull him inside the cabin, and find something to put over that window?"

"Yes, sir."

I linked my arms under the navigator's shoulders and pulled him out of his chair and through the door that led into the interior of the plane. As I laid him out on the floor, I closed his eyes, which were staring with the stark shock he'd felt just before death. If death brings peace, why had I seen agony in those eyes?

I shook my head to clear my thinking and began searching for something to cover the smashed window to minimize the loss of pressure in the cockpit. By the time I returned to the cabin with two thin oblong sheets of steel and mechanics tape, the cabin was bitterly cold. I began taping the steel sheets over the broken window. The force of the wind made it difficult to hold the steel against the smashed pane. I had to press my shoulder against the sheets to hold them steady as I taped each in place.

Major Martin alerted the rest of the crew of our plight, and Seth Barrett tossed four wool blankets inside the cockpit.

We were now flying below the rest of the formation and well behind. The major had leveled off at ten thousand feet and backed off our speed. The *Lydia Sue* was more than an hour later than the other planes landing. An ambulance and stretcher-bearers were waiting when we pulled to a stop in front of the main mechanics hangar.

In silence once again, we waited on the tarmac until the body of Lieutenant McDougal was removed from the plane, and we saluted smartly to attention as the sheet-covered stretcher was lowered through the door. Major Martin, his face stoic, climbed into the ambulance for a final ride with his fallen navigator. He would see to the burial arrangements and write the letters of condolence to McDougal's wife and parents, the second such letter he had written in less than two weeks. It would be long after midnight before the major returned to our barracks. The next morning, his eyes rimmed with fatigue, Major Martin walked over to operations headquarters to find a new navigator.

Thick fog draped itself around the island overnight. There would be no bombing missions over Japan this day, a welcome respite for the Japanese from the death and destruction that had been raining down on them, day and night. And a welcome day of quiet for the crew of the *Lydia Sue*, a day to mourn for Harper and now McDougal.

25

Saipan was lashed by high winds and drenching rains for three days. There was fog in the mornings, scuttling any movement on or off the island by air, then replaced by a thick, humid mist in the afternoon. Visibility was minimal. But it was enough time to repair the *Lydia Sue* and overhaul her engines. The day she was rolled out of the hangar was the first morning sunshine returned to Saipan. Her silver sides glistened in the sunlight, and her engines were purring.

Major Martin ran his hand over the plane's gleaming sides, pleased to have her back. The entire crew stood around the aircraft, complimenting her facelift and welcoming her back like an old friend much missed.

"Let's go see if we have a navigator yet," said the major, leading the way briskly across the tarmac to the operations area, where new airmen checked in for assignment to a crew. If we had a new navigator, his name would be posted on the personnel board. The major scanned the assignment list.

"We've got one. Lieutenant William Thomas Deems."

Deems. The name hit me like a brick. "Did you say Deems, sir?"

"Yeah, why?"

"I joined up with a Bill Deems. We're friends from back home. They separated us in Reno. He was assigned to navigator school."

"Well, let's go see, Rookie. He's billeted in our barracks."

When we came into the barracks, Bill was sitting on the side of his cot, sewing the unit's insignia onto his uniform shirts. He looked up while biting a thread from the arm of a shirt, and he spotted me, his face lighting up in a broad grin.

Bill Deems was the last person I expected to see on this godforsaken island, but the one person I was most pleased to see. When he held out his hand, I pulled him to me instead.

"How the hell did you get assigned here?" I asked, after releasing him from my fierce hug.

"Just good luck, I guess," he said, his face flushed by my unabashed show of affection. "I told them I wanted a tropical island with lots of those hip-swinging hula dancers, and they said no problem; we aim to please. So here I am."

"You came to the right place, Lieutenant, didn't he, boys?" The major stepped forward to shake hands, just as Bill's right hand went smartly to his forehead in a salute.

Major Martin waved off the salute. "Meet some of the crew, Deems. Obviously, you know Winstead. This is Sergeant Derrick Lawrence, our tail gunner. This here's Sergeant Hap Simpson. He's the left gunner. On the right side is this guy, Sergeant Will Chandler. Over there is the bombardier, Les Akers," he said, pointing to the airman first class who was still waiting for the sergeant stripes Major Martin had requested several weeks ago. Akers grinned and tipped his fingers in an off-handed salute.

"And this is the other bombardier and sometimes gunner, Sergeant

Barry Steinmetz, who also doubles as our procurement officer." That brought laughter. Steinmetz was from the Bronx and spoke with a thick New York brogue that elicited a lot of "What was that again?" from his fellow crew members. Steinmetz could locate, confiscate, steal, or barter just about anything the wing needed, talents that made him public enemy number one to the quartermaster unit— and indispensable to Major Martin.

"Hi ya, Deems, welcome aboard." Steinmetz extended his hand warmly.

"Seth Barrett, our other gunner, is still outside making sure the mechanic types followed his instructions to the letter when they put our bird back together. He wields a bigger wrench around here than Mr. Boeing." Laughter greeted the major's comment, which left Bill looking puzzled. "Inside joke, Deems," explained the major. "You'll understand when you meet Barrett."

Bill seemed overwhelmed by seeing me and by the generous welcome from his new crew. "Glad to meet all you guys. I'm looking forward to working with you." Bill smiled and lowered his head shyly.

"We'll leave you two to get reacquainted. See you in the mess hall at noon. Come on, guys, we've got a set of wings to get reacquainted with." The crew members followed the major noisily out the door, leaving us alone in the long, narrow barracks.

"How did you manage to get sent here?" I asked, still incredulous at our being back together, five thousand miles from where we parted.

"The assignment captain at the base just said navigators were needed on Saipan. And I told them, okay, send me."

"Mom and Dad sure will be surprised when I tell them you're here with me."

"I got a letter from them just before I left for Hawaii." Bill fished in his duffel bag for the crumpled letter on top of a stack of letters bound in a rubber band. He handed it to me. It was full of the usual hometown news with which Mother filled her letters to me—who got married, who had a baby, what had happened to some of the people we knew in high school. Ann McClelland was engaged to a boy from New Jersey stationed at the army base outside Gadsden. My parents were planning to attend the wedding, which, from the date on the letter, had already happened. My Ann, my dearest Ann—I could still see her, framed in the screen door of her grandmother's house in Anniston, tears trailing down her cheeks, waving good-bye. That day seemed so long ago now. Maybe marriage would prove as kind a refuge for her, as her grandmother had been.

And there, in the last paragraph of the letter—a mention of Sylvia. Mother wrote that she was engaged to a fellow from Birmingham, a professor at the University of Alabama. Doc Cunningham said they were to be married in the fall and live in Tuscaloosa. Each word I read was like a staggering blow. I wondered bitterly if she had received my letter professing my love and asking her to marry me. Had she shown it to her fiancé? Had they both laughed at the poor, lonely airman, trying to line up someone to whom to come home?

I stood staring at the drab green barracks wall, the letter crumpled in my fist. I loved her, wanted to protect her from the pain life so often dealt her, to hold her in my arms, to cherish her. And she wanted someone else.

"Are you okay?" Bill's voice seemed to come from far away, intruding on the hurt ripping my heart.

"Sure."

"Hey, I didn't know you still had a thing for Sylvia, or I wouldn't have shown you that letter. I'm sorry, real sorry, Johnny."

"It's okay, Bill. I should've been over her a long time ago. Now's as good a time as any, hey, buddy?" I tried to sound flippant, unconcerned. "Let's get some chow," I suggested, laying the letter on top of Bill's cot before turning to walk ahead of him out of the barracks.

Conversation was batted back and forth around me at the long dining table. I would nod occasionally to feign normalcy but did not allow the lunchtime banter to invade my withdrawal. I was alone with my hurt, and that's the way it would remain. I had never discussed Sylvia with any of the crew. I had no picture to put on the wall above my cot, no letters to share with the other guys in the way they passed around letters from their wives and girlfriends. Intimacies were a shared commodity in our wing, but I declined.

By evening, we had our orders. A dawn raid on Osaka—what was left of it. Early lights out for the oh-two-hundred reveille gave me the quiet sanctuary of darkness.

Rejection is always a trial—one that many cannot bear. For me, it meant lying in the dark barracks, hearing the soft snoring of the men around me, seeing Sylvia on the cot in back of the dry cleaners, undulating beneath me, moaning softly, her soft skin dampened with sweat. Oh, God, I wanted her, missed her. Was she in his arms tonight, moving in sexual rhythm with the professor? I pictured him in my mind—an older man, balding, with glasses, his groping hands fondling her firm breasts, his heaving breath in her ear. I twisted in agony.

I was still awake when a sergeant's shout shattered the stillness along the line of cots. It was two o'clock. The wake-up call was greeted with stirring and the usual sullen grumbling as the airmen put their feet on the cool wood floor and fumbled for towels and razors. Death would dog the wings of some of us this day, but we would meet that fate with clean-shaven faces and clean-smelling armpits.

At oh-four-hundred, the *Lydia Sue* was rolling down the runway, her bomb bays crammed with the makings of a really loud, rude awakening for the residents of Osaka. We would arrive with the sunrise—the first wing in, the first to feel the flak, the first to head back to the safety of the blue Pacific waters.

It was Bill's first time at the navigator's console. He smiled and flashed an okay sign as he put his headset on and strapped himself into his seat. Major Martin clapped him on the shoulder as he passed through to the cockpit.

"Get us there in a straight line, Deems, and on time."

"You got it, Major," replied Bill, giving the wing commander a thumbs-up.

Bill had the maps and coordinates spread out in front of him. He and the other navigators attended a briefing separate from the pilots, where they poured over the latest intelligence information and target coordinates. They were the eyes of any successful mission.

The night sky was a maze of star groups that sparkled like rhinestones under stage lights, all the brighter with the moon only a silhouette. By the time we reached the western outskirts of Osaka, the flak from anti-aircraft guns was already menacing our approach.

"I thought those intelligence guys promised a soft approach to the targets," I recalled to Major Martin. "I'd say the Japanese have a little warmer welcome in mind for us."

"You're right, Rookie. Keep her steady. Deems, how much further to target?"

Before Bill could respond, a flak bomb burst off our left wing, sending a shudder through the *Lydia Sue*. It was apparent that the old girl did not like bombs going off so close to her.

"Target just ahead, sir, about two degrees to the left."

"Roger, Deems. Pack Leader to all wolves. Target ahead two degrees east. Happy hunting."

Major Martin banked the plane slightly to the left and ordered the bomb bays opened. The other planes in the formation followed his new direction. When Bill confirmed the target was nearly below us, the major turned the plane over to the bombardier, Akers. Seconds later, he shouted, "Bombs away!"

The payload of incendiary bombs glided toward a factory complex in the center of smaller buildings. That arrangement was the same heartless strategy employed by the Japanese throughout the empire, camouflaging war plants in the center of residential areas. Bombs tended to find their own path, many straying from the assigned target. Some would provide a loud and fatal greeting for many of those in the homes surrounding the factory complex.

The flak explosions intensified as we drew closer to the target. There were no signs of Japanese fighter planes.

Just as quickly as the bombs were headed to their destinations, the major ordered the leading formation to bank the big bombers east, away from the worst of the flak concentration. We had completed the turn and were headed south toward the Pacific when a gunner on a plane on our left wing shouted the warning: Zeros at three o'clock. The Japanese planes were approaching, level with our formation; then they quickly rose above us and began diving toward the nearest bomber.

The Mitsubishi A6M fighter had been designed for agility, which was displayed now. The little fighter packs hunted and singled out bombers on the far edges of the formations.

The major ordered all pilots to ascend to twenty-five thousand feet, out of range for the Zeros, which had a lower cruising range, but it was too late for a bomber on our west wing that had smoke pouring from its right engines.

"Major, we're hit bad." It was the pilot, Lieutenant Mitch Eden. "I can't control her. I'm ordering everyone out. See ya, Major." Seconds later, the plane erupted in a ball of fire, splintering the huge bomber. It's severed parts began plummeting downward. There had not been time for the crew to bail out.

Eden had shaved next to me this morning, creasing the white lather that covered his cheeks and chin with a half smile as I nodded hello. He had finished shaving before me, smiling cheerfully as he rinsed out his shaving cup. "Good hunting today, Lieutenant," he said as he lifted his shaving cup in a salute.

"You, too, Eden." The last time I saw him was as he walked back into the barracks.

The hunter had become the hunted and the prey. Our rapid assent spoiled more kills for the marauding Zeros. They broke off and the B-29s set course for Saipan. Only one plane lost but two others hit. One of the damaged planes was left with only two working engines. The pilot reported he would try to make it to Kadena Airfield on Okinawa.

As soon as we reached the relative safety of the open ocean, the major ordered the entire formation down to ten thousand feet to take stress off the disabled planes and conserve fuel. We had been over the Pacific about fifteen minutes when the sun reflected off two dots in the sky ahead. Instinct is often quicker and more accurate than the eye. Before we could visually confirm it, we knew they were enemy planes, approaching head-on. They may have been off a carrier making for a land base and had the bad fortune to cross flight paths with a formation of American bombers. Whatever the case, we would never know.

The two A7Ms, the next step up from the Zeros we'd just eluded, were coming right for us and making no attempt to veer away, despite being greatly outnumbered.

"Enemy, dead ahead," warned the major to the other planes beside the *Lydia Sue* and behind her. The two disabled bombers had taken up positions within the center of the formation for protection.

The gap between the approaching Japanese planes was closing quickly, and still the enemy planes did not veer. They would be within gun range in moments. I glanced over at the major, mentally trying to anticipate what he would order us to do. If he took us up quickly, the two damaged planes would be left vulnerable. One of the planes was barely maneuverable and running low on fuel because of leaks. The second plane had two wounded crew members and was also short an engine.

"Hold steady; let's call their bluff." The major would not abandon the two disabled planes. Still, the Japanese planes refused to budge from their certain collision course with our planes.

The forward guns on the *Lydia Sue* and the other planes around us were now cracking. A whiff of smoke came from one of the A7M's engines. Still, they came straight for us.

"Hell, they're gonna ram us! They're goddamn kamikazes!" screamed Major Martin. "Get the hell out of their way." The major's warning sounded over the headsets as the two enemy planes were closing to within a thousand feet, still headed straight for our front formation. The B-29s on both sides of us swung out from the formation, ascending above the path of the oncoming planes. But the realization of the Japanese strategy came too late for the *Lydia Sue*. The nearest A7M, with its right engine now ablaze, was nearly in front of us before the major could try to veer the *Lydia Sue* away. The fighter brushed our right wing, tearing part of it off and shearing off its own wing in the collision. The enemy plane spiraled out of control toward the ocean.

The *Lydia Sue* shuddered in shock. It took all of Major Martin's strength to hold the rebellious throttle to maintain even minimal control of the big plane. Luckily, the aileron was intact, or the *Lydia Sue* would have followed the Japanese fighter into the Pacific. She was losing altitude rapidly.

"Everyone bail out. I can't hold her much longer." The major looked over at me. "You, too, Rookie. Take along a raft. You'll need it." He grinned. "And Rookie, save a spot for me, okay?"

"The best seat in the raft, Major. We'll hold the champagne until you're aboard."

"Thanks a bunch. Good luck, Rookie."

"You, too, sir."

Major Martin had already turned back to his task, looking intently ahead, his hand tightly gripping the spastic throttle. It was the last time I saw him. It is a picture of courage I still remember vividly.

Bill Deems was waiting by the hatch that separated the cockpit from the body of the plane. He ducked under the frame; I was right behind him. Bill pulled two inflatable rafts from the stow rack, handing one to me.

Steinmetz was standing by the open doorway, the wind forcing him to grip the sides of the inside doorway. He looked pale.

"Everybody else out, Barry?"

"Yes, sir. Akers got away first, then the gunners."

"Better bail out, Barry. You don't want to keep the sharks waiting. From what I hear, they love kosher."

"I hope not, sir." Steinmetz turned to me, fear mirrored in his dilated eyes.

"It's okay, Steinmetz. We'll be right behind you." Relief replaced the panic and fear as he looked out at the blue expanse of ocean below him.

"What's that damn Indian's name?"

"Geronimo."

Steinmetz stepped into wind yelling, "Gerrrronnnimo, ohhh shit!"

The *Lydia Sue* was down to three thousand feet and losing altitude rapidly. Bill hesitated only briefly in the doorway, his lips forming good luck as he leaped out. I jumped right behind him, the force of the cooler air in my face taking my breath away momentarily. I could see Bill's chute opening below me, and behind him, Steinmetz's open chute floating toward the ocean. I yanked the cord on my chute and it unfurled on cue, the thrust of the wind under the expanding parachute jerking me upward so hard that I nearly dropped the folded raft. The force of the parachute's release also triggered my life vest to inflate, impairing the view directly below me.

I was floating now, the fully opened chute slowing my descent. Ahead of me, the *Lydia Sue* was being jostled dangerously by the winds. Then, suddenly, the big plane nosed downward and into a rapid spiral toward the ocean, spinning like a huge, winged top. The plane cut a swath of churning white foam where it entered the sea, a grave site marked only for a moment before the white foam dissipated.

There had not been time for Major Martin to parachute out after holding the doomed B-29 steady enough for the rest of the crew to escape. He loved the *Lydia Sue* and always gave her an affectionate pat for luck before entering the cockpit. She would now be his tomb.

The ocean was rapidly approaching my feet. I tossed the raft that should fully inflate on impact and land right-side up, if I was lucky. It did, filling noisily with air as I hit the water a hundred feet away. The life jacket kept me bobbing on the surface of the smooth Pacific. Although it was the hottest period of the summer, the water was cool. I swam toward the raft and heaved myself into its belly with the help of the side ropes. Safe. I could not linger long in the euphoria of that word. I had to find Bill and Steinmetz and the other crew members, all scattered over a mile stretch of ocean—and, I hoped, alive.

26

I was oblivious to our rescue, oblivious to how Bill must have struggled to keep my limp head above water, how he pulled himself into the spare raft that had miraculously escaped damage from the spitting Japanese machine gun. Bill later told me he gripped the Mae West the way airmen were trained to do and pulled me in beside him, cradling my bleeding head in his arms. And he said he prayed. Not a formal prayer. Not the kind I memorized in Sunday school. He just asked God to let me live, and if he did, Bill said he would never ask for anything again, and he meant it.

Despite the gentle coaxing of my parents, Bill never attended church with us. If he had a relationship with the Almighty, it was something he never shared with me. He recalled later the minutes ticking away slowly as I lay prone in his arms, blood still pumping from the places penetrated by the bullets. It was then he said his pleas to God were replaced by an angry rant, cursing the navy plane that had spotted us much earlier for not sending help. Hope began retreating as despair overcame him.

Bill had not seen the periscope circling, so he became aware of the submarine only when the sub broke the ocean surface, a football field's length away, and rocked the small raft.

"Steady, buddy" were the reassuring words spoken by the sailor who first reached down to grab Bill's Mae West. Other strong arms pulled me into the rescue raft. "We thought you guys were goners."

Later, much later, we would learn that only one other crewman survived the mortal wounding of the *Lydia Sue*. Sergeant Derrick Lawrence had been plucked from the ocean on the second day, his exposed face severely sunburned. He lay in the bed next to mine for three days, until he was put aboard a plane bound for Hawaii. I never knew he was there.

Even at the urging of the chaplain and against a direct order from the head nurse at the field hospital, Bill refused to leave my bedside. The base commander relented, giving in to Bill's recalcitrant loyalty, and ordered the pouting nurse to provide him a cot next to mine. He would doze with his hand on my arm, in case I stirred while he slept.

A week after our rescue, I was put aboard a hospital ship bound for the States, still unconscious.

Bill went back to his war, flying two of the final bombing missions against the Japanese before a B-29, baptized the *Enola Gay*, took off from Tinian with only one bomb aboard—a bomb that would change, forever, war as the world had known it. The awesome, destructive force of the atomic bomb brought the proud Japanese to their knees. They surrendered the same day that I walked down my hospital ward for the first time.

The day after I awoke from the coma my appetite returned. I woke up famished. That seemed to please the nurse and Major Drummond, both hovering over me. "Anything but Jell-O," I said.

The doctor nodded and barked an order for a plate of solid food to be brought up from the galley.

The worst of the pain from my three wounds had eased during the merciful coma, and my body, while at peace in its limbo state, restfully repaired some of the damage done by the bullets.

The major looked down at me, offering a thin smile, and announced in his thick New England brogue, "Winstead, I think it's time you get out of this bed and take a few steps, just to get your sea legs back. Maybe a trip to the head for your first outing. But first, let's take a look and see how your wounds are progressing." He scowled as he scrutinized the crude surgical entries made to remove the bullets. "I hate to admit this, Lieutenant," he observed with a wry smile, as he probed for any sign of new infection, "but I think I did a better job carving on my first cadaver at Harvard than I did on you. You think I might be a little out of practice?" His tone was thick with self-deprecating sarcasm. I knew, just looking at the dark circles under his eyes, that any problem he had surgically repairing my wounds was not caused by a lack of practice but more likely a lack of sleep, because there were too few doctors to care for too many wounded patients.

Major Drummond signaled to an orderly standing patiently on the opposite side of the bed. Together, they lifted me by the shoulders to a sitting position, then placed my feet on the floor.

"Dizzy, Winstead?" the doctor inquired.

"A little, sir." My response, only a hoarse whisper, stung my throat.

"Just sit there a minute, son, and let your head clear." Drummond's lips pursed in a brief smirk that passed for a smile. "You've been a troubling case, Winstead. I wouldn't have given you a snowball's chance when you were brought aboard this ship. You'd lost a lot of blood. One bullet pierced your lower chest and another one tore a hole through your shoulder. Both wounds were already infected." The doctor's grip tightened around my arm. "Let's get you moving."

As we walked slowly down the narrow corridor between beds, the doctor kept up a steady banter in an effort to keep my mind focused on moving and not passing out. He described yellow puss mixed with blood in the drainage tube from my chest wound, alerting him to the extend of the infection. With penicillin in short supply and reserved for only the most critically wounded, he had only sulfur to battle the infection.

Maybe it was my youth, he speculated, or just good luck, but I had rebounded more quickly than he expected. And I could hear the grudging admiration in his voice when he recounted taking the drainage tube out of the wound in my chest shortly after I came out of the coma. "You gripped the bed, but you didn't holler. That takes courage, son," he said, describing the agonizing procedure yesterday. "I know it hurt like hell." He was right on that diagnosis.

Dizziness threatened to overwhelm me as the orderly assisted me out of the head.

"You steady now?" asked Major Drummond.

"Yes, sir," I answered weakly.

"Let's put him back in bed, Corporal. Better let him sit on the side of the bed longer before he ventures out the next time. He's still pretty weak."

The two men assisted me back onto the bed, just as my stomach revolted against the movement. The next thing I felt was a cold ceramic bedpan being pushed under my chin. The retching spasm passed quickly, yielding only brackish bile in the pan. I welcomed the feel of the pillow under my head, which was still reeling from the unaccustomed motion.

Black dots danced in front of my eyes, fading as the spinning finally slowed. When the food tray arrived minutes later, I waved it away. My weakness was an embarrassment. Earlier, a sailor without legs in the adjacent ward had pushed his wheelchair through the narrow lane between the doubled-decked beds. I mentally chided myself for having two good legs and not being able to stand on them any longer than I had.

"Glad to see you awake. You had the doc going for a while, wondering if you would come out of it. You know, the coma."

I glanced across to the next bed in the direction of the voice and into a face as young as mine, with bandages wrapped around the head and under the chin.

"Hi. Airman Dunn Edwards." The airman winced as he said his name. "It still kinda hurts to talk," he explained somewhat sheepishly in his slow, deliberate speech, as he extended his right hand to shake.

Even with the beds in the ward so close together, it took some effort for me to turn on my left side and grasp the hand Edwards extended toward me.

"Lieutenant John Winstead. Nice to meet you." Even that movement brought back the dizziness, so I eased back on the pillow.

Edwards was watching me sympathetically. *Stow the conversation,* I demanded silently.

He didn't. "Where you from, Lieutenant?"

Irritation rose like bile as I turned back to look at the eager young face in the next bed. The exasperation receded. "Gadsden, Alabama. Where you from?"

"Utica, New York. I could tell from your accent you're from the South."

I nodded and turned away, hoping to discourage further conversation.

"I got hit during a run over Osaka," he continued, undeterred. "Where'd you take your hit?"

"My plane was downed coming back from a bombing run," I replied, staring straight above me. "A Jap plane shot up our raft." It was only then that I realized I did not know what had happened to Bill Deems, if he was alive or dead, or maybe wounded and even aboard this ship. "I had a buddy with me." Agitation now pushed my voice above a whisper for the first time. "How do you call someone? I've got to find out about my buddy," I said, looking imploringly at Edwards.

"There ain't no buzzer to call anyone," Edwards replied.

My frantic concerns were only partially answered by the duty officer later that day. Bill was not aboard the hospital ship. It was not until the week before our arrival in San Francisco that I finally learned Bill had been unscathed in the Japanese attack on our raft and was reassigned to an air group on Okinawa. The news buoyed my languishing spirits for the first time since being wounded. By the time we docked, I was able to walk the length of the ward without the orderly's support.

A crush of people packed the huge, glass-enclosed building adjacent to the dock in San Francisco, jostling for a view of those being brought down the gangplank on stretchers from the gleaming white ship. The noise was deafening.

I was among those who walked down the gangplank with assistance, leaning on the arm of a pretty young lieutenant not much older than I. My left side ached, rebelling against the steep incline of the gangplank. Sensing my discomfort, the nurse nudged me to the side so others could pass, and she called for an orderly to bring a wheelchair.

"Good-bye, Lieutenant," she said cheerfully at the bottom of the gangway. "I hope you have a speedy recovery."

She directed the orderly toward a stand of army ambulances just outside the reception building. Ahead of us, stretcher-bearers carried their wounded burdens slowly through the building, as eager faces on both sides of the roped-off aisle tried to recognize their loved ones.

"You expecting anyone to meet you, Lieutenant?" the orderly asked.

"No, my family is back in Alabama. It's a long way to come. I'm not sure if they know I've been sent home."

"The army usually notifies your folks. You married?"

"No."

"Leastways, the army tells the wife if her husband's been wounded. Looks like a lot of wives here today," he observed, scanning the crowd.

"Yeah."

It was then I saw Collier, his face alight in a broad grin of recognition. Ann McClelland was beside him, and both of them were now waving at me. Collier appeared taller, his face less gaunt than when I'd last seen him. Ann wore a stylish felt hat that partially covered her eyes. She continued waving as they walked parallel with my wheelchair, making their way slowly through the throng to the entrance.

Just outside the doorway, free of the restraining rope, they rushed over—Ann throwing her arms around my neck, Collier grasping my right hand. Men seldom cry, guarding through their lifetimes against this outpouring of emotion that women find so cleansing. The tears springing to my eyes surprised even me, rolling down my cheeks as I held Ann close with my one free arm.

"Welcome home, flyboy." Ann's face was awash in tears. I gently halted a teardrop poised to slide off the end of her nose.

"This is quite a welcome," I told them, beaming my delight that they were there. "I didn't even know if the family had been notified."

"We got a telegram three weeks ago that said you were on board a hospital ship headed here. Dad pulled some of his War Department strings, and here we are."

"I hate to interrupt this homecoming, folks," said the young orderly, ducking his head somewhat shyly, "but I've got to get the lieutenant into one of them ambulances."

In the excitement of the welcome, none of us took notice of him as he stood patiently behind the wheelchair.

"Oh, sure," I said, acknowledging his presence.

Collier released my hand and stepped back from the wheelchair. Ann gave me a soft kiss on the cheek before relinquishing her embrace.

"We'll meet you at the hospital in Palo Alto. They're having a reception for families there this evening. The army is even providing a bus for us."

"Okay, see you there." I waved to them as the orderly pushed the wheelchair toward the nearest ambulance, where he strapped me into a cot. The men above and beside me nodded a greeting but lay silent on the hour-long trip to the army hospital. Several of them puffed on cigarettes provided by the lone orderly riding with us.

Anticipation of this homecoming had been high among the men in my ward aboard ship. They talked incessantly about getting back to the States, to home, to parents, to wives, to sweethearts, to women, to sex. Now, instead of the expected jubilation, there was quiet introspection among the men around me. I was content to be left with my thoughts.

Ann was lovely—radiant, even. Marriage apparently agreed with her, even though her husband had shipped out for England right after their nuptials. My mother mentioned in one of her letters that Ann had put her plans to attend college on hold and had gone back to live with her grandmother, who was now bedridden with crippling arthritis.

I was anxious to hear about Collier's new wife, the nurse, who, from the looks of him, was giving him sterling care. His emaciated frame had filled out. His limp was almost undetectable. If love is the best therapy for all that ails us, then my brother was being lavished with affection.

Some family members were waiting for the ambulances at the hospital entrance, reaching for the hands of loved ones as they were borne inside. The more critically wounded were taken to the medical wards. Those like me, who were more healed and ambulatory, were escorted to a large room just inside the entrance, where a painted banner declared "Welcome Home." USO volunteers were handing out sandwiches and donuts from tables at the rear of the room.

Collier and Ann were waiting there, sipping cups of steaming coffee and balancing paper plates filled with food. I was instantly hungry and wolfed down the plate of sandwiches Ann handed me.

"Peanut butter and jelly," I laughed. "It reminds me of the lunches Mother used to pack for school. Remember how she always put a big dill pickle in Addison's lunch, and the faces he made eating it? I don't know how he could stand those things."

The laughter faded from Collier's eyes, even before the smile left his face. "Sorry, John. I still miss him a lot. Funny how little things like pickles bring him back to us."

I had thought a lot about Addison during those periods when Bill fell silent while our rafts swayed in the swells, as we strained to hear the sound of a ship or plane. And of Collier, too.

Growing up, I had never been close to either of my older brothers. I had hero-worshiped their fabled pranks and basked in the reflected ardor for their athletic abilities, but I was too young to know them as they knew each other, as siblings bonded by age. Mother often declared, in her rare moments of anger or frustration with her two oldest children, that they were more like twins than single births and certainly as much trouble. Matured by war—and wounding—the years separating our births and youth no longer separated us now.

"Anyway, little brother, you had us worried for a while, didn't he, Ann? Taking off on a cruise and not telling anyone where you were going." He gently jabbed my uninjured shoulder.

Ann took the empty plate from my lap, put in on a nearby table, and sat down next to me, taking my hands in hers. "The doctors here are going to check you out thoroughly, tomorrow. And as soon as you can travel, they'll let us take you home. Won't that be great?" She looked at me, the smile radiant on her pretty face. "Your mother and I are going to get you back on your feet so you can live up to this tall, dark, handsome person I told my husband about—I tried to make him jealous enough to marry me quickly without my having to get pregnant."

"Hey, I almost forgot to tell you," Collier said, striking his forehead with the palm of his right hand. "You're going to be an uncle."

"I learned that in a letter. When?"

"Right around Thanksgiving. Mom and Dad are really happy."

Me, an uncle. I liked the sound of the word. A little Collier to take fishing on the Coosa River and swimming in the hole below Noccalula Falls.

Collier, at times, had been a brooding child, whose happiness was often dependent on moving in lockstep with Addison, his mentor since their playpen days. The brooding returned with the loss of Addison and the loss of a leg. A quiet darkness enveloped his spirit, a despondency that the salve of his family's love could heal only to apathy. This was a new Collier, happy and optimistic, looking forward to the birth of his child, a man who reflected love and obviously was well loved in return. I was looking forward to seeing again Collier's wonderful Katie, who had resurrected my older brother's buoyant spirit.

An hour later, a nurse with lieutenant's bars announced visiting hours were over, and the patients must return to their wards. I opened my arms to Ann, pulling her tight against me.

"Thanks for coming all this way. It sure means a lot to have you here."

"Hey! Remember me? I'm the one who owes you so much. And we aren't leaving without you. So hurry up and impress those doctors that you're ready to go home. See ya tomorrow."

Collier gently gripped my shoulder. "Take care, baby brother. I've bribed a luscious nurse to tuck you in tonight, so sleep tight."

"Will do, big brother." Laughing, I shook Collier's hand. "Is she as cute as your Katie?"

"Not even close, but I didn't think you'd notice after those long months of enforced celibacy."

"See ya," I said. Collier turned to leave and then turned back, putting his arms around me in an awkward hug before finally pulling away. "Tomorrow, after breakfast, okay? See ya then." He turned and walked out with Ann.

As I watched them pass out of the large room, down the hall and disappear out the front glass doors, I suddenly longed to be back in Gadsden.

My return to Gadsden was put on hold two days later, when a surgeon reopened the wound in my side to stop new bleeding and repair the area ravished by a fifty-caliber machine gun bullet. It had ripped into my right side and exited out my back, tearing muscle and chipping the lower ribs.

Collier and Ann came daily, staying as long as the nurses would allow. They chatted about friends back home and passed along the latest messages from my parents, who were given daily updates on my recovery.

A letter arrived from Bill. He was still on Okinawa. His wing expected to be reassigned to an air base in Japan soon. He was learning a little Japanese from a prisoner who'd attended Oxford University in the 1930s. The former naval captain was now cleaning up the barracks and helping in the officer's mess while waiting to be expatriated to Tokyo. Japanese officers were the last prisoners of war to be returned to their homes and families.

A week after the surgery, I was able to walk around the ward without Collier's help. The side wound still ached, rebelling against any quick movement, but each day brought less painful movement and more time out of bed.

Ann had gone into San Francisco on a bus to shop at that city's famous department stores, leaving Collier and me to spend a quiet afternoon in the activities room, playing gin rummy. It was a game at which he excelled, and I was down to my last toothpicks when the mail cart came by.

"You, Winstead?" I nodded to the orderly, and he handed me a letter. I stared at the handwriting. Sylvia's. My finger slid slowly under the flap, noting the return address was a post office box in Tuscaloosa. There was no mistaking the fluid handwriting.

My dearest Johnny,

I heard you were wounded, and I hope that if this letter reaches you, you will be much improved. Your mother gave me your address. She looks well, despite her obvious concern about you. I spoke briefly with your father, and he was as kind as ever.

I received your letter, and I will cherish it always. I am married to a nice man I met in school. We could be moving to a new location shortly. He is a widower and has a son who is entering the Naval Academy this fall.

I have been carrying more hours and went to school this summer, in an effort to get my nursing degree in fewer than three years. The university is expecting a flood of returning servicemen, now that the war is over and because they can get help with tuition through the GI Bill.

Please let me know how you are doing. Send the letter to the post office box number, and I will get it.

Please know how much I care. If there had been a way we could have been together, I would have worked to see it happen. You are young, and your life is still ahead of you. Go to college, get a degree, and be successful and happy. Somehow, I will know how you are doing because I care for you deeply.

I will love you always,

Sylvia

She loved me; she cared. But not enough to hold off marrying a man maybe twice her age. Why? The answer was not in this letter.

"You okay, brother?"

"Sure."

"Is it a 'Dear John' letter from Sylvia?"

"Sort of. She got married to some guy with a son old enough to enter the Naval Academy. Says she loves me but still married this other man." I crumpled the letter savagely in my hands. "It doesn't make sense. I was willing to borrow from Grandmother's trust to have the money to get married. I could take care of her and still go to college." I turned my head away from Collier to shield the tears smarting in my eyes. "She's all I think about. She's all I ever wanted. She just never wanted me, not even after Bubba was killed. God, I wish I could wipe her from my mind!" I cried through clenched teeth, slamming my fist on the table, scattering the cards dealt there.

Collier reached his hand across the table and placed it on my arm. He grimaced at the pain on my face as I lifted my head and looked across at him.

"Why couldn't she wait? If she really loved me like she says, she would have waited for me, not bury herself with an old man." My words were tinged with bitterness at her rejection, rejection being visited on me yet again. "Goddamn her."

27

I would curse her often, in silence, on the long flight back to Birmingham, while staring out the window of the army cargo plane at the diversity of the western landscape. Through the middle states it melded into a checkerboard of fields of different shades of green and tan whose variety was not unlike the mosaic of my feelings for Sylvia. Would I ever be over her?

Only Collier remained to make the trip home with me. Ann returned by train, days earlier, to Anniston to be with her grandmother, whose health was failing rapidly. Her death, just hours before our arrival in Birmingham, tempered the joy of being back in Alabama. Back home.

I spotted my parents through the small, dusty window of the aircraft, looking far away and forlorn, in the small crowd standing behind the chain-link fence between the airport terminal and the runway.

War changes all it touches. I had left an exuberant teenager. I was returning, less than a year later, a man, aged more by the horror of death and loss of war than by time. My parents had given more than most to the war: three sons. Now, two were returned to them, to be welcomed with the love and concern that had been the primary ingredients of their parenting since our birth.

My sister, Sarah, was with them, and Collier's Katie, looking radiant, despite her protruding stomach. The two sisters-in-law broke away from my parents and ran toward the plane, smiling and waving as the portable stairway was fixed in place. Collier barely had one foot on the tarmac before Katie's arms were wrapped around his neck in a strangling embrace, tears streaming down her flushed cheeks. Sarah's welcome for me came appropriately with less ardor, a peck on the cheek and a careful hug. "Welcome home, John. Come on," she said, tugging at my sleeve and pointing in the direction of the area behind the fence. "Mom and Dad are waiting over there."

Mother and Father were not there. They were already hurrying toward us, Mother waving her gloved hand. I can't remember seeing my mother without gloves on any dress-up occasion. They went with her to church, to choir practice, shopping. A pair could always be found in her bottomless pocketbook, ready to be put on if the occasion demanded. It is a part of women's fashion I miss in my own generation.

Her white cotton gloves felt soft on my cheeks as she held my face in her hands, her tears flowing, her lips quivering. "Oh, Johnny, I've been so afraid you would not come home to us. Welcome, welcome, welcome."

I kissed both her damp cheeks and held her close before relaxing my hug long enough to stretch out a free hand to greet my father, who was standing patiently behind my sobbing mother.

"Glad to have you back, son." His eyes misted as he held my hand in both of his large, strong hands.

"Thank you, sir."

"You look too thin and pale," my mother observed. "Have they not been feeding you enough at that army hospital?"

That prompted a spirited laugh from Collier, who was standing behind us. "Mom, he eats like a horse, and he's almost as healthy as one," he added, trying to mollify her concern about my injuries.

Turning to me, Collier pulled Katie gently forward into my view. Her large blue eyes were like two bright galaxies in a universe of freckles that dotted her satiny skin, all of that prettiness crowned by a mass of unruly, curly auburn hair. "Welcome home, John," she said softly, smiling warmly. "You have been much missed by all of us."

"Let's see—you're the pregnant one," I teased, glancing down at her stomach.

"That's me," she threw back, laughing. "You can identify me by my stomach dimensions. Welcome home, brother-in-law." She threw her arms around me with only slightly less vigor than she had embraced Collier.

"Whoa, girl, unhand this man, or he'll be put on the permanently disabled list for sure. These Yankee rowdies take some getting used to, little brother." Collier beamed indulgently at Katie.

"Excuse me, Lieutenant. We must get you to an ambulance," ordered a brisk voice behind me. I looked around at the pretty face of a young army nurse, her lieutenant's bars pinned on her starched white nurse's cap.

"We were just headed that way, Gretchen. This is the wounded brother-in-law I told you about," said Katie.

"Oh, hi, Katie, I didn't see you." The young nurse lowered her head shyly.

"Gretchen, Lieutenant John Winstead. John, this is one of the best nurses at the hospital, Lieutenant Gretchen Bostick."

"Pleased to meet you, ma'am," I said, formally extending my hand.

"Nice to meet you, Lieutenant." She lowered her head again, as a blush radiated over her face. "Can you take him to that ambulance by the gate, Katie?" she asked, pointing toward the edge of the airfield.

"Sure. See you later, Gretchen."

"I wouldn't mind having that taking care of me," Collier remarked, his eyes following the slim-waisted nurse hurrying toward an airman being carried on a stretcher. The remark drew a punch to the stomach from Katie. He bent in mock pain. "Lead us to the ambulance, my little pugilist."

The army hospital stood back from the road, a tall white edifice of antebellum style, with the patients wings reaching out like four large fingers from the main building. I had had enough of hospitals in California, enough of being bound to a bed by my injuries. I would get well here—and quickly.

My mother was there every day, waiting patiently during my daily physical therapy. She provided her own therapy by tenderly massaging my legs and arms to ease the pain in the joints from the rigorous sessions.

Collier came every day after his classes, effusive with his encouragement, the darkening circles under his eyes betraying the long hours he now spent bent over his engineering books, trying to make up for the classroom time lost while he was with me in California. While in California with me he had arranged to transfer to Samford University in Birmingham. He and Katie wanted to be closer to Gadsden and my parents when their child was born.

I redoubled my efforts to be well, spurred by a gnawing restlessness to be free of the army, to go to college, to find Sylvia. In all our conversations, my mother never mentioned her, and I never asked, knowing what Mother's answer would be: that Sylvia was gone from me, and I must never see her again.

By the end of the second week, I was walking a mile on the hospital grounds. By the end of the fourth week of my hospital stay, I was pronounced fit enough to go home. My headaches persisted— agonizing and debilitating at times—and before the onset of the pain, they were preceded by blurred vision. Doctors said they were the legacy of the severe concussion caused by the bullet that grazed my skull and deadened my senses for nearly three weeks. The doctors had no answers, only a insouciant prediction that the headaches would go away in time. They did not, but over time, they came with less frequency.

Collier drove us to Gadsden on the day of my release from the hospital. My discharge papers would follow. I was returning home a civilian. Tucked in my duffel bag was the Purple Heart awarded with minimum ceremony the day before. While Katie and Mother chatted casually in the backseat, Collier and I sat silent up front, wrapped in the poignancy of coming back to the place we had left as whole men and to which we were returning less whole.

I saw the house a block away, its wide front porch sweeping gracefully around the side opposite the portico, the sun gleaming off the fresh coat of white paint. My father repainted every ten years, scrapping and sand-blasting the old paint away to provide a virgin surface for new paint. He was waiting for us at the curb as Collier pulled the car in front of the house; my sister and Ann were just behind him.

In the exuberance of my arrival in Birmingham a month ago, I had failed to notice how Father had aged. Maybe being away from him nearly a year made the changes more noticeable. His thick black hair was now heavily threaded with gray, the temples already fully white. There were deepening groves in his face that made him look more drawn and gaunt. The hard work, the long weeks away from home, the loss of a son—all these had taken a discernible toll. He embraced me as I stepped from the car, tears glistening unchecked in his eyes.

"Hi, Dad. It's good to be home."

He nodded, this rare display of emotion preventing words, and gently loosened his grip.

"Let's get a look at you, boy," said an unmistakable, booming voice. "How have they been treating you in Birmingham?" It was JB Stevens. The druggist took my hand, his mammoth paw giving his usual death grip. I was glad I never wore rings. "Sure good to see you home safe, son. Maudie and I have really missed you."

The ever gentle, gracious Maudie was at his shoulder, smiling her welcome and taking my face in both her hands as she planted a kiss on both cheeks. I was the son she never had; the little boy she doted on with cookies and milk every afternoon; with homemade stuffed animals every Christmas; and every birthday, with silver dollars placed inside miniature fire trucks and steam shovels that whistled and smoked. She held me with the proprietary air of a favored aunt. To me, she was exactly that, and more.

Doc Cunningham and his Laureen were there, too, along with neighbors and old family friends and high school classmates. They flooded out of the house onto the lawn, clutching my hand, patting my back, each offering a warm welcome.

When the milling people thinned around me, Ann approached, wrapping her thin arms around my neck, laying her head against my shoulder. I could feel her tears dampen my neck. I held her tight against me, knowing she was one of those I had missed the most.

"I was sorry to hear about your grandmother," I whispered in her ear.

"Thank you, Johnny. I miss her a lot."

"Come on in the house, boy!" boomed JB. "Maudie and some of the ladies have laid out a feast you won't believe. I've worked up a mighty hunger waiting for you to show up."

Millie Thomas was behind the dining room table, setting out bowls filled with food of every variety. She had aged. Her large warm eyes looked weary, and the creases in her smiling cheeks had deepened since I last saw her. She tucked me inside her ample arms for a moment, then released me slowly, looking into my face as she slipped her arms away.

"You is all growed up, Misser John. And what a fine young man has come home to us."

I smiled down at her round face. "How is Jeb, Millie? Mom wrote the leg injury hadn't healed well."

"Tha's right." She shook her head slowly. "My Jeb ain't never gonna walk again, and it's a killin' him. He ain't the same, young John. He just ain't the same, my Jeb." She pulled a large hanky from the voluminous pockets of her apron, sniffing away the tears that had formed.

"I'll come out to see Jeb next day or so, Millie. Maybe we can perk him up; what do you say?"

"He would like that, Misser John. Promise me you'll come. It would mean a heap to my Jeb."

"I promise, Millie." It was a promise I kept two days later.

An old mongrel dog watched me with rheumy, incurious eyes as I ascended the several wood steps to the porch of the sharecropper shack in which Jeb had lived all his life. The dog barked no welcome. And there was no response from inside to my rap on the door. I opened it slowly and peered into the gloom of the large single room that comprised the shack, where the only light came from a rear window.

"Jeb. You here? It's John Winstead."

"Dat you, Misser John?"

As my eyes adjusted to the dim light I saw Jeb on the bed, his dark face elevated by two pillows with feathers poking out of the worn ticking. A smile creased his large mouth briefly when I grasped the bony hand he extended to me, then quickly faded. His face was gaunt and his black eyes sunken in their sockets.

"It's good to see ya, young John. My Millie told me youse home."

I pulled a rickety wood rocking chair near the bed and sat down. "How you doing, Jeb?"

"Not so good, Misser John. Not so good," he repeated in a raspy voice. "My leg got broke and it ain't healed. Can't do nothin' but lay here like dis."

Tears glistened in his eyes. I took his hand back in mine. He was now a shadow of the man I saw shortly before leaving to join the Air Corps.

"Doc Cunningham was out a bit ago," Jeb said, looking at me with those stark eyes. "He didn't know I could hear, but I did, Misser John. He said to my Millie der ain't nothin' kin be done." He turned his head away as tears spilled down his shallow cheeks. "I knowse I'm dyin.'"

My throat caught at his words. Seeing him, I knew he was right. I stayed with Jeb for an hour. There wasn't much to say. He seemed content just to have me there. When he drifted off to sleep, I slipped out.

I went back to visit Jeb again before the morning after

Thanksgiving when we received a call from Doc Cunningham telling us Jeb had passed away.

His funeral was a tribute to the respect in which Jeb had been held by those who knew him and for whom he worked. Among the several dozen people who attended his burial in the Negro cemetery just outside Gadsden, there were as many white faces as black.

Millie was surrounded by her seven children and just behind the family stood the commander of the several squadrons which made up the courageous Tuskegee Airmen, Lieutenant Colonel Benjamin O. Davis, under whom two of Jeb's sons had served.

Shortly after Jeb's passing, Millie left Gadsden to live with her oldest son. Her children would all attend college and forge successful careers even before such opportunities were insured by national civil rights legislation. The grit instilled in their offspring by Jeb and Millie in the small space of that drafty sharecroppers shack would lead two of her sons to march beside Dr. Martin Luther King, Junior in Selma. The oldest daughter would help lead the bus boycott in Birmingham.

Millie lived well into her seventies, in Birmingham, her days filled with caring for her ever increasing number of grandchildren, then great-grandchildren. And I would always be welcomed warmly when I occasionally paid her a visit.

As the Christmas season approached following Jeb's death, welcome home celebrations similar to mine were extended to returning veterans throughout Gadsden. Many of the returnees would march in a place of honor in the annual Christmas parade, and that Christmas would be made more special because they, like my brother and I, had returned to enjoy it with our families.

The city we returned to had changed, hardened by the reality forced on its factories and people by the war. The efficiency demanded by war production brought more mechanization to the rubber and steel plants, even to the large textile plant.

Women had replaced men in those plants. Some were reluctant to give up their jobs to the returning men, demanding job protection from the unions and getting it, as the unions flexed muscles long weakened by hard times and the Great Depression. There would never again be enough jobs in the factories for the younger men to join their fathers. This sent many of the returning veterans to college, with tuition paid by the benevolence of a grateful nation. I would be among those college students that winter.

Much to my dismay and chagrin, doctors at Birmingham Veterans Hospital insisted my injuries precluded playing football. My dream of quarterbacking for the Crimson Tide had been dashed in the blue waters of the Pacific.

A week before I was to leave for Tuscaloosa for the start of classes, Bill Deems came home to bury the mother he had seldom seen since moving in with my parents. The death was listed by the empathetic medical examiner as natural causes. No mention was made on the death certificate of the alcohol poisoning that resulted from downing a quart of hundred-proof gin in less than two hours. Her funeral was delayed until her son's return.

Bill stood staring at the death-hardened face in the cheap casket, a face grooved with deep lines, chiseled there by excesses. As I pulled him gently away, his face was expressionless, devoid of any grief, his emotions erased by the loveless relationship with the woman who had borne him. His connection to her was only biological. Bill's father did not even bother to acknowledge the telegram my parents sent him in Louisiana, where he was a roughneck on an oil rig.

It had taken Bill nearly two weeks to return to Gadsden from Japan. He never went back to Japan. Instead, he opted for an early discharge offered to less experienced airmen no longer needed in the newly independent Air Force. A career in the flying branches of the armed services had lured many war-seasoned pilots to choose a military career over the uncertainty of civilian life. But Bill had no such reservations. We both enrolled at the University of Alabama a week after classes started, he in pre-law, me in pre-med, a choice I made based as much on admiration for my long-dead country doctor grandfather as for what I really wanted to do with the rest of my life. My grandfather died when my father was still a boy, but Father never ceased missing the man who had left him to spend his remaining young years under the roof of a tyrannical and abusive stepfather, whom he despised and left home at fifteen to escape.

My father seemed elated by my choice of careers. Doc Cunningham was equally pleased at the choice. I spent a leisurely afternoon in his small, dimly lighted private office, discussing the pitfalls of medical training. It was an afternoon I would reflect on often in the eight years ahead, wisely following the advice of this man who would practice his healing trade until he was well past seventy.

We arrived in Tuscaloosa in Bill's Ford coupe that he purchased with the proceeds from a life insurance policy, the only thing left to him from his mother's meager estate. We registered for classes, were assigned a dorm room, and began the search for our classrooms in the buildings scattered around the sprawling campus. That first night after classes, I began the search for Sylvia.

28

My search ended two days later. She was walking slowly toward me down the wide steps leading from the building that housed the campus bookstore and post office. Engrossed in reading a letter, she didn't see me until nearly bumping into me at the bottom of the steps.

"Johnny!" The surprise was evident on her face.

"Hi," I responded with a forced casualness.

"How are you?" Simple, straightforward, so much like Sylvia. "I read in the Gadsden paper that you were back home after being injured."

"Yes. I'm a lot better now." She knew I was home but hadn't called or visited.

"Are you a student here?" I asked, trying to sound nonchalant.

"No, not now. I was picking up the mail for my husband. He's been teaching here." Straightforward again. Sylvia's eyes were remarkable. They mirrored her thoughts, and she looked away in confusion under my unyielding inspection.

I felt anger burn within, irrational anger that made bile rise in my throat, choking off speech. Married. She reminded me so quickly, so casually.

"Please, won't you come and meet Richard? He's waiting in the car just down there." She pointed to a newer-model station wagon parked at the curb. A man in the front passenger seat was looking up at us. How much did he know about Sylvia and me? Had she told him anything of our relationship?

We walked toward the car, and I could see the man inside was older, his thick, wavy gray hair worn longer than the style of the day, his hazel eyes framed by steel-rimmed glasses. They were kind eyes, paternal in their assessment of me.

"Richard, I would like you to meet an old friend of mine from Gadsden, John Winstead. John, my husband, Richard Barrington."

"How do you do?" he said, extending his hand through the open window. His friendly manner disarmed my anger. He was much older than Sylvia, near fifty, I guessed. He had to be, with a son old enough to attend Annapolis.

"Sylvia told me you had been wounded in the Pacific. I'm glad to see you appear to have recovered from your wounds. Are you attending the university?"

"Yes. I'm in pre-med."

"Good field, but a long haul through school. The world could use a lot of caring young doctors. It's a field that has gone wanting during the Depression" His words were soft-spoken, and his voice held the kind of authority one expected from a professor.

"Do you teach here?" I asked, directing attention away from me.

"I did, but I'm leaving. Sylvia and I are moving to Ann Arbor, Michigan. I've taken a position at the university there." He must have discerned some of the anguished surprise his announcement elicited. I had just found her, and he was taking her hundreds of miles away. I quickly corralled my rebellious thoughts. "It's a great opportunity for us. I'll be heading up a new program for disabled veterans. Sylvia's going to work on a master's degree. We're looking forward to it, aren't we, dear?" It was the first time he addressed her.

"Yes. Yes, we are," she said. "Richard will be starting a pioneering program for returning veterans who have physical handicaps." She looked up at me for the first time and offered a brave smile.

How beautiful she was, her eyes luminous in the sunlight. The smile drifted briefly over her face, softening it. Once again, she lowered her eyes under my unrelenting gaze. The awkward silence that followed was broken by Barrington.

"Will you be playing football in the fall? Sylvia told me what a terrific player you were in Gadsden." As I turned back to him, I saw it, in the back of the station wagon—a wheelchair. "Sylvia said ..." His voice trailed off as he realized the object of my attention. "I lost the use of my legs several years ago," he explained quietly, answering the question forming in my mind.

"I'm sorry. That must be rough."

"One gets used to it. I think it may be what got me the job in Michigan. They think I can identify more with those young men who lost limbs in the war and have to train for a career."

I leaned my arm against the top of the car, staring at the pavement beneath me. Why had Sylvia married a man so much older than herself, a man confined to a wheelchair, a man who would be a burden to live with, needing her assistance in almost everything? She was young, vital. Her beauty, her energy, could be a passport to the kind of life, the kind of marriage, she had yearned for with Bubba. Now, she was tied to a cripple, however kind.

"I love her, John." He seemed to read my thoughts, and his answer came simply, quietly. "Sylvia has told me about you … and her. I understand how you must feel about her, because I feel the same way." His words, so softly spoken, jolted me. When our eyes locked, Barrington's did not flinch. His eyes were gentle and searched my face for my understanding that he could love her as deeply as I did.

I looked away and stared across the top of the car at the cafeteria, at students coming and going or stopping to chat on the steps, and at men holding the door open for female students. They were all so carefree, so unaware of the pain gripping my insides. I had just found Sylvia, and she was already lost.

The logic of that deduction seemed so simple. She was married, and she was moving, leaving for a distant state, leaving a home much removed from that which she had known and much removed from me. I had lost her. Every instinct ingrained in me since early childhood molded what I must do, must say. I stood away from the car and looked down at Barrington's pleasant face.

"I hope you'll both be very happy in Michigan." I offered my hand to Barrington. He gripped it warmly.

"Thank you."

I turned to Sylvia, standing quietly beside me. "Best of luck. I hope we'll meet again sometime."

She looked up at me, a faint smile creasing her lips. "Thank you, Johnny. Thank you for everything."

She held out her hand to me. I took it, turning the palm up slowly as I bent to kiss it. She drew in her breath. So the feeling was still there. That, at least, was left of what had been, of what might have been. I would never again feel her writhing in ecstasy under me, feel her fingernails raking my back as I spent myself within her. She was now for another man to enjoy, a man with severely limited abilities to give her pleasure.

"Good-bye, Sylvia."

I turned abruptly and bounded up the steps of the supply building two at a time, hearing the motor start as I entered the building; I did not look back as she drove away.

We are told that time eases pain, but it's a slow process. I preferred a more rapid easing of the grip on my gut. I threw myself into my classes, loading up with all I was allowed to carry, and I began a strenuous physical workout program. I also decided to try out for the football team in the fall.

"You're nuts" was Bill's response when I told him my plan. But he decided if I could do it, so could he. We began running three miles a day. By spring, we were up to five miles. With permission from the unsuspecting football coach, and because I was a veteran with a Purple Heart, we were allowed to use the weight room under the guidance of a weight-training instructor. Alabama had one of the more progressive weight-training programs among American colleges, developed in the late 1930s by an assistant football coach who utilized techniques well ahead of his time and his peers. Muscles that had semi-atrophied because of the trauma of my injuries and inactivity began to painfully reactivate.

We both planned to walk-on for spring football practice, though the chances of two walk-ons making a team as fabled as Alabama were slim. We knew that, but it did not deter our determination to make the team.

Sylvia was still with me, haunting me at odd times, which pushed me to work harder to purge her from my thoughts, my memories. Only in sleep was I free of her, and not always then.

Exhaustion helped, and so did hunger. The vigorous training program increased our appetites. We were continuously hungry. That forced us back through the cafeteria line a second time for most meals, draining our finances at a rapid pace. The government check we got each month paid for tuition and books. The room and board came out of our pockets.

Fear of poverty promotes petty larceny—at least it did in our case, and Bill was the genius behind the scheme. Cafeteria tickets could be purchased in advance for different amounts. Students presented the paid meal tickets to a cashier, who rang up a paid receipt and handed it to the students, who then handed it to another cashier as they exited the cafeteria and Bill noticed that all the receipts were placed in a box near the cash register.

Before we put our grand larceny into action, Bill got acquainted with the exit cashier, a student he knew from French class. The flattery he lavished on this somewhat homely but receptive classmate was almost cynical, coming from someone as naturally shy as Bill. It left the gullible girl always believing he would be calling her shortly for a date. Of course, that never happened. Diverting her attention was almost always successful, and it gave me time to stealthily retrieve a handful of slips from the box.

Back in the sanctuary of our dorm room, we would sort out the paid slips and use them at the next meal to pay for our food. The scheme proved the salvation of our dwindling savings accounts. It also brought us unwanted attention and accolades from some of our dorm mates who were more attentive to our actions than the cashier.

We were nearly caught once. Just as my hand went into the box, the cashier's attention was drawn my way by the conspiratorial laughter of two students from our dorm in line behind us. Bill's genius for quick thinking saved us. He quickly asked the girl for a date, and that brought her attention instantly back to him and away from my culpable hand.

It was that date that proved the undoing of our free food. The cashier became infatuated with Bill, who made the mistake of having sex with her on their first outing. She was hell-bent on an encore, which Bill was hell-bent on avoiding. Spring football practice came to his rescue.

29

My rigorous training paid off. I made the team, although not as quarterback.

Harry Gilmer had come to Alabama, like a cavalry charge in a John Wayne western, and the offense moved to his bugle call. I was an end with the primary job of blocking for the halfback. Alabama was a running team in those days. Passing was less frequent, almost an afterthought and only used to surprise or in a third-and-long situation.

An undetected hernia, probably a legacy of his hard drop into the Pacific Ocean, sidelined Bill's hopes of playing for the Crimson Tide. He did get a job as assistant team manager, which paid free room and board in the athletic dorm.

Our food problems were over. Not only was the food free, but it came in bigger servings and with better quality and variety than the menu offered in the cafeteria. Steaks replaced hamburgers. The University of Alabama took care of its prized athletes' culinary needs.

We were the only vets in the athletic dorm, which tended to isolate us from the other athletes. They were more deferential than friendly. The chiding camaraderie among the other players was never extended to us. No invitations were proffered to be at one of the late-night, clandestine beer-drinking gatherings or any of the rowdy parties hosted by players in their dorm rooms. Such activities had the tolerant blessings of the dorm mother, who somehow kept these strictly prohibited goings-on from the coaching staff.

I was surprised, late in the season, when a reporter from a Birmingham newspaper approached me as I was heading to the showers after practice.

"Hey, Winstead, can I talk to you a minute?" A friendly smile spread across his chubby face. "I'm Don Brandt from the *Appeal*. Coach Thomas says it's okay for us to talk. In fact, he said we could use his office." He hesitated, uncertain when I did not respond. "Really, Coach said it was okay," he quickly offered reassuringly.

"Look, we're not supposed to talk to reporters. What's this all about?" I asked, my tone skeptical.

"I heard you were in the Air Corps and wounded. That's kinda unusual to be wounded and then come back and play football. I sure would like to do a story on you." His round face looked up at me, somewhat pleadingly. I never had much dealings with reporters except for the several instances the lone sports reporter from the *Gadsden Times* talked with me after one of our games. That was different. Here, contacts by athletes with the press were strictly controlled by the athletic department. Again, that pleading look.

"Okay, I guess, but I'll have to check with Coach first. Come on." I waved to Brandt to follow me. "Let's go to his office."

Brandt wrote his story. It was picked up by the Associated Press and United Press International and ignited a barrage of telephone calls and inquiries from all over the nation. The university's press office ran interference for me, screening the requests for interviews. Movietone News cameras came to the final game of the season. They filmed my parents sitting with the university president and his wife, my mother looking slightly uncomfortable with this newfound fame.

Late in the third quarter, playing in a driving rain and down by a touchdown, "Cavalry Charge" Gilmer called an end around. That was me. I cut outside, then turned into the center of the field about twenty yards from the goal line, just as the ball dropped into my hands out of the dripping sky. The opposing safety, a burly, mud-covered defensive back, barreled my way, his arms stretching menacingly toward me, but the mud took his feet from under him, and he plummeted to the ground as I scampered, untouched, into the end zone. My first and only touchdown of that season was recorded for nationwide replay on movie screens, garnering me unlikely and undeserved hero status. Despite my celluloid fame, we lost the game.

The end of football season brought an end to the media attention that had been fueled by a combination of my age—twenty—my Purple Heart for three bullet wounds, and my being the youngest of three brothers who served in the war. Coming from what the Movietone announcer described as an All-American family that had sacrificed its oldest son to the cause of freedom, and welcomed home another son who lost a leg helped frame my new fame.

It was a heady time. Bill and I were now getting invitations to occasional late-night dorm parties. We were seasoned beer drinkers, with fresh opportunity to display our ability to hoist bottles and remain ambulatory, however wobbly we both might be when we left. If my status was still uncertain among the other athletes, following all the attention over my "wounded veteran goes to college and plays football" publicity, my stock definitely rose among the jocks, firmly cemented by my epic beer drinking at parties.

I found solace in the weekend drinking, in burying myself in my studies, in running five miles a day. I was exhausted at night, exhaustion I welcomed, if it kept me from thinking about Sylvia. The pain of losing her still flooded over me at times, and I wanted to incise the pain of longing, permanently.

By the time we returned to Gadsden for the Christmas holidays, the pressure of football, partying weekends, and long hours of study were evident to my mother. She fussed in the kitchen all day long, determined to banish my leanness with pies, cakes, and a daily offering of some of her best cooking. It was irresistible and despite my melancholy, she succeeded in adding pounds to my frame.

JB Stevens had his own remedy—women—and the use of his car whenever we wanted it. That offer proved irresistible. I renewed some old acquaintances, and so did Bill, who had lost some of his instinctive shyness with girls. We would avail ourselves often of the druggist's hospitality during our college years.

But it was never enough to banish the melancholy, a sadness I vowed to erase by continuing a grueling academic schedule and football, efforts that would earn me a double degree and being named an honorary All-American. Then, I decided, before entering medical school, I would find Sylvia. She could not be happy with her invalid professor, not my Sylvia of the backroom cot, the woman who could fire my senses in a way no other woman came close to doing. I would have her again. It was that promise to myself that drove me through those undergraduate years.

* * * *

That determination to find Sylvia was almost immediately made a distant priority by Ann. She returned to Gadsden from New Jersey without notice, renting a room and taking a job as a receptionist at a small construction company. It was Doc Cunningham who told Mother that Ann was back, pregnant and alone. I had just completed my mid-term senior finals when my mother called. We had a four-day break before classes resumed, and Bill and I drove to Gadsden that frigid January afternoon.

Ann was behind the desk in a cramped, dingy office, housed in a converted modular army barrack. Emotional pain had dogged her most of her young life. It was there still, in her eyes, in her wavering voice, as she rushed into my arms.

That evening, we sat in a back booth at a small café on the outskirts of town. The hamburgers we ordered remained untouched, as the grief of her four-year marriage spilled out. Like so many veterans, Peter Hammit returned from the war a changed man. His family was dismayed he had married while stationed in Alabama. Ann found a glacial Yankee welcome from the Hammits—she could have dealt with that, but not the drinking. Her husband's growing alcoholism was condoned by his family—they excused it as an outcome of his marriage, rather than his own weakness. In his sober moments, he felt trapped by a marriage he claimed he entered into without thinking.

In his drunken moments, he moved from verbal abuse to hitting her, in the stomach, the chest, but never in the face, where his fists would leave visible marks of his cruelty. In a drunken rage one night, he raped her. Two months later, when she told him she was pregnant, he struck her in the stomach so hard it had knocked her doubled-up to the floor, gasping for breath.

She left Newark the next morning by bus, taking only her clothes and the small amount of money she found in her husband's billfold, arriving in Gadsden two days later with seven dollars. The three thousand dollars she received from her share of her grandmother's life insurance had been squandered by Hammit within months of his return from the war. On what, she was not sure.

Her sad eyes held a hint of desperation, the same look I had seen the night she told me of her father's sexual abuse. At my parent's insistence, Ann moved into one of our upstairs bedrooms and would make her home with them until she was on more stable financial footing. Bill went with me to pick her up the next day from the rundown home where she was rooming. All that she owned was in a small suitcase.

The next day, a Saturday, Collier and Katie and little Addison arrived for one of their clamorous visits. The house was filled with the squeals and laughter of the toddler playing hide-and-seek with his equally boisterous father and grandfather. The child had endeared himself to my father in a way that none of his own children had. Neither Collier nor I could remember our father on the floor, on his hands and knees, playfully wrestling and laughing with us. He was a changed man.

Ann, like Bill, was gathered into this family circle and made to link with each of us. Bill had long ago accepted his place in that circle, and Ann was being quickly welcomed back. At the early Sunday afternoon feast Mother lavished on the dining room table, she looked around at each of us, smiled, then requested we hold hands. It was the first time we had done so in offering the dinner blessing. Ann was sitting next to me and squeezed my hand gently. Despite the overtures from my family, Ann remained quiet and withdrawn. Only little Addison seemed sometimes to bring Ann out of her sad shell, into which she would once again withdraw when he bounded off to pursue a new distraction.

As we were relishing the chess pie my mother passed to each of us for dessert, Collier announced that Katie was expecting again.

Addison clapped his hands from his highchair and chirped happily, "A baby in her tummy." And then he expanded, "I was there."

"That's right, Addy."

"Mommy's tummy big." The child held his chubby arms wide to demonstrate how big, to the indulgent laughter of the adults around the table.

I glanced at Ann. She was smiling. This is the way news of an impending birth should be received, with joy, blessed by the love of those hearing the news. How differently her announcement had been received. I took her hand and held it under the table. She was my friend, the friend I seemed never able to protect from the cruelty inflicted upon her so often.

The next weeks sped by. I came home to Gadsden every weekend. Most of my time at home was spent at the desk in the parlor, with my books on an array of subjects spread out before me. I was close to completing my undergraduate work. Ann would sit near by, sewing or knitting quietly. She and Mother were making clothes for the new baby.

A tranquility finally settled over Ann as her stomach enlarged. She would join in more during the dinner-table conversations, which sometimes became quite animated, especially when Collier's family was in residence for the weekend.

Alone, as we were now in the parlor, she was content to sit without conversing, never intruding on my studies. I would look up at times to watch her bent over her sewing. She seemed to feel my attention and would glance up with a warm smile. There was a growing comfortableness between us.

Bill was the first to place his hand on her protruding stomach and get a swift kick in the palm. It had to be a boy, he declared. No girl would kick a guy that hard. Strangely, Mother agreed, although her opinion on the sex of Ann's child was drawn from her experienced observation of how boy fetuses were positioned.

It was a boy, born the week after my graduation, eight weeks premature. He lived only an hour. A pall hung heavily over all of us who stood silently as the tiny white casket was lowered into the grave. Ann was still hospitalized, deeply sad and even more withdrawn. My parents, Bill, Collier, and Katie stood beside me as we watched the infant Ann tearfully refused to name laid to rest.

Mother made Ann her personal challenge. The new baby clothes, so lovingly hand-sewn, were boxed in tissue and put away, high on a closet shelf. She plied Ann with her favorite soups and desserts and nursed her frail spirit with endless good nature and kindness.

With me, Ann remained polite but withdrawn, unresponsive to my attempts to engage her interest in a book, a movie, a newspaper article—anything to turn her mind from its sad meanderings.

In July, Ann returned to her job at the construction company and enrolled in business-college night classes. It was my mother's idea, and little by little, Ann returned to us.

That same month I purchased a car with money from my grandmother's trust, and announced one evening I would be gone for about two weeks. I needed to get away and had no itinerary. Bill knew better, and Father suspected something but said nothing.

The trip had been taking shape in my mind for weeks. Father's old road atlas helped me map the route. My longing demanded the trip. I left for Ann Arbor on a sultry, wet Sunday.

30

The address in the telephone book led me to a small, wood-sided bungalow in a neighborhood of similar homes near the campus. There was no doorbell, so I knocked twice.

A young woman with her hair in pin curls, bound up in a scarf, stood inside the screen door, holding a small child in her arms. A look of consternation greeted me.

"Whatever you're selling, I don't want."

"No, ma'am, I'm not a salesman. I'm looking for some folks who are supposed to live here—Professor Richard Barrington.

"They used to live here, before us."

"Do you know where they live now?"

"I don't know. They didn't leave a forwarding address. We got some mail for them after we moved in. I just gave it back to the postman." The girl shifted the baby to her other arm. "He's a year old now and getting to be a load to tote around," she explained, gently prying his chubby fingers from a beaded necklace around her neck.

"I'm a friend of the Barringtons, from Alabama."

"Well, I can only tell you what the neighbor told me. When Mr. Barrington passed away, his wife and little girl moved out of town. She didn't know where. That's why I just gave their mail back to the postman." The shock of what she had just said must have reflected on my face. "Oh, I'm sorry, mister," she stammered contritely. "I just thought you already knew—about Mr. Barrington, I mean."

"No, I didn't know. That's all right. You had no way of knowing. Thank you, ma'am." I turned to leave.

"I'm real sorry you didn't know." She shifted the squirming child back to her other arm, away from the tempting necklace. "I'd invite you in, but the house is a mess. You know how it is when they start walking. They're into everything," she said, looking fondly at the squirming toddler.

"Thank you anyway, ma'am. I have to be going. Thanks again."

"Sure."

She was still framed in the doorway, holding the child behind the screen door, as I pulled away from the curb.

The secretary in the Veteran Services Department was brusque, letting me know with body language that I was intruding on her busy day. "Professor Barrington died of pneumonia in April," she curtly informed me, reading from a folder with his name typed on a white tab. "I know he was hospitalized for a time. He had multiple sclerosis, you know."

I didn't, but I nodded my head. "Do you know where I could get in touch with Mrs. Barrington?"

"She moved away, back to where her family was in Georgia or Alabama—somewhere down South." She closed the folder, officiously signaling an end to our conversation. "Sorry I can't be of more help," she said, dismissing me.

Barrington dead. Sylvia, a widow with a little girl. Gone again without telling anyone where. I had rehearsed what I would say to her all the way from Gadsden to Ann Arbor, how much better her life would be with me than her invalid husband, how much I would do for her to make up for the years we were apart, how financially secure life would be when I was finally a doctor. Plans and promises she was no longer in Ann Arbor to hear.

I drove back to the street with the rented bungalow. A next-door neighbor was outside in her yard, watering some pansies in a window box. I stood at the end of the sidewalk leading to the front porch. She had not seen me approach, and I did not want to startle her. "Excuse me, ma'am, my name is John Winstead. I'm a friend of your former neighbors, the Barringtons. Could I talk with you a minute?"

She looked at me from underneath a wide-brimmed straw hat that shaded a thin, freckled, middle-aged face. Wisps of gray hair were matted to her damp brow. "I really didn't know them very well. He passed away in the spring. It was quite sudden. Very sad. His wife was a young thing, and they had a little girl. Cute little thing. Used to run over and talk to me when I was out in the yard." She stopped and observed curiously. "Are you related to them?"

"No, ma'am. I'm just a friend. I talked earlier with the lady next door. She didn't know where Mrs. Barrington had moved to. Did she tell you where she was going?"

"No, not really. My husband and I went to the funeral home. I asked her what she'd be doing. And she said probably she'd move back down where her folks were. Somewhere in Alabama, I think. They moved here from Tuscaloosa, as I recall."

"Yes, ma'am."

"Will you come in and have a cup of coffee, Mr. … Winston, is it?"

"Winstead, ma'am. I'd be pleased to, thank you. I could use a cup of coffee."

I followed her into the small living room, its modest furnishings reflecting a worn, rumpled, comfortable look. The fireplace was flanked by floor-to-ceiling bookcases crammed with books and old magazines. Over the mantle hung a large beveled mirror encased in a faded antique gold frame.

It was early afternoon. The steaming coffee she brought on a tray from the kitchen was welcome. I had not eaten since the night before.

"By the way, I'm Anita Carlisle. I don't believe I introduced myself."

I stood and held out my hand. "Pleased to meet you, Mrs. Carlisle. You're very kind."

"Not at all, young man, not at all," she mused, taking a seat in a well-worn leather chair across from me. "I liked the Barringtons. Nice folks. He seemed happy, despite being in that wheelchair. You knew he had multiple sclerosis?"

"I learned that earlier today. I knew he was an invalid, but didn't know why he was confined to a wheelchair. I met him only briefly at the University of Alabama. His wife is from my hometown."

"And where is that, Mr. Winstead?"

"Gadsden, Alabama, ma'am."

Mrs. Carlisle chatted on about the Barringtons while I sipped coffee. When she fell quiet, there was an awkward silence.

"I guess I'd better be going, ma'am," I said, setting my cup on a coffee table. "I appreciate all you've told me. I'm heading back to Alabama. I'll try to look Mrs. Barrington up there. Her mother still lives in Gadsden."

"I hope I've been of some help."

"You have, ma'am. Thanks for the coffee."

The highway stretched before me in the glare of the oncoming headlights. In those long, tired miles of driving, I rested my search. I had wanted Sylvia more than anything else in my life. She had been with me since I was a teenager. I loved her deeply; I would always love her in the hidden recesses of my heart. It was now a part of me that I must close off and move on. Instinctively, I knew, however long or far I searched, I would not find Sylvia in Alabama.

Sylvia had a nursing degree. That information came from the first neighbor. Mrs. Carlisle volunteered that Sylvia just completed a master's degree in nursing. She could now teach, as well as work as a nurse in a hospital. She would be amply able to support herself and her daughter, finding higher pay in northern hospitals. Another reason not to return to Alabama.

In September, I would enter medical school in Birmingham. Many of the male students with whom I had just completed my undergraduate work had married, were even fathers. I envied their focus and contentment at a time when I felt an escalating need to enervate the restlessness that seemed constantly astir within me since leaving the Air Corps. More than anything, I longed for a measure of contentment in my life. And I knew now I would not find that contentment until I ended the search for someone who would never be mine.

As the ribbon of dark concrete evanesced behind me, another face began replacing Sylvia. Ann. Gentle Ann. The only one to whom I confided the reason for my trip. She seemed always to understand, never to question. Ann floated in and out of my thoughts as I began to accept Sylvia as finally lost to me.

I had been obsessed with finding Sylvia, to once again pull her into my arms and cloak her in the protection of my love. Dwelling always on Sylvia, I had moved Ann to a distant and safe place, emotionally. Friend, confidant, companion—Ann seemed always there without ever intruding. My sense of her renewed as the miles sped by.

I arrived back in Gadsden the next afternoon, weary and hungry. I ate, and mother steered me to the bedroom to sleep, summoning all of her considerable self-discipline to avoid asking where I had been and why.

I awoke the following morning, rested and famished and knew there was one final thing I must do that day before I excised Sylvia from my mind and heart. After wolfing down several of Mother's freshly baked biscuits heaped with blackberry jam, I drove across town to a neighborhood I had never visited. The homes were set back from the unpaved, dusty street, each sadly neglected by its tenant, probably reflecting the condition of the people living inside. There was an almost funereal gloom draping the home I approached, with a screen door hanging precariously on two of three hinges. The woman summoned by my persistent knocking peered at me suspiciously from behind the crooked screen. Her face was a worn mirror of her home.

No, Sylvia had not returned to Gadsden. Yes, she was certain of that, her mother said in response to my persistent questions. Sylvia's mother looked at me with increasing impatience and finally admitted gruffly that she had not had any contact with her daughter since Sylvia left Gadsden. Without another word, she slammed the door shut abruptly.

As I turned to walk back to my car, I wondered if she would even care to know her daughter had married and made her a grandmother. Probably not, I speculated, as I slipped behind the wheel of the car. I tried to picture the little girl as I would have pictured Sylvia as a child—blonde and blue-eyed, with soft creamy skin and a ready smile. I gripped the steering wheel and forced that image from my mind. The search for Sylvia ended here. But there was one more stop I needed to make before heading back to my parents' home.

Ann was at the kitchen table, sharing coffee with Mother when I returned. She smiled, her green eyes warm with welcome. "Hi, stranger. We missed you."

That evening, I proposed to Ann while we sat in the swing on the back porch. Even the back-and-forth of the swing did little to stir the humid air of that early August evening. Ann looked at me searchingly. "Is this for real, Johnny?"

"Yes, it's for real," I assured her, smiling as I wiggled a ring box out of my pants pocket and slipped a small solitaire diamond engagement ring onto her finger.

Snuggling her head against my shoulder, she whispered her affirmation as tears welled in her eyes. I had always found an insouciant comfort in her friendship, never more so than that evening.

Three weeks later, we were married. Standing in front of the mantel in the parlor of my parents' home, arms linked, we listened to the stern-voiced Reverend Hillard P. Coates read the vows we then repeated. He made no effort to soften his scolding voice as he admonished Ann and me on the sacredness of the pledges we had just exchanged, before pronouncing us man and wife.

It was this same mantel where, as children, we would find our stockings hung on Christmas morning, filled with apples, oranges, and Mother's homemade fudge and divinity. I lifted Ann's chin and kissed her lips, which tasted as sweet as that candy so many years ago.

Bill stood beside me, while Katie held Ann's small bouquet of roses from Father's prized bushes. Just behind the flinty Reverend

Coates was Mother, clutching Collier's arm and dabbing her eyes with her free hand, glancing over occasionally at my sister, Sarah, who looked elegant in a pink suit. Sarah's husband looked bored, as he always did at any Winstead family function.

My father was clearly pleased with my choice. Ann had long ago been accepted as a daughter and had been lovingly harbored in our home. Now, she had repeated words that officially bound her to our family.

31

I do not know when I knew I no longer loved Ann—or if I ever loved her in the way I had promised on that late August evening four years ago. She was always my friend, comfortable, supportive, and there. I had retreated to her in despair. She welcomed me unquestioningly. If she expected passion, she never complained when it was lacking, seemed never disappointed. We were comfortable, even in bed. She seemed content in a marriage that substituted politeness and kindness for the love she had every right to expect.

In those four years, Ann had never mentioned Sylvia. Nor had I. Not until the night she told me she was leaving. Ann looked away, her eyes fixed on a picture of the two of us taken on our wedding day. Tears threatened as she struggled for control. "I'm going to Indianapolis, John. I'll stay with Katie and Collier until I find a job. Katie is certain I can get on in a clerical position at the hospital where she works." She turned slowly back toward me, away from our wedding day photograph. It was a day that held such promise. "Russ

Dennis will take care of the divorce for me. It will be a year before it's final. It's the best he can do."

I was stunned by her announcement. She had given no hint it was coming. I felt suddenly helpless, blindsided, at a loss for words. All I could say was, "Is this what you really want, Ann?" A stiff, lingering silence followed my words until I finally asked, "Why?"

Ann was silent for some time. She turned away from me so I could not see the tangle of emotions playing out on her face. When she turned around to face me, she said simply, "It doesn't matter why. What matters is, it's over." She sighed and looked down. "Maybe this will allow both of us to find the happiness we're missing."

I had no response. Despite my surprise and the instant hurt and anger it aroused, I knew she was right. "Is there anything you need? Anything I can do to change your mind?" I asked lamely, in an effort to shift the guilt I was feeling for the failure of our marriage to Ann, knowing at that moment it was too late.

"No, John. This is for the best. For both of us," she added. "There's a bus leaving at eight tomorrow morning. Can you take me to the station?"

I nodded silently, and Ann disappeared into the bedroom.

We rode to the bus depot in silence the following morning, Ann staring ahead, her thin hands tightly gripped in her lap. My perceived rejection by her bore into me like a hot iron. I wanted to be angry, as angry as I had become during the night, alone in the big overstuffed chair in the living room—angry we ever married, angry I was losing my friend, mourning the end of a friendship with a woman I had known since high school.

Somewhere in the deep recesses of my guilt, I blamed Sylvia. If I had found her in Michigan that fateful summer, four years ago, I would never have married Ann, and I would not be losing this woman I so cherished as a friend, so neglected as a wife. Now, they would both be lost to me.

The two large suitcases seemed light as I pulled them from the trunk. All that Ann had or wanted was inside. "You don't have to stay here until the bus comes," Ann said, averting her eyes from mine.

"I'll wait with you. Anyway, we haven't talked about money. You'll need some to get started on your own."

I handed her five hundred dollars. It was most of the money we kept in the apartment for monthly expenses. She stared at the white envelope, thick with tens and twenties.

"I don't want this money, John." For the first time I heard an edge of bitterness in her voice. "You can pay the attorney his fee for the divorce."

"Look, take this money." I reached for her hand, placed the envelope into it, and pressed her fingers over the contents inside. "I'll pay Dennis. And I'll tell him to transfer $25,000 from my trust fund to your account when you get settled."

"No, John, no," Ann said emphatically. "I don't want your grandmother's money." She shook her head adamantly. "She gave that to you, not me."

"She left if for my future, and there will be plenty left for me. I want you to have it, Ann. You can buy a home, make a new start. I sure as hell haven't given you much else."

She answered my admission of fault with a silence I knew was deserved. Despite all that had happened to her—her father's sexual abuse, her first husband's alcoholism and brutality, now this—she seemed quietly forbearing. I almost wished she would lash out at me, make me angry, make me feel less guilty, but that was not Ann.

We walked toward the depot, checked her luggage, and sat, silent and introspective, on the hard, rounded wood seats, waiting for the bus to begin boarding. When the bus's departure was announced over the public address system, Ann did not move. She remained seated as she had in the car, with her hands tightly folded in her lap.

"You need to find Sylvia, John." Her voice was barely above a whisper. "When you find her, you'll find your daughter." She said it so softly, I wasn't certain I heard what she said. She read the incredulity in my face. "Sylvia's daughter is your child. I was in Gadsden two weeks ago and happened to be at your folks' house when Sylvia brought her to see your parents. Sylvia wants the child to know your mother and father, but only if your parents won't tell you until Sylvia is ready. She didn't want you to feel burdened or the child to come between us. I promised her I would never tell you either. But you need to know."

I stared into her eyes. "My God" was all I could think to say. I buried my face in my hands. How could this be? I had assumed the child was Barrington's. How old was she? Where was she? My mind was spinning. Sylvia, the mother of my child. But when? There had always been a telepathy between Ann and me, as if we could read each other's thoughts, each other's emotions.

"She learned she was pregnant right after you enlisted in the Air Corps. Your mother said Sylvia called, but never said why she was trying to reach you." Ann looked over at me for the first time since we sat down, her soft eyes brimming with tears. "You should know your daughter before she grows up. She looks so much like you."

"Why the hell didn't you tell me?" I whispered, an edge of rage in my voice. "I had a right to know. You and Mom and Dad had no right—you most of all. Damn you!"

The tears spilled onto her cheeks, but her voice remained surprisingly steady. "I love you so much, and I knew if I told you,

I would lose you. Then I finally admitted to myself that I've never really had you," she said sadly. "You were always hers."

The shrill voice on the public address system announced a final call for the bus leaving for Nashville, Indianapolis, and Detroit. Ann turned away from me as she rose. "Don't get up. I would rather go to the bus by myself. Anyway, you know how I hate good-byes."

Anger, blind anger, fired within me as Ann began walking toward the double doors leading to the boarding area, looking small and forlorn. I wanted to hate her, to scream my pain at her, pain she inflicted on my pride that I had let her down, disappointed her, failed her. But the sudden realization I might never see her again erased my anger. I caught her elbow just as she was pushing one of the doors open.

"I'm sorry, Ann. I don't want us to part like this. I was really stunned by what you told me. It just needs to sink in." She raised her hand and gently stroked my cheek to ease the distress she saw there. Ann, gentle Ann. I held her hand against my cheek for a moment, feeling its softness. "Stay my friend, Ann. It's how I love you."

"Always." She disappeared inside the bus. I saw her walking down the narrow aisle toward a vacant seat by a window. Her tears glistened in the reflection of the dusty pane. It was my last image of Ann before the bus pulled away from the parking dock.

I was reeling from the disclosure that I had a daughter as I drove back to our apartment—my apartment. If what Ann said was correct, the child would be about nine years old. In my agitation, I forgot to ask the child's name. I tried to picture her in my mind. All I could see was beautiful Sylvia, her long blonde hair blowing softly about her face and shoulders, her chin lifted high against the breeze, her face alight with a smile that preceded a ripple of throaty laughter. How much I still loved her. Ann must have known, must have harbored that knowledge and buried the hurt it caused for much of the time we were married. It was then tears stung my eyes. Why, God, could I not have loved Ann, reciprocated even a small measure of her feelings for me?

The next morning, I left early for Gadsden to confront my parents about my daughter and find out if they knew where I could find Sylvia. They were startled and saddened when I told them Ann and I had parted. And they were more startled when I told them I knew about their visit with Sylvia and my daughter.

Her name was Elizabeth Ann, my mother revealed, as she dabbed at the tears springing from her eyes, but she preferred to be called Bethann. The child was nearly ten, she said, and beautiful, with my dark hair and blue eyes. When I asked where I could find Sylvia and the child, Mother shook her head. "I don't know," she replied, her voice choked with sobs.

Father sat silently across from me, waves of guilt and sorrow vied with embarrassment on his taut face. He averted his eyes from my harsh scrutiny. "They're somewhere in Nashville," he admitted tersely.

Mother shot him a shocked look. It was obvious he had not told her of their whereabouts. He explained he had just set up a college fund for Bethann at a Nashville bank. He looked across the table to me, his eyes pleading for understanding. "We had to promise not to tell you, John. Sylvia was fearful that your knowing about Bethann would bring conflict between you and Ann. She made Ann promise not to tell you." His gaze wavered, and he dropped his head. "We didn't know what to do, son. We love you, and we love Ann. We never meant this to cause such hurt."

I knew that was true, and that acknowledgement diffused my

anger. Mother was still crying when I left an hour later, promising to let them know as soon as I located Sylvia and Bethann.

My residency at the University of Alabama-Birmingham hospital would be completed in a week. That gave me a week to search for Sylvia before I had to report to a small hospital in eastern Tennessee, where I had committed to work in a medical outreach program for indigent Appalachian families.

With no street address or telephone number to work from, my week in Nashville became exhausting. Despite being a relatively small city, Nashville was a major medical and education center, boasting more hospitals and universities than Birmingham. I spent each day calling on hospitals and doctors offices to ask for Sylvia under her variety of last names. I even drove to several smaller suburban hospitals in the counties ringing Nashville. No nurse by that name. The telephone directory yielded no Sylvia Barrington, or Moss, or Barnes, nor did the information operator.

At the end of the week, I left, tired and discouraged. I had come to Nashville with the same high hopes as many young musicians and singers—to find the end of my rainbow—a rainbow's end that still remained, for me, out of reach.

My parents agreed to get her address when Sylvia next contacted them and to tell her Ann and I were divorcing. They expected Sylvia to call soon. She had promised to try to bring Bethann to see them before school started. I left for Birmingham the next morning full of hope that my search for Sylvia would end soon. That hope was dashed when the promised telephone call did not come before I left for Appalachia.

32

The mountains of eastern Tennessee were crowned by thin, multi-shaped clouds giving the appearance of Indian wigwams with smoke wafting from the summits. No matter the season, old timers said the smoky look was always there, at its thickest in the morning when a soft mist spread over the lowland valleys, which lay like grassy outstretched palms to the timber lines. Only in winter were the rich variations of green interrupted by the purity of new snow. I never saw the white of winter, only the lush green of summer, often from far up mountain trails, as I ministered to the farmers and coal miners who populated hollers that reached from the valley's palm, like many long, narrow fingers upward through the timbered heights.

Health care for these hardy, isolated families was sporadic, coming too late to many in those remote, mountainous areas. Tuberculosis was still a problem among these mountain families, even as it was being eradicated from most of the nation's population. Emphysema and cancer further emasculated lungs already lined with coal dust. Doctors were paid by the Public Health Service to bring healing to the mountain residents, who would drive down from their mountain cabins in dilapidated trucks to the medical clinics manned by young physicians like me, or we would bring those skills directly to these residents in their remote cabins. Either way, we doctors honed our skills, to be used in the future on less backward patients who could well afford to pay handsomely for our services.

I came to quickly admire the handful of doctors who labored year round in those mountains, overworked and drawing far less pay than a sedate urban practice would provide. I had gone back to different areas of Appalachia for the past three years as a volunteer, fulfilling something that first drew me to medicine, a practice of healing that would seldom be called on in the upscale Birmingham practice I was to join in the fall.

Doc Cunningham had invited me to become part of his growing practice. I was highly flattered but was committed to the Birmingham practice, with two medical school friends, after completing my surgical residency.

The work that summer began at dawn and lasted well past dusk. Each week, the doctor-and-nurse teams took turns driving up the rough roads into the mountains, and when the roads narrowed to trails, they'd walk, sometimes miles up steep hollers, to bring basic medical care to families who rarely came to town—perhaps only two or three times a year, if then.

Children had to be inoculated to attend school in the fall, something parents resisted doing because of decades-old taboos against the preventive shots. Whooping cough—triggered by a bacterium and highly contagious—and diarrhea had been particularly prevalent this summer. Parasites were common because drinking water often came from untreated water taken directly from mountain streams or uncovered wells.

It was well water, contaminated by an old outhouse dug too close and slightly above the well, that brought me, along with a clinic nurse, on a humid late-August afternoon, to trudge along a narrow, rough path to the side of a critically ill three-year-old boy. It was the first case of typhoid fever I had seen, even in these remote mountains. The boy's fever was 104 degrees. Bathing the child in cold water was keeping the fever from raging higher.

The nurse working at my side agreed the child needed to be hospitalized quickly. We wrapped his painfully thin, shaking body in a blanket, and I carried him along the narrow path through the dense woods. The path was hardly wide enough for the deer, who used the trail to reach the water pooling under a waterfall, halfway down the mountain. Nervous squirrels scampered up trees, chirping their irritation at our intrusion, as we headed toward the rough road at the foot of the holler, where we had left the car.

The boy's mother walked silently behind us, the rapid pace giving a pink flush to her otherwise sallow complexion. The characteristics of her thin face were all too familiar in these parts, evidence of poor nutrition and decades of marrying cousins not far enough removed for genetic safety.

She looked much older than her twenty-eight years. The husband had stood on the rotting wood porch, following our progress down the mountain path, his other five children standing around him or sitting on the rickety steps. I learned something during those summers spent in one of the poorest regions of America. The residents of Appalachia—despite being removed from the mainstream of American life and culture by geography and illiteracy—cherished their children above all else.

Once we'd reached the car, it took another hour to reach the nearest town and still another half-hour by ambulance to get to the nearest hospital, which was run by a group of stalwart Catholic nuns. The grieving mother held her son's hand the entire way as we sped along the winding rural highway with the siren wailing. It may have been the mother's touch, more than my ministrations, that kept the child alive long enough to get the help he needed. By the time we arrived at the emergency entrance of the small hospital, the boy's breathing was rasping and shallow. He was very near death.

I wanted this child to live. My whole being seemed intent on achieving that. It was an unspoken promise I made to this shy, backward woman each time our eyes locked on each other, as we tried to keep life in her child's frail, little body during the drive to the hospital.

A short, plump, take-charge nun with warm hazel eyes joined us as the gurney was pushed down the corridor toward the emergency room. "This way," she said, pointing to a side corridor with windowed double-doors halfway ahead. "We have an isolation room already set up with an oxygen tent."

The child looked so alone inside the plastic tent, which was draped over his upper body. The boy's respirations were shallow, and his breathing was becoming more labored. Breath was being squeezed from his small body, and I seemed helpless to keep the inevitable from happening. For an hour I watched the labored breathing, hoping oxygen would nullify the need for what was becoming inevitable. It would take another twelve hours for the penicillin to begin eradicating the life-threatening infection. I called for the nun.

"We'll have to do a tracheotomy, Sister, to ease his breathing. Is there an emergency OR available?"

"Yes, Doctor. I'll call the head nurse, and we'll be ready by the time you prep." She flew out of the room, her white robe flapping around her swift heels. She perceived the danger of the procedure on a child in such frail condition but did not question for a moment my decision to operate.

The young nurse who stood on the other side of the boy's bed went to get the gurney still parked in the hall outside the room. We lifted him gently, and the nurse and an orderly, commandeered from down the hall, hurried the gurney toward the lone elevator just outside the double-doors.

"You won't let m'boy die, will youse, doctor?" The mother's eyes were pleading, and her hand, languid from exhaustion, held my arm.

I could not bring forth words to comfort her. I wanted to promise her that the child would live to return to their mountain home, well and happy, to grow to manhood in the loving environment of that drafty cabin. But I had to face what every doctor must, many times. I was not God. I had not been inside a church since leaving the Air Force. For the first time since choosing medicine as my life's work, a prayer formed in my mind. Please God, give me the skills to save this child.

"I don't know, ma'am, but I'm going to try. Pray for us both." I patted her shoulder and rushed toward the elevator.

The nun was true to her word. An anesthesiologist was already giving the child a sedative. The nun was donning a surgery robe, and a nurse was standing by to help me into mine and to push my hands into surgical gloves after I quickly scrubbed up with antiseptic soap.

"The head nurse will assist you, Doctor. She's on her way now."

"We can't wait, Sister. Let's get started."

I had just completed the incision for the trach tube when the head nurse came into the small surgery room, still securing her face mask. She hesitated, stopping just steps from the surgery table. I looked up. "Something wrong, Nurse?" I demanded sharply.

"No, Doctor, I … I'm sorry."

"Trach tube," I barked.

It was in my hand before I ended the order. I slowly forced the narrow tube down the opening in the child's throat. If we could relieve the stressful breathing, maybe—just maybe—we could keep him alive long enough for the antibiotics to battle the typhoid fever. The total procedure took less than ten minutes. I clipped the last strand of suture to secure the tube. The little boy was already breathing more easily.

"Let's get him back to the oxygen tent. I'll stay with him tonight. Thanks for all your help."

The nun and two nurses nodded their acknowledgment of my gratefulness. One of the nurses began wheeling the gurney out of the OR, back to the isolation room. The head nurse, who had arrived late, walked behind the gurney as it was pushed through the double-doors leading out of the surgery.

The nun touched her arm. "One moment, Mrs. Barrington, I would like you to meet Doctor Winstead. He brought the patient here from the clinic at Pisery."

The nurse stood still, her back to me. With her hand holding the right surgery door open, she turned slowly in the doorway, in response to the nun's introduction of me, pulling the mask down to reveal her face. "I already know Dr. Winstead," Sylvia said.

I could not speak. All of the years of looking and longing for this woman, who now stood only feet away, came washing over me. I had searched so hard, only to be disappointed. And here, on this humid evening in August, in the center of a small hospital surgery, I'd found her.

"I didn't know you knew each other. Well," concluded the nun, looking somewhat awkward, "excuse me while I get your patient situated, Doctor, and I'll let the two of you visit for a few minutes."

She left Sylvia and me, still standing, unmoving, staring at each other across the several feet that separated us, a distance measured both in space and time.

"Hello, Sylvia." I spoke barely above a whisper, venturing to bridge the chasm of silence between us.

"It's good to see you, Johnny." The years had changed her little. She was still slender and beautiful, with strands of rebellious blonde curls slipping out the side of the stiff nurse's cap that partially hid her long hair, tamed in a bun at the nape of her neck.

"I didn't know you were working here," I responded lamely.

"I've been here two years. Doc Cunningham gave me a sterling recommendation, and the sisters believed him." She smiled slightly. "Contrary to popular belief, nuns are very gullible," she added, her smile broadening, lighting up her face.

"They're also good nurses," I noted.

"Yes, they are," she agreed, "especially Sister Clare."

There was so much I wanted to say, not just these stiff pleasantries. I wanted to rush across the space that separated us and take her into my arms. My legs remained locked in place.

"Well, I had better get back to my floor," Sylvia told me. "We're short a nurse this evening. I'm filling in. Can I have someone bring you some coffee or a dinner plate?" Her voice trailed off.

"Thank you, no food. But I could use some coffee. I'm going to stay with the little boy. He's in isolation. That will minimize exposure to anyone else on staff."

"I'll see that someone brings it right away." She turned to leave, pushing the door wider with her hand.

"Sylvia." She turned in the half-open doorway. "I searched for you after your husband died. I couldn't find you. Please come see me before you leave tonight. Please."

"I will, Johnny, as soon as I finish my shift."

She stayed that whole night as I sat by the bedside of the child I so wanted to live. The boy's exhausted mother was tucked into bed in a nearby vacant room by the ever-present Sister Clare.

Sometime during the night, Sylvia knelt on the floor beside me, laying her head in my lap, falling asleep as I stroked her hair. When she awoke, we began to talk as the young boy slept quietly under the oxygen tent, his breathing more even and less labored, his life force returning as we kept vigil at his bedside.

She had been alone when Bethann was born, unmarried and out of work. Her small savings, along with money Doc Cunningham loaned her, sustained her long enough to finish nurse's training.

Sylvia had met Barrington in one of his classes and later took a job cooking and cleaning for him and his son. Barrington was considerate, knowing that he had only a few years to live. Bound to a wheelchair by lifeless legs, he could not be a husband, but he had been an affectionate and caring friend and stepfather. His death had been expected but still had been devastating. He had been the only constant, the only security in her life since she had left Gadsden.

It was in response to questions from Bethann, Sylvia explained, that prompted her to bring the child to Gadsden to meet my parents. The only father Bethann had known was Richard Barrington. She had accepted his parentage without question. Expressing a sad curiosity, the child did not understand why she had no grandparents like other children at school. And she questioned why she had no aunts or uncles or cousins. Even why she had no siblings. Sylvia had no answers for her daughter until the evening she picked up the telephone and called my parents to arrange the visit.

They had welcomed her warmly and unquestioningly embraced Bethann as their grandchild. When my parents told her I had married Ann, she insisted they not tell me about her visit, fearing Bethann could become a wedge between Ann and me. Then Ann arrived unexpectedly. Stunned and embarrassed, Sylvia feared she had made a terrible mistake, despite Ann's graciousness. She admitted being circumspect when Mother asked where she lived, but she offered no refusal when Father suggested setting up a college account for Bethann at a bank in Nashville. Tears gathered like azure pools in her eyes. "I'm so sorry, Johnny. I should never have taken Bethann to see your parents."

"Don't be." I lifted her chin and bent to kiss her moist lips. "Ann left me. She wanted to make room for you."

"Oh, God, Johnny, I never meant that to happen. Please believe me," she pleaded.

"You're not to blame. I am. I took advantage of Ann's sweet nature and our friendship to find a refuge after losing you. It was wrong. Now, maybe Ann has a chance to find the happiness she deserves."

Sylvia looked up at me searchingly, her eyes awash in tears. She seemed to find what she sought in my face. "I love you, Johnny. I always have."

She slept then, more soundly, until the first pink traces of the new day were etched in the eastern sky. By the change of nursing shift at seven, the boy's fever had dropped. The antibiotic was finally prevailing. I offered a silent prayer of thanksgiving.

Sylvia slipped out to get us both a cup of coffee. When she returned, the boy's mother was sitting by his bedside, holding his small hand in hers, waiting for him to awaken.

"Dr. Winstead, you look very tired," Sylvia observed, handing me the steaming cup of coffee.

"I am, Nurse Barrington."

"Then drink this coffee, and we'll go meet your daughter."

EPILOGUE

We've come back, all of us, aboard this cruise ship, back to the blue Pacific waters where so many we knew had perished so long ago. The cruise line provided a floral lei for each of us to throw over the side of the white vessel this afternoon. Some of the ringed flowers are still floating on the quiet seas, gliding up and over the calm swells, stubbornly resisting the apodictic pull of the ocean, only to eventually be swallowed by a distant swell.

"Is this where Major Martin went down?" Sylvia's voice is soft as it drifts into my reverie. She stands beside me at the polished brass railing, looking out at the endless expanse of the Pacific. Its landscape is uninterrupted by land and bordered by a cloudless summer sky.

"I don't know. It might be near here. I'm not sure where the sub picked us up. We probably drifted miles from where we hit the water."

I'd thought a lot about Jimmy Bob Martin during the five days we'd just spent in Japan and Okinawa at a reunion of the old war horses of the Seventh Air Force. The smell of Juicy Fruit never failed to bring him back to me, even now. I smile recalling his right jaw always plumped with a wad of the chewing gum. His widow is here, with her two sons and their families.

Lydia Sue Martin never remarried, choosing to do what she and her husband had always planned to do—raise a family from the provisions of their rich Georgia soil. It has made her wealthy— Martin pecans are marketed throughout the nation. They taste best in one of Sylvia's prized pecan pies, which I blame for the ten additional pounds now spread over my frame and which daily jogging and endless hours in the hospital wellness center have failed to diminish.

"When we get home, I want a pecan pie. Could you whip one up for this old flyer?" I slipped my arm around Sylvia's waist, still slim in defiance of her age, and pulled her close.

"I believe I could do just that, Rookie." Sylvia looked up at me, smiling at the use of the nickname I had managed to keep a close secret until the welcoming reception at the base on Okinawa, revealed in the greeting Derrick Lawrence shouted across the crowded room.

Sylvia's eyes are as blue as the ocean reflecting in them, her flawless complexion framed by gray hair, is worn short now. She looks far younger than her sixty-five years and is still beautiful. Lawrence thinks so, too. He flirted outrageously with Sylvia throughout the first evening, finding courage in bourbon highballs that increased the crimson hue of his face and energized his mouth. Sylvia deftly deflected his harmless attention.

Recognizing his loneliness, she welcomed his company into our family group. He has remained attached to us at each of the week's events, having come alone to the reunion, the only surviving member of the *Lydia Sue*'s crew besides Bill Deems and me.

Bill chose not to come, despite protestations and downright

begging from me and his beautiful Caroline. Still less than a year into his post as Alabama's attorney general, Bill insisted he could not leave so soon into his term, even for this reunion. But I know it is not the job that kept him away. Sadness dogged his young years. The war, for him, was just one more pillager of the natural ebullience we should all enjoy in our youth.

It was Caroline who changed his lingering demeanor. He was thirty-three when he met Caroline Clippinger at a Washington reception, hosted by the Birmingham law firm he joined shortly after graduating from law school. Within five years, the name Deems had been added to Billingsly, Drapper, Cox & Associates, a prestigious firm in Birmingham's legal establishment, which maintained an office in the nation's Capitol.

Caroline was a tall, leggy Junior Leaguer, with flowing auburn hair and a spirit to match. Her family traced its beginnings in the fox hunt country of Virginia, back nearly three hundred years. The sudden death of her father shifted the responsibility for running his sprawling estate to her.

From the moment Caroline and Bill were introduced by the congressman representing her Virginia district, her goal was crystal clear: to marry the shy, soft-spoken attorney from Alabama. Bill was a confirmed workaholic bachelor who skillfully eluded numerous efforts to win his attention—efforts put forth by some of Birmingham's most tenacious mothers of socially prominent, eligible young women.

Witty and intelligent, mercurial and stubborn, vivacious and charming, Caroline Clippinger succeeded where all others failed. Since both her parents were dead, and she was an only child, I had the honor of walking Caroline down the long center aisle of the majestic and cavernous National Cathedral in Washington, while

Bill stood alone, awaiting her arrival in front of the altar. Then I took my place beside him as best man, and Sylvia stepped up beside Caroline as the bride's only attendant.

Following the wedding, Bill resumed leadership of his firm's Washington office, growing it into one of the Capitol's top legal bastions.

When he and Caroline returned to Birmingham ten years ago, following the unexpected deaths of two of the firm's managing partners, we made up for lost years on the golf course. The golf games became fewer when he was drafted to run for attorney general. He won by a landslide, and he and Caroline moved to Montgomery.

I miss him not being here, almost as much as I missed him during his many years in Washington, when we saw each other just two or three times a year, usually in Gadsden, during his pilgrimages to my parents' home. Bill's two children called them Grandma and Gramps. They long ago replaced the parents to whom Bill had been born. His children never knew and never questioned their bloodlines to the endearing old couple who welcomed them as grandchildren.

It was Bill's daughter Sylvia, named for my Sylvia, who took leave from her law studies at Georgetown to nurse my mother during the final weeks of her losing battle with cancer.

My father, bent with age, his face deeply creased by his nearly ninety years, sat with his beloved honorary granddaughter at Mother's bedside. A month after we buried Mother, Father joined her in the cemetery, next to their oldest son, Addison, lost on the sandy dunes of North Africa in an earlier and more distant conflict than the one fought over these waters in the waning days of World War II.

The deaths of my parents were the mournful catalyst that brought our family together. My brother Collier came home for an extended stay with his Katie, still a picture of Irish vivacity. Her generously freckled face and good humor were only lightly touched by the years of raising her brood of six. The youngest is a daughter, an impish mirror of her red-haired mother, fondly welcomed and vociferously protected by her five older brothers. Collier's family remained with Father in the days following Mother's burial and was still there when Father joined his beloved Ada.

Even Ann came with Collier and Katie for Mother's funeral. Gentle Ann, her hair grayed by the passing years, had remained in Indianapolis following our divorce and never remarried, choosing instead to be a doting aunt to Collier's children. None of us knew until later that she was waging her own battle with cancer. In less than a year, we would all make another sad journey to Anniston, to bury Ann near her mother and grandmother.

Our three sons are here with us, at Sylvia's gentle insistence, along with our seven rambunctious grandchildren, Winsteads all. For this week, they have been part of my world, a world in which I was barely older than most of them, a time they know about only from history books.

Our oldest, our daughter Bethann, is covering for me while I'm here. She joined me in the clinic several years ago, bringing a fresh approach and new leadership as our head pediatrician. Her three children are with us, which she laughingly insists is the best vacation she could have.

She was nearly twelve when her first brother was born. For all of their formative years, Bethann was more mother than sister, and she continues to dote on her three brothers with a mix of motherly indulgence and discipline. She and Sylvia were a formidable matriarchal alliance that stemmed the boys' Winstead-bred rowdiness more than anything I could say or do.

"Excuse me. Are you Lieutenant Winstead?"

"I was forty years ago. Now I'm just John," I reply, smiling back at a face that sweeps me back in time, despite the gray hair accented with a round bald spot at the back of the crown.

"I'm Jacob Steinmetz, Barry's brother. I was in Hawaii, waiting to be deployed with the Seventh when he was lost. He mentioned you a lot in his letters home." His dialect betrays his New Jersey roots.

"Good to met you, Jacob," I say, extending my hand. "This is my wife, Sylvia." Sylvia smiles warmly and extends her hand to the stocky little man standing before us. He is a middle-aged mirror of his brother, with the same ingratiating smile.

"Barry called you Rookie in his letters and said you were kinda Major Martin's favorite. The major looked out for you 'cause you were so young and all."

"I'm flattered if he did. I needed looking after in those days. I was greener than the jungle when I arrived on Saipan. The major was my real flying instructor, but he depended on Barry a lot," I said, shifting the subject away from me. "Barry could find anything we needed, anywhere it could be found. We used to call him our procurement department." I laugh, recalling the little sergeant who managed to hustle, borrow, or just plain steal whatever our air wing needed.

"Yeah, he was that way at home, too. Like a squirrel. Coming here for this reunion has sure brought him back to me." The broad smile drifts slowly off his face.

"I'm glad, Jacob. He was a helluva man. I was proud to serve with him. Wish he'd made it home."

Steinmetz looks at me thoughtfully, then extends his hand again and pumps mine. "Thanks, Winstead. He sure would have enjoyed this, and God only knows what would be missing from this ship when he got off." Laughter shakes his stocky frame and dances in his dark eyes. "Glad to meet you, Mrs. Winstead. See ya 'round." Still chuckling, he drifts off toward another group of old airmen.

I turn back to the ocean, the afternoon sun shimmering on its surface. I can see them, their faces reflecting in my mind like slides projected on a screen: Les Akers, with his eyes peering down the bombardier sights. Will Chandler, strapped to his machine gun, its barrel spitting flashes as the bullets rip toward their target, and Will, yelling a warning to Hap Simpson to aim his machine gun at a Zero coming from one o'clock high. Seth Barrett, running his hand under the engine for any telltale sign of leaking fuel. Kevin McDougal, with his head resting on the maps he had been navigating from, as his life's blood spills out. Jim Harper, his body covered with a white sheet as it is lifted down from the *Lydia Sue*. Barry Steinmetz asking who is that damn Indian, as he hurls himself toward the ocean. And Jimmy Bob Martin, his strong hands locked on the spastic joystick, a big wad of Juicy Fruit bulging in his right cheek, as he guides the plane he lovingly named after his wife to its grave—and his. All so young and lost so long ago.

I felt Sylvia's lithe fingers entwining around mine. "Sorry you came, Johnny?"

"No. I'm just glad you're here with me."

If, as one writer opined, war is the quintessence of man's primeval need to assert himself, then the vicissitudes of peace, for however long it lasts, must be all the more treasured by those of us who survive war. Our oldest son served in Vietnam during the final months of that war. He returned to us unscathed. Our peace returned with him. And now, on this gleaming ship, lapped by the swells of the softly undulating Pacific, I finally put my war and its losses to rest.

I wrap Sylvia in my arms, my chin resting gently on her head, and feel her warm back against my chest. A floral lei drifts leisurely by just yards from the ship, another reminder of this day of farewell. I have come, these forty-some years later, to reconcile in my mind why they—and not me—were claimed by this watery battlefield and to bid them a final farewell.

I said good-bye to Gadsden many years ago, a place too painful for Sylvia to live. We chose a place with no past, just a future. It is only now that the dark memories of war, with all its horror and loss, once relegated to my distant memory and long obscured, can finally be acknowledged.

As I stare out at the sinuous waves, I kiss the top of Sylvia's head and a quiescent cape of my deepest feelings for her wraps itself around my senses. There is no greater feeling.